DANGEROUS

LEGATUM - BOOK 3

LULU M SYLVIAN

GRIFFYN INK

Copyright © 2018 by Lulu M Sylvian

All rights reserved.

No part of this book may be reproduced in any form or by any electronic or mechanical means, including information storage and retrieval systems, without written permission from the author, except for the use of brief quotations in a book review.

❦ Created with Vellum

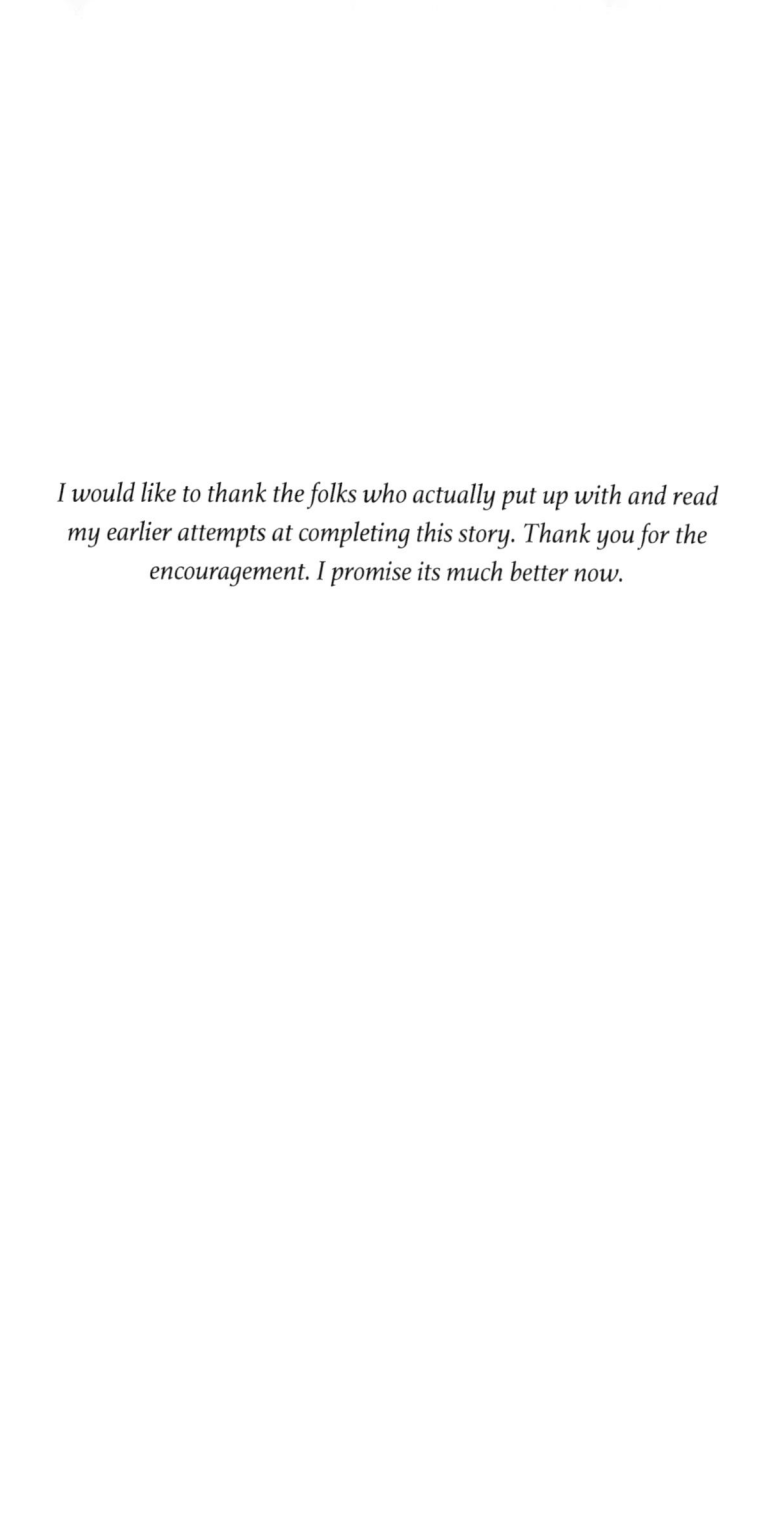

I would like to thank the folks who actually put up with and read my earlier attempts at completing this story. Thank you for the encouragement. I promise its much better now.

PROLOGUE

Dante stomped his feet. His breath turned to steam. Damn, it was cold.

He glanced back at the woman in the station wagon. She beat ineffectually on the door. "Let me out," she whined.

Dante was sick of Cindy's whining.

His coat was not warm enough for this climate. He thought of different ways he could help the salesman who sold it to him experience this level of bone-deep chill. He was tempted to shift so that he could have some fur protecting his body heat.

It was almost two hours past time to give her another dose of medicine. Dante thought maybe it was time to let her fully wake up, especially since he was passing her off to her alpha. Let him take care of her. For once.

From the sounds of things, the Meyers's alpha had disregarded and underestimated Dante's reluctant guest. Cindy pretty much wreaked havoc on his cousin Julia's plans for finding a science-minded wolf to help understand the ramifications of wolf-shifter DNA showing up as an ethnicity in ancestral DNA tests. Cindy had managed to render a local

Meyers wolf incapacitated, steal her plane ticket, and arrive in her stead at a genomics conference in Nashville.

Cindy was working on the misconception that killing an alpha would transfer all their powers to her, and thought she would be able to accomplish this at the conference. Had she received a proper education from the existing hierarchy of her family, she would have known better and possibly not caused harm to Dr. Kimbro.

Cindy started yelling and rocking the car back and forth trying to get out. Dante chuckled; child safety locks were a beautiful thing. He pushed hard against the car, causing it to lurch. Cindy stopped her thrashing.

A dirt-covered SUV rolled to a stop in front of Dante. The window lowered.

"Palatine?"

Dante nodded. "Meyers?"

The SUV pulled over, and a broad older man got out of the car. "Thanks for delivering the package."

"I should thank you for picking her up. She is a pain in the ass."

The station wagon started rocking again, and Cindy screamed curses.

Dante hit the window with his elbow, effectively shutting Cindy up.

"How did you get her all the way up here without causing an issue at the border?" Meyers asked.

"Benadryl. Told the border guard my girlfriend was asleep in the back. She was so groggy it didn't occur to her to not answer the guard's questions: name, birthdate, where we were headed."

"What did she tell them?"

"Home. You have something to keep her restrained? She flails about a lot otherwise."

"Yeah, we're good." Meyers turned and leaned into the back seat of the SUV. When he straightened, Dante was looking at the barrel of a pistol.

"Well crap, I thought you guys didn't do those up here." Dante sighed and stood up from his relaxed posture against the station wagon. "Let me guess; you're not Meyers."

"Good guess, asshole." Not-Meyers waved the pistol at Dante. "Release the girl."

Dante slowly turned and opened the car door. He reached in. Instead of releasing Cindy, he instantly shifted into wolf form and plunged through the back, breaking out the rear window of the station wagon, running as fast as he could for the woods off the side of the road. A gunshot rang out behind him, but he kept running.

Dante circled around in the underbrush. Not-Meyers leaned into the car. Dante ran. In seconds he was out from under the trees and on the other man's back, his teeth buried into the thick sweater at the man's neck. *Stupid appropriate cold-weather wear.*

Not-Meyers threw Dante from his back and turned with alpha-like speed, shifting into a light brown timber wolf. From the noise and the rocking of the station wagon, Cindy was still restrained and struggling against her bonds. Dante ignored her and faced off against the newly shifted wolf.

Not-Meyers apparently had access to Meyers's information. How else would he have known to meet Dante and Cindy here? *Did Cindy have more support in her efforts of undermining the local alpha? Who was this guy?*

The two wolves continued to snarl and circle. Finally Not-Meyers lunged. Dante countered with a snarling bite for the throat. Claws scratched, teeth gnashed, fur flew as the wolves rolled over each other, broke away, then attacked again.

Three large black SUVs stopped with squealing tires, blocking the first SUV in and surrounding the fighting animals. Several men spilled from the vehicles.

"Stop it," a loud, commanding voice barked, followed by the ratchet sound of a cocked shotgun. "Jesus, Graham, I told you what was going on with your daughter, not so you could be an idiot, but so that you knew she was one." The big man with the shotgun stomped over to the Not-Meyers wolf and kicked him back away from Dante.

"You must be Dante Palatine." He nodded to Dante. "Someone find him some clothes."

Dante stayed in a crouched defensive position. Jeans and jacket dropped in front of him.

"Turn, man. I'm Jeff Meyers. We need to talk."

Dante slid into the passenger seat of the Escalade, grateful the heater was on full blast.

"My people have a lot of cleanup thanks to those two. I thought I could trust Graham; he's my wife's brother. Went Smith on us after his wife died, and unfortunately for the girl, she was neglected and ended up with a lot of misconceptions regarding her own kind and who to trust. She made a real mess of things for you folks down in Nashville, didn't she?"

"She certainly tried. She's smarter than you think, but not as smart as she thinks she is."

"Ain't that the way?" Jeff Meyers chuckled. "How did you get her across the border? After we couldn't arrange for the Cessna, I wasn't sure you weren't going to be stuck with her for longer."

"Creative applications of allergy medicine. Look, she has some seriously bad information on how pack structure works. I don't know, and I don't want to know your plans for dealing with her. But if rehabilitation is on the list, she needs wolf-shifter 101 on an epic scale. Most ten-year-olds know more than she does," Dante said.

Jeff Meyers nodded thoughtfully. "This has been an eye-opener. We are a fairly closed-off group, never thought we needed to think of what kind of influence vamps would have on our family. They got some prime manipulative fodder with Cindy. I can only blame myself."

"The vampires are stirring up something on the West Coast," Dante started. "From something Cindy mentioned, it sounds like its having a ripple effect across the continent. And they are dragging wolves in, but no one knows exactly why. They tried to rekindle a family feud between the Palatines and the Aventines. You might want to consider reaching out to your nearest neighbor, and make sure you're all on the same page when it comes to how to handle any influx of bad from the vamps and their daywalkers."

Meyers nodded.

"How is Dr. Kimbro?" Dante asked. "Last I heard, you had found her, unidentified, in a coma in a local hospital."

"She's on the way to a full recovery. She had some memory issues, but with each change she recovers more memory and more capability. She was never a strong wolf, so the change was always a slow process for her, and now apparently it is exhausting for her as well. She's only shifting every few days or so. You know, we can handle cuts and shots and even broken bones, but traumatic brain injury in one of our kind isn't something I think any of us have any familiarity with. Her skull was broken up pretty good; if she were a typical human, she would be damaged for the rest of her life. That's if she recovered." He huffed. "Remedial wolf-shifter 101 is the least of Cindy's worries. Now that she's delivered, what's next for you?"

"Someplace warmer. But first I have to return to the store

and the jerk who sold me this coat, telling me it would be plenty warm for Canada."

"And do what?"

"Get a full refund. He lied. I'm freezing."

Jeff Meyers laughed.

1

Geena woke. She was in the rental RV with her face smashed into her pillow and her arm flung out, hanging over the edge of the bed. She felt a tightening in her chest, her arms were like cement weights. A shadowy figure loomed behind her. She tried to explain away everything on not being fully awake, but when she struggled and still couldn't move, and the shadowy figure drifted closer, she began to panic. Her voice didn't work, and she couldn't suck in the air she needed. She fought as the fear rushed in. It wasn't working; she couldn't breathe. Everything went black.

Her face was still half smashed into her pillow, and her arm still hung over the edge of the bed. She felt sleep drunk. Same exact position; apparently waking up earlier had been a dream. Geena couldn't hear anyone else in the RV with her this time. Hannah and Brooke must be up already and in the bathhouse. She didn't understand why she couldn't move anything except her eyes. She tried to close them and go back to sleep, but she couldn't move her lids. That's when she sensed the presence behind her. Figuring it was either of her friends, Geena tried to call out, asking for help. She made no sound. The shadowy presence moved, slowly getting closer. She told herself it must be Brooke, too tall for Hannah. She tried to relax. A sense of malicious intent overwhelmed her as the figure moved closer. Geena started panicking. She couldn't breathe; she couldn't get enough air.

Move, Geena. Maybe if she could only move her arm, she could make it stop. She focused all her energy on lifting her arm.

Geena woke up again. The sun streamed through the window of the RV. She was in the same position. Remembering she had just had back-to-back sleep paralysis dreams, she attempted to twitch her finger. *All right, I'm probably still there. If I can move my arm, it will all be fine, and shadowy Brooke will stop creeping me out.* At least this time Geena wasn't panicking.

Lucid dreams and sleep paralysis, great. Geena figured it was the stress from closing the plant and everyone losing their jobs, including herself, finally catching up with her. The shadowy, malicious form glided around just out of Geena's line of sight. She couldn't move her head. She remembered if she tried to move her neck now, when she actually woke up, she would have a neck cramp. Geena focused on keeping her breathing even, trying hard to not panic.

A warm, fuzzy muzzle with a wet nose nudged at her face. A dog; that was new. The shadowy figure retreated. Geena relaxed and tried to reach up to pet the animal, but the effort exhausted her and she fell back asleep.

The next time Geena woke up, she wasn't on the RV bed but on the fold-out couch. She lay on her back with her arm thrown across her eyes. The only similarity to her dreams was the light streaming in. Someone had made coffee. Geena sat up, inhaling the pleasant aroma.

Reality.

She had no sense of smell in her dreams.

"Sleep okay?" Hannah asked. It had been their first night out. Her best friend, Hannah, had taken the overhead bunk, and Hannah's cousin Brooke had the main bed, leaving Geena on the couch.

"Not really." She scratched her head and rolled her shoulders. Physically she had been comfortable enough. "I did that sleep paralysis dream thing."

Brooke came forward into the front section of the RV. "Do you always have sleep issues?" she asked.

"Yeah, but I haven't had an episode like this for a long time."

"Was it bad?"

"Not too bad. I kept thinking the shadowy figure was you." Geena nodded at Brooke. "And I had at least three false wake ups."

"Did you just say I was the creepy shadowy figure?" Brooke asked.

"I didn't say creepy," Geena replied.

"The shadowy figure is always creepy, Geena," Brooke retorted.

True, the shadowy figure was always sinister. It always felt malicious. The large dog was new. He had given Geena a sense of calm and protection she hadn't experienced with her sleep paralysis before.

Hannah sat next to her and handed her a cup of coffee. "I remember when you first told me about these in college, you honestly thought someone was coming into your dorm room."

"The ones my freshman year scared the crap out of me.

They felt so real. They were terrifying. This wasn't scary like those." Geena held the coffee in front of her face, letting the warm, aromatic steam revitalize her.

"You thought you were crazy until you talked to a counselor." Hannah sipped her coffee. "You were so happy when you found out it was just stress-induced weirdness with your sleep."

"Why is it my sleeping brain knows I'm under stress before the rest of me does?" Geena looked back and forth between the other two women. She began tapping herself in the middle of her forehead. "All right, brain, clue in—this is vacation, no stressy-stressy time."

Brooke poured herself a coffee and leaned against the counter. "You need one of us to drive the first leg so you can do some catch-up sleeping?"

"Yeah, I think that would be good." Geena rubbed sleep out of her eyes.

∼

Hannah leaned out the window. "What do I do now?"

Geena stood outside. She had just connected the sewage pipe to the RV outlets and plugged the other end into the campsite's sewage hookup. Their camp neighbor, a middle-aged man who made no bones about announcing he was looking for a trophy wife and wondered if the statuesque, blonde Brooke was interested in being his next missus, had provided Geena with useful advice, such as don't leave the RV sewer hookup open overnight, because rats could climb up into the rig's system. Getting rats out of the system is incredibly difficult; plus no one likes the idea of a rodent having a sneak attack on "your hiney when you go to take a dump in the middle of the night."

He definitely lacked charm and charisma. Geena totally understood why Brooke wasn't willing to leave everything behind and take off with him. And why she was currently in hiding.

The bugs also liked Brooke. Neither Geena nor Hannah received one bug bite, but Brooke looked like a chew toy. They determined it had to be something in her lotion that attracted the bugs, so she took an early shower in the bathhouse. She had returned to the RV with her arms covered in pink calamine lotion spots.

"Give me a second to stand on it, and pull the thingy. Now you have to dump a garbage bucket of water down the toilet." Geena twisted the black plastic handle opening the connection to the sewage pipe. In two quick steps, she was standing on the pipe as it snaked its way into the ground sewage connection. "All right!" She raised her voice so Hannah could hear her. "Dump the water!"

Water made slushing noises as it moved through the pipe. "Do it again!"

Hannah's face appeared at the window. "More water coming right up!" She disappeared, and a minute later more water swished down the pipe.

Geena stepped off the pipe and switched the black handle to close the connection.

"All right, Hannah, fill the bucket again, and then let the water run down the drain for like five minutes."

Geena danced around the area, shaking her hands and high stepping in her own personal this-is-gross-I-don't-want-to-be-a-grown-up dance. The sewage hookup had been everyone's nightmare job, and Geena had lost the lottery they played that morning with broken spaghetti noodles. Again, thanks to their neighbor, Geena knew to go up to the office store and buy a box of disposable gloves.

Having purple nitrile hands made this process a tad less "ewy."

Hannah leaned out the window again. "I think it's ready."

"Thanks." This time Geena opened the gray water valve, letting all the non-sewage water clean out the pipe. The pipe jerked about as a large quantity of water slushed down its length.

"All right, now the bucket of water."

Brooke walked around to the service side of the RV. "Hey, Geena, how's it going?" Apparently paying more attention to making sure their neighbor was not around than to where she put her feet, Brooke kicked the hose. It popped out of the ground connection, and water spread all around her feet, sloshing over the toes of her UGGs.

"Oh gross!" she cried.

Geena wanted to laugh; she couldn't help it. She knew it wasn't nice of her to find humor at Brooke's expense, but part of her mind couldn't help but think it was karmic payback for all the crap she had put up with from Brooke over the years. Besides, what was a grand RV adventure without at least one sewage mishap? And here they were getting it out of the way on the very first morning.

Hannah leaned out the window. "What happened?"

"I'm going to puke," Brooke cried, obviously thinking that sewage had just surrounded her.

"It's just water. It's just water." Geena bit her lips together, and breathed heavily through her nose to suppress the laugh that wanted out. "We had already finished flushing the pipe; it's gray water. Basically, it's clean."

Brooke collapsed into herself, her shoulders pulled up and in, her hands like claws under her chin, as if she could pull her upper half away from her lower half. "Ew ew ew ew ew."

She pranced away from the water. "I need a shower, and I'm tossing these boots."

Brooke muttered "gross" and "ew" as she gingerly walked back around to the front of the RV. Geena followed.

Hannah met them at the door with a towel, soap, and a pair of flip-flops. "We'll finish up."

As soon as Brooke was out of sight in the bathhouse, Geena and Hannah started laughing. They laughed until they cried. "What a way to start the trip: panic attacks and sewage spills."

"I know," Geena agreed, wiping at her eyes, "but if I didn't laugh, I'd be crying."

"Poor Brooke."

"She's gonna be so mad."

"I think she already is. She just bought those boots."

∾

Geena decided she was awake and alert enough to take the first driving shift, and that she would nap later. The highway stretched out flat and straight in front of them. "I can almost understand why some people think they can put the RV on cruise control and go take a nap or make a sandwich."

"The road is hypnotically the same, isn't it?" Hannah agreed.

"At least we are out of critter suicide alley; that was gross."

"Hey, Brooke, were you able to look up why that section of highway had so many dead things?" Geena called behind her. "Brooke?"

Brooke sat at the dining booth, now converted into her

work space with her laptop, a notebook, and phone. Her fingers flew across the keyboard as she transcribed the words in her headphones.

"She can't hear you; she's plugged in," Hannah said, looking back at Brooke. "I've meant to ask, how's Gran?" Her phone buzzed.

"She knows who I am about half the time. Another text from Tim?"

"You know how he is," Hannah began. "Timmy worries about me; he's protective."

"Yes, I do, and the word you want there is possessive. He's got to understand you are allowed to have a life separate from him. What would he have been like if Ashley had come? Would he be constantly texting you—or her, expecting her to spy for him. He's protective to the point of..."

"Being overbearing." Hannah gasped and covered her open mouth. "I can't believe I just said that out loud." She giggled. "Yeah, the closer the wedding is, the more in my space he is."

Hannah leaned back in the passenger seat. "I think if Ashley had come, he would still be texting me. Too bad she changed her mind. I think this would have been one of those amazing bonding experiences for us. I really want us to be the kind of sisters-in-law who are good friends too." She sighed. "Then Tim wouldn't have to worry about either of us, and not have to keep tabs on me all the time."

Geena scoffed. "It's 'cause he thinks we are lesbian lovers or something. Let's make a sex tape and send it to him. And watch his head explode!"

"Geena! I can't believe you just said that!" Hannah gasped.

"Seriously, why can't we have time with you without him

constantly barging in? And don't say because he's being protective or because he loves you so much. It's not my sparkling personality he is seeking out. He's made it pretty clear his opinion of me."

"What did you do or say to him for that?" Hannah asked.

"I breathe, Hannah. That's it. I've known you longer, and I'm your friend. That's all he's ever needed not to like me."

"But he's tried to set you up with his friends."

"His friends? I think he found the most desperate guys in that frat to take me out to get me away from hanging out with you."

"They weren't all bad. What was that tall, good-looking one's name, Dax?" Hannah typed a reply to Tim's text.

"Right, Dax the date rapist?"

"He did what?"

"He did nothing, made it real clear he wasn't attracted to thick girls. He said I wasn't even worth date raping. He was a real charmer. Tim set me up with some of the meanest, rudest, biggest, ugliest jerk faces ever. His choices trump the losers Brooke always tries to introduce me to. At least he hasn't even bothered to get any get-Geena-out-of-the-way dates since you got engaged. I love you, missy, and I will support you because you love him so much. But Tim doesn't like me."

Hannah shrugged. "Maybe you'll meet someone on this trip. Someone not from Atlanta."

"That's what I need, a fling, someone not looking for the trifecta of southern-belle female perfection." Geena scoffed.

"You mean thin, white, and rich?" Hannah asked.

Geena nodded. "You're already taken, and Brooke with her two out of three always meets guys."

"Oh come off it, Geena. You're"—Hannah paused—"well, one out of three?"

Geena shook her head. "Oh-for-oh, especially if Gran is counting. You know how proud Gran is that her ancestors bucked the system. These days she remembers the past better than the present. I mean I know it's not like a third of Atlanta doesn't claim Cherokee heritage, but you'd be surprised how many poop heads there are out there about it—"

"Fuck him! Motherfucking asshole!" At that moment Brooke threw off her headphones and slammed her phone to the floor before stomping to the bathroom. She had to slam the door several times to get it to close and stay shut.

Geena and Hannah looked at each other with wide eyes. Hannah undid her seat belt and rushed to the back of the RV to talk to Brooke through the bathroom door. Hannah's cell phone, left on the passenger seat, buzzed with another text. Geena picked it up and glanced at it.

Love you, Hans. My bad texted that to work buddy comedy ensued.

Geena harrumphed. Tim engaging in office comedy—she would only believe it if she saw it. Even then it would probably be drier than an old-school British TV comedy. Tim didn't have a sense of humor.

Geena sort of felt bad for Brooke. This trip had mostly been Brooke and Ashley's idea. So far Brooke had had to work, endure flying biting bugs, get propositioned by annoying old men, nasty sewagey water on her shoes, and now whatever this was about. Brooke was not used to so many things going awry. She tended to have the easy road in life.

2

The RV campground spread out in a large, wide-open, flat parking lot. Brick bathhouses were scattered at regular intervals. It was spotlessly clean, with no trees or shrubs. This was camping in a luxury parking lot. The night before they had camped under a canopy of trees. Geena loved how each place was different. Tonight would be an easy night, with time to sleep in in the morning. And hopefully Brooke wouldn't complain about bugs, neighbors, or sewage.

Geena, Brooke, and Tim's sister, Ashley, had worked hard to sell Hannah on an RV road trip for her bachelorette outing. They'd wanted something epic and truly different. Geena had wanted to have some fun after the layoffs at work. Brooke had needed something she could weave into her flexible work schedule. Ashley had mostly wanted to get away from her parents and brother pre-wedding.

Geena knew they had sold the trip when their pitch equated "glamping" with money.

"Glamping? You're making that up," Hannah had said.

"No, she's not. Look it up; it's a thing," Brooke explained.

"Still sounds cheap. But glam-camping could be fun." Hannah sighed.

"Real glamping takes money. This is far from cheap. Do you have any idea how much these things cost?" Geena asked.

"They can't be that much." Hannah resisted her friend's sales pitch.

"Ashley, pull up the Prevost site," Geena said.

A large silver and black bus displayed on the laptop screen. "The ones like this run way over a hundred grand new. So this involves having some serious money."

"Oh, go to Pinterest and show her glamping pictures," Brooke added.

Money talked around Hannah, and her friends knew that if there was something she was on the fence with uncertainty, just tell her it was expensive or that of course the rich did it. Hannah had been raised to equate expensive with quality.

"Okay, I'll ask Daddy. Who knows, maybe he will even offer to pay for it since its officially part of the wedding activities." Hannah's father owned one of the largest hot tub retail and installation companies in Georgia, Harris Hot Tubs and Spas. Hannah had been featured in his television commercials since she was born. She was the much loved and highly spoiled only child of a wealthy man.

The cost, while somewhat reasonable, was still a stretch on Geena's freshly laid-off income. When Daddy Harris picked up the tab on the RV rental, Geena was beyond thrilled. Unfortunately Ashley bailed on the trip at the last minute. Geena had secretly been relying on Ashley to serve as a buffer between herself and Brooke. Hannah was Geena's oldest friend; even though sometimes Hannah was clueless, she would put up with a lot for

Hannah—including dealing with her possessive fiancé Tim and her narcissistic cousin Brooke. Hannah's father covering the cost had been a game changer for this trip as far as she was concerned. Geena would definitely put up with dealing with Brooke for a free trip to the Grand Canyon.

Hannah popped her head back in the open door. "Hey, Geena, the bathhouses are swank. They have those huge waterfall showers. Nice and big. And doors that lock!"

"Oh good, that bathhouse last night was gross."

Brooke stepped into the RV. "All hooked up; let me wash my hands." Geena moved out of the way so Brooke could reach the sink to wash up. She seemed to have calmed down substantially after her minor meltdown on the road, explaining her outburst as a reaction to work suddenly requiring extra hours while they knew she was traveling.

"That hot tub has my name on it," Brooke said to Hannah after she turned and climbed back down the stairs. "Wanna come, Geena?"

"No, I'm going to lie down for a bit. I swear I can see highway stripes when I close my eyes. I never did take that nap."

Hannah and Brooke said "okay" and "bye" before they left to head over to the brick-enclosed patio area that featured the pool facilities.

Geena stretched out on the sofa. Just fifteen minutes. Then change for the hot tub. Getting into a tub of warm water right now would put her to sleep. She didn't think that drowning on this trip would be much fun.

The RV park was wide open, and the facilities people were kind enough to put three to four spaces between the different rigs. Louder, closer rumbles told her that someone was pulling into a nearby space. The distant swish noise from the freeway filtered in through the open windows, lulling Geena to sleep.

Geena dozed off. She realized she had slept when she awoke to voices. Two familiar female voices and an unfamiliar male voice. She focused in on the male voice. It had a lovely deep timbre, sounded like a man in his prime, not too young, not too old. She listened for other voices, another man, kids, a female traveling companion. She didn't hear anything. The voices trailed off, and she heard thumps and clanks and grunts. Brooke stepped into the RV. Geena sat up and rubbed her eyes.

"Looks like we have another chatty neighbor. This one is obsessed with his motorcycle. It gets old real fast," Brooke said to Geena as she headed back outside with their picnic setup.

Geena turned and looked out the window. Hannah and Brooke were setting up the picnic table and attending to something on the grill. Hannah's hair was wet. Geena had slept longer than expected. Hannah and Brooke had already been to the hot tub and back, and now set up for dinner.

She couldn't see their neighbor, but she heard his voice again. It wasn't clear, but Hannah was smiling and shaking her head. "No, really, I don't think so. Motorcycles make me nervous."

Ah, Brooke had said he was obsessed with his motorcycle. Geena formed a picture of a rugged, burly, bear man with a long, scraggly beard and a leather jacket in her head. That was until she heard his voice again. Her mental image of him got younger, skinnier, and took on a more hipster flair with the beard—still full but more groomed.

It wasn't until Geena stepped out of the RV that she could see this mystery man. She stood at the bottom of the door and held to the frame of the RV for balance; she didn't quite feel fully awake. Their neighbor did not meet either of her predetermined mental images. This man was gorgeous. Well, what she could see of his broad back and behind certainly was. His shoulders were wide, and his tight, faded red T-shirt showed off a chiseled back and arm muscles that a superhero would be jealous of. His thighs were long and lean and encased in faded jeans that pulled tight across his legs and shapely rear end. He squatted down next to an elaborately painted customized motorcycle, a chopper.

The bike was a citrusy orange color with licks of lime-green flames and paler pin-striped scroll details. The chrome work looked new. Geena wasn't usually a motorcycle enthusiast, but she didn't need to be one to admire excellent artistry when she saw it. This looked like it had come from one of those TV shows where they made customized choppers, maybe even more beautiful. No wonder he was obsessed with it.

She hoped the man was half as attractive as the bike. *Please, oh please, oh please be as gorgeous when you stand up.* She caught a glimpse of curling dark hair, but his head was tilted forward and away from her. When he straightened up, he unfolded taller and taller. He stood well over six feet tall with thick hair that brushed his collar.

When he turned around, Geena stopped breathing. He was glorious. She continued to lean against the RV, as any stability she did have vanished as she admired the man. His jaw was square and sculpted, his nose long and straight with the slightest arch, his cheekbones high and sharp. He had thick black eyebrows that topped large, deep-set hazel eyes in a slightly olive complexion. He smiled. It caused the slightest creasing at the corners of his eyes. His teeth were perfectly straight, and his skin set off their Hollywood-dentistry white. Geena was too dazzled to think that maybe he was too unrealistically perfect, but Brooke was not impressed.

"She said she's not interested. Why don't you just drop it?" Brooke snapped.

"No offense," he said. "I really was asking if either of you wanted to take a ride."

Geena found her voice. "Does that offer include me?" She paused to catch her self-confidence. "'Cause I'd love to be taken for a ride." She would take any ride this man offered. If she had to describe her ideal dream lover's looks, this was the picture she would expect to see.

The man angled toward her, seeing her for the first time. He paused and slowly looked at her. Geena felt his gaze rake up and down her form as if he made physical contact. If it was possible, the broad grin he sported grew even larger. "That offer most definitely includes you, pretty girl."

Geena watched as he licked his teeth, running the pink tip of his tongue along the edge of perfect white teeth. The unexpected sex appeal in that one swipe of tongue made her mouth go dry. He gave her a predatory gaze the likes of which she'd never received before. The gaze identified her as a woman he was interested in doing manly things with. She desperately hoped she was reading him right or she was about to make a fool of herself. She had to remember how to flirt and not just throw herself on him.

"It's a pretty bike," she said, approaching him. She tried not to sway her hips as she walked toward him, but something in his gaze made her want to swish everything she had in his direction.

"Don't be naive, Geena. He's not talking about a ride on his bike. He's being a perv." Brooke had clearly taken offense at this guy.

"Ya know, Brooke, sometimes an offer for a ride on a

motorcycle is just that, an offer for a ride on a motorcycle. He's got the pretty bike out; he obviously plans on using it. I'm sure this is just what it appears, an offer for a ride on the motorcycle." She emphasized each word for Brooke, and then turned back to the man. "Right?"

He sighed. "Yes, this is what it appears to be at face value, a ride on the bike this lovely evening."

"There isn't room for your butt on that bike, Geena. Get real." There it was. Brooke had lasted almost two days before letting the weight comments slip. Brooke always seemed to want to deflate her joy. Geena wasn't going to let her take this moment from her. She gritted her teeth and grinned as if she hadn't heard a word.

"Oh, there is plenty of room for her," the man replied. Geena decided ignoring Brooke worked. And to think, she'd thought Brooke had gotten over her earlier foul mood. This went beyond having a bad day at work. Usually Brooke went after the tall, good-looking ones, but for some reason this evening she was on the verbal attack. Hannah was just being Hannah. She barely talked to men now that she was engaged. Geena couldn't help but think, fine, they were not interested, then more for her.

"You don't even know him."

Geena leveled a glare on Brooke. After turning back to the gorgeous man, she stuck her hand out in greeting. "I'm Geena Davies."

He folded her hand into his larger one. She felt small and dainty around him. Geena never felt dainty; she liked this feeling. "Like the actress?"

"Daveez, not Daviss." She emphasized the *eeez* and the *iss*. "I get that a lot. I think she was kind of a big name actress when I was born, not really sure. My parents don't pay much attention to movies and things. They probably heard her name and thought the combination sounded good."

"Fair enough. Dante Palatine." He held her hand longer than what was politely necessary.

"Dante? Well, aren't you Italian?"

"Not as much as my name would suggest. I use spaghetti sauce from a jar." He winked at her.

Geena's insides did a flip. "Somewhere you have an Italian grandmother spinning in her grave."

"I'm sure I do, spinning at high velocity." He laughed. It was a deep, warm sound.

Geena decided she could listen to him laugh forever.

"I'd love to go for a ride if the offer stands."

"It sure does. I even have an extra helmet." Dante left to rummage in the cab of his truck, giving Geena an excellent view of his backside. He returned carrying two helmets: a large white helmet with full-face coverage and a smaller black one. He placed the white helmet on the seat of the bike and strode over to Hannah, who had been watching the exchange but not interfering the way Brooke had. He handed her a business card and another piece of paper. "This is my phone number, and this is the pink slip to my truck. I'm not going to hurt your friend. I'm not some serial killer. I'm just going to take her for a ride. The card is yours to keep, the pink slip I get back when I return your friend safe and sound."

Returning to Geena, he began placing the smaller helmet on his own head. "So you like to ride?"

"I've never been on a motorcycle. I just figured if you were really offering rides, then this would be a pretty bike to ride on."

"Okay then, let's get this helmet on you and get you situated on the bike."

As he snugged the helmet strap under her chin, she asked, "What do I hold on to?"

"Me." He grinned at her.

"That's it?"

"That's it, and put your feet here, not there," he said, flipping down some pegs and pointing at a pipe.

He balanced the bike and helped her onto the seat. Geena watched as Dante awkwardly straddled the bike to mount in front of her. It was clear it would have been easier for him to get on first. But he was a gentleman, and he'd helped her first. *I bet he makes sure the lady always comes first in bed too.* Geena closed her eyes and hoped she hadn't started blushing.

"You're gonna give that bike a flat tire."

Geena ignored Brooke's quip.

Geena tentatively placed her arms around Dante's waist. He pulled her in closer as if he was tightening a seat belt. Her breasts pressed into his hard back, and her arms circled a set of rock-hard abs. How could she not think about sex pressed up against him like this? Glad he couldn't see her, Geena was sure she blushed now.

The motorcycle roared to life, and everything between her legs started rumbling with a rhythmic vibration. No wonder boys with bikes got girlfriends. Dante eased the bike forward. With the motion, she realized she wasn't holding on tight enough. She tightened her grip, and Dante patted her hand as if to say, *tight enough, I need to breathe.*

He navigated the bike slowly out of the RV park and headed north on the main road. The road was long and straight and headed away from the rest of civilization. This was exhilarating. Geena began to giggle. The giggling caused her to jiggle. Dante shifted his back against her. It created a delightful friction, and Geena's nipples responded in a positive sexual fashion, hardening into peaks.

They sped up the road for what felt like a minute before Dante pulled onto the shoulder. He swung his leg forward and over, dismounting the bike. "I need to visit those bushes for a minute," he indicated with a nod of his head.

Embarrassed, and not wanting to get caught being some peeper-creeper, Geena carefully and purposefully looked the other direction.

"Want to try going a little faster?" he asked when he returned. "You will need to hold on a little tighter."

"I thought I was maybe squeezing you too tight," she said, her cheeks warm with flush from the excitement.

"I don't think you could hold me tight enough." He winked.

This time she was tempted to see if she could sneak a feel of his chest while holding on.

The ride back to the RV park was even more exciting than the first part of the ride. His wink when they turned around made her breathless. He didn't seem to mind her squish. And he hadn't made a single comment about her breasts against his back, or the size of her butt causing a flat tire. It felt like the bike flew. She closed her eyes and held on tight. She had to admit this might be a little too fast, so she focused on the feel of his body and his smell. He smelled clean with a hint of pine. She was so focused on holding on that she barely noticed the bike slowing down. She didn't want to let go when the bike stopped, more from fear than from enjoying the feel of him. Even though she thoroughly enjoyed the feel of him.

Dante slowly peeled her arms from around his waist. Geena was disappointed she had to let go. He helped her off the bike and steadied her as she found her land legs again.

He removed his helmet, then stooped down to help her off with the one she wore. "You survive?"

"That was great!" she gushed. "But..."

"A little too fast?"

"Yeah, at the end, it was a bit too much."

"Well, next time, not so fast."

Geena mentally spun in joy; he had just said *next time*. Of course this was a chance meeting with a handsome camping neighbor. There wouldn't be a next time.

They parted ways after their return to the RV park. Dante made excuses and carried off a bundle toward the laundry facilities near the pool. Hannah and Brooke had already finished dinner, and waited for her. She sat and ate the small piece of grilled chicken and the salad that was left. Lunch had been such a large affair that a small dinner was all that was needed. Besides, Geena's stomach was full of butterflies from the ride and meeting Dante. She couldn't eat much.

"So where did you go?" Hannah asked.

"He just drove up that way." Geena pointed, indicating the road. "Then we came back. Oh my gosh, it was so much fun." She took another bite of food. After swallowing, she continued. "He's really sweet; he made sure I held on tight. And didn't go fast until I said I was willing to try it."

"I can't believe you did that. Geena, he could be dangerous," Brooke chastised.

"Yes, he could, but he wasn't. Brooke, it was just a ride on a bike." Geena defended her actions.

"You've done worse," Hannah added.

"I have not," Brooke huffed indignantly.

"Spring break, senior year, Cancun. You took off on a pontoon for three days and didn't tell anyone you left,"

Hannah stated. "I got a text about four hours after you left, saying you were off with a new friend, see ya later, bye."

Geena stared pointedly at Brooke.

"Fine, fine," Brooke sighed. "I'm just trying to look out for you."

Geena dropped her gaze. If she said anything now, she would be the one to come across as the bad guy, not Brooke. Not protective, worldly Brooke.

"Men like that are predatory. You aren't used to them. You usually date such nice guys."

"I usually date turds, Brooke. He's different, but you have already decided he's not one of the good ones, and frankly, I think he is."

"Can't be; he's too attractive. A guy that good-looking is entirely too self-centered to be a nice guy. He's built; he clearly spends too much time working out to look a certain way."

"Oh, and you don't?"

"Well, yes, I do, so I have to deal with guys like him at the gym. You don't." Brooke gave Geena a sneer.

"I don't know, Brooke," Hannah cut in. "He seemed actually quite friendly and nice. I really don't think he was hitting on either of us. And once Geena agreed to go on the bike, all his attention was on her. That seems pretty decent to me."

Brooke snorted through her nose. It was clear that she thought neither Hannah nor Geena would understand.

"Well at least," Geena said to Hannah, "she didn't say he was gay."

"True." They both laughed. "Boys who look like that tend to like boys who look like that," they said in chorus.

They laughed harder. Brooke softened and grinned.

"Well," Geena said as she picked up her dishes and

headed to the garbage, "if he's gay, sign me up for a sex change."

∽

Geena awoke at a grossly ridiculous hour for someone who did not have to go to work. She felt refreshed, with no sleep paralysis issues this morning. It was too early to make coffee and wake the other two. After getting dressed, she quietly left the RV and headed to the bathhouses.

"Good morning, Geena," a deep voice said from behind her. She turned to see Dante leaning against the side of his Airstream. It appeared he had just been unhooking it, getting ready to head out.

"Hey, Dante." Geena's heart beat faster. She tried not to be terribly flustered. But she was. This morning his hair was pulled back under a bandana, his chin covered with a heavy dusting of beard. "You leavin'?"

Damn, she didn't want him to go. She didn't know how to ask for his phone number. She was always so bad at this.

"After a morning ride. Care to join me? Do you have time?"

"Sure, they're still asleep. We don't have plans to head out until ten-ish."

"C'mon, I'll buy you a coffee. There's bound to be at least one coffee shop or doughnut place that way." He indicated toward town.

"Sure, let me put this up." She hadn't showered. She could take one later. Heck, missing a shower to be with Dante would be worth it. She hurried back to the RV and made sure she had on plenty of deodorant—just because she hadn't showered didn't mean she needed to smell like it.

Dante was already waiting on the bike with it rumbling

when she came out of the RV. She stood patiently next to him as he secured the helmet for her. She managed to swing herself onto the back of the bike. With time this could be easy. "I left the girls a note; they can text me when they wake up if we aren't back yet."

The morning was sharp and clear. Geena didn't typically enjoy this time of day. Of course when she was awake before seven a.m., it was in order to go to work, not exactly an enjoyable process. She had a few weeks of sleeping in allowed, she reminded herself, so why wasn't she asleep now? Maybe she'd subconsciously heard Dante and woke to find him. For whatever reason, she was glad she'd woken up early. Having her arms around Dante was a great way to start her day.

They didn't ride very far before Dante pulled into a doughnut shop with an outdoor patio. Geena cleared off a table while Dante ordered coffees. He surprised her by bringing out half a dozen doughnuts. "I didn't know what you liked, so I got a variety. Please tell me you eat doughnuts."

"Heck yeah, I eat doughnuts." Geena leaned forward and grabbed the chocolate-covered one first.

He smiled and stretched in his chair. He really was tall, and long, as she watched him reach back over his head.

"Just how tall are you? Your arms seem to stretch out there for miles."

"I'm six-three-ish. I come from a tall family. My cousin—that's his Airstream I'm pulling—he's six-five or so. I'm positively short compared to him."

"I can't imagine you as being short. I mean, I'm short. Hannah is short. Six-three is not short."

"Height is all relative. It doesn't matter if you're tall or short. We're all pretty much the right height when we're on our backs." Dante waggled his eyebrows at her and gave her a leering grin.

Geena's jaw dropped, and her cheeks tightened and felt warm with a flush. "Dante!"

"Sorry." He sat up, placing his coffee on the table. "That was lewd; my apologies."

"That was lewd." She grinned at him. "Accurate but lewd."

He laughed. Geena like the way the sound rumbled deep in his chest.

"So now that we have established that I am lewd, what's your story, Geena Davies?" He took a long pull on his coffee. "What's with the traveling princess road show?"

"Princess road show? Excuse me?"

"No offense, Geena, but the three of you are some kind of road trip wet dream: the blonde, the brunette, and the redhead. Three beautiful women, each one more beautiful than the next. You're like a collection of movie princesses. Hannah, small, delicate, brownish-red hair. I bet she's really bookish too. She's the one from *Beauty and the Beast*. Then your Amazon friend, the one that wanted to castrate me on sight yesterday."

"Brooke."

"She's like some warrior princess, but she looks like Cinderella, slender, tall, blonde. And then you." He paused to inhale.

"Me, I'm there to make the other two look good."

"No." He shook his head. "You're the gem, with that raven hair, blue eyes..." His voice faded off. "And those pink lips." He paused, staring at her. He held her gaze for a full minute before shaking his head again. "You're Snow White."

"I may have been Snow White once, but I've drifted."

Geena took a large bite of a glazed doughnut and munched at him, unsure what to make of his gaze.

He laughed.

"Hannah is getting married. This little vacation is her bachelorette party on wheels. There were supposed to be four of us, but her future sister-in-law ditched us. So it's me, Hannah, and her cousin Brooke. Hannah and I always talked about seeing places around the country together, and with her getting married, it just seemed like this was our one shot at doing it. We've flown off to Vegas a few times, but that really is never as much fun as everyone tries to make it. You know, too much stress to have a good time. Too much"—Geena raised the pitch of her voice—"'This is us having a good time.'" She let her voice return to normal. "This way, we get to see things like that Cadillac Ranch just up the road, with the cars planted upright like some Detroit Stonehenge but in the middle of Texas. Today we head over to Santa Fe. We'll see the Georgia O'Keefe Museum and hopefully get some good tamales. Then it's the Grand Canyon. Four do-whatever days at the Grand Canyon. Then back on the road home."

"Hey, me too. I'll be at the Grand Canyon in a couple of days. I will come find you there."

"I'd like that." She knew she smiled too much, her cheeks hurt. She actually didn't care if she was foolish. Dante paid particular attention to her, and she planned on enjoying it while she could.

"What about you?"

"I'm multitasking. I have to head into the reservation today to see about finding some missing family members."

"Oh jeez, I'm sorry. You have family that's missing?" Geena sat upright. A pit formed in her stomach. She felt here she was, wasting his time, and he had to help locate someone.

"Oh no, not like that; I said that wrong. Genealogy stuff. I'm looking to fill in the gaps in the family tree type of thing. My branch of the family believes we have some relatives in the Navajo tribe, and I'm going to meet some possible cousins."

"Oh, that scared me."

Dante rubbed her forearm soothingly. "I'm sorry to cause you alarm; bad word choice."

"And what's your other task—you said multitasking? That's your cousin's Airstream, right? Taking it for a tour?"

"No, technically I'm working."

"This is work?"

"Yep, this is work. Morgan likes to have his own trailer on job sites and not stay at hotels. You know, the comforts of your own stuff and all. So I'm hauling it back to him in California. Sonoma."

"You had to drive your truck out here to pick it up?" Geena asked, mindlessly tearing off bites of doughnut as she listened.

"No, I flew out to New Orleans, where Morgan had been. He and his wife were doing some Habitat type work after some floods. Just bought the truck; it still has that new car smell to it."

"What about your bike? How did you get that there?"

"Oh, the bike is new too. I hadn't expected to get that, but when it showed up as being available on an online chopper board I follow, I couldn't resist. The guy who had them do that build out, in the end, couldn't pay for the work. So I bought him out. That's why I got the truck, so that I could haul both. Otherwise I would have just used the old SUV Morgan hauled it out with."

"You just bought a custom bike at random? Isn't that expensive?" She bit her lip. Money wasn't something you should talk about with someone you just met. She realized that was a bit rude.

"It can be." Dante nodded. "I put it all on Morgan's American Express, he'll end up taking it out of my expenses or pay or something."

Geena's phone began buzzing. "Looks like they are awake," she said, checking her text messages.

Dante stood up. "Let's get you back before they can get out of the bathhouses, so they can't be too upset that I swept you away for some alone time." He winked at her.

Dante and Geena returned to the RV park with plenty of time to spare before either Hannah or Brooke returned from their morning ablutions. Geena watched as he loaded the bike onto the back of the truck using a ramp made of boards. She moved out of the way as he backed the truck up to the Airstream and hooked up the trailer.

She wanted to throw her arms around him and kiss him goodbye. This morning's coffee break had been one of the best dates she'd been on in a very long time. Even though she knew it wasn't a date-date, she certainly wished it had been. She stood next to him in front of the truck door. Geena stuck out her hand to shake his. "Goodbye, Dante Palatine. Thank you for the ride on your bike."

Dante kissed the back of her hand. "This isn't goodbye, pretty girl. I'll come find you at the Grand Canyon. I'm a good tracker when I need to be."

Geena watched as Dante climbed into the cab of his truck. Making sure she was safely out of the way, he pulled out of the RV park. *And out of my life.* The pang of disappointment in Geena's chest hurt a bit more than she expected.

Hannah approached from the bathhouse. She waved as Dante drove away. "He's pulling out already?"

"Yeah, he would have left earlier but I was outside, so we got to talking."

Brooke joined them, watching Dante drive away. "Why do you look sad?"

"Because, Brooke, he is one of the nice ones, and he just left."

"Oh my God. Did you have sex with him this morning?"

"No, Brooke, he fed me doughnuts."

3

Dante eased the truck onto the freeway. He'd started the day behind schedule. Then again, he didn't mind. When he had been ready to load up the bike, he spotted Geena sashaying toward the bathhouse. Geena, glowing Geena. Did that woman not know how much va-va-voom she put into her walk? She reminded him of a line from an old Marilyn Monroe movie, "like Jell-O on springs." Maybe she had seen him and was being tempting on purpose. He'd planned to watch her backside work its way into the bathhouse, but then he had an overwhelming desire to be between her thighs again. Even if it was innocently, on the back of his bike, and he was facing the wrong direction. His thoughts would never be innocent when it came to Geena.

Dante was not looking for any female distraction on this trip. But it had certainly found him. The redhead in New Orleans had been a bit too crazy. She had said she was only interested in a good time. So was he. What she was doing was window-shopping for a baby daddy. Fortunately, Dante had been prepared, even when she had stated a preference for going "bareback." Dante preferred bareback as well, but not when the girl in question was apparently working on an agenda that would end with the word *paternity*. He wasn't in need of another complication so soon. Nothing about Geena had been complicated. Her smile was genuine, and her sex appeal natural. And a soft pink aura surrounded her.

The small one with fine bones had commented on his chopper first. Dante was still proud of his new purchase and happy to show it off. It really had just been part of natural conversation to ask her if she wanted to take a ride on it. That's when the tall blonde amazon attacked, jumping down his throat. She had been overly protective in a stay-away-from-my-property kind of way. She'd treated him like scum who dared to talk to her in a bar, which was interesting because he hadn't been talking to her. She had been attractive until she opened her mouth. Looks were not everything; attitude and personality could make or break a pretty face.

That's when the sassy, cute one stepped out of the RV and onto the back of his bike. First, he only heard her sweet, soft voice. The voice of an angel forthcoming with one hell of a come-on. "I'd love to be taken for a ride."

Of course, she meant the bike, but that was not the kind of ride his body immediately wanted. Not when he heard that soft Southern accent. Her voice went straight to his balls. Her girlfriends were good-looking, but they couldn't compare to her. Her long raven-black hair emphasized her pale features. Geena had the sweetest heart-shaped face, the bluest eyes framed in impossibly long black eyelashes, pink lips with a natural pucker that spread into the warmest smile, curves for miles, and she was not afraid to flirt. He had not missed the barbs her friends shot at her. She seemed to ignore them, brushed them off as good-natured teasing. No, she was not thin, but that didn't matter. He liked women—all shapes, all sizes, all colors. He wanted to know what her hair would feel like in his fingers. He could image all too well kissing those full lips. She didn't need the obvious mate aura for him to be attracted to her. But it didn't hurt.

And then there had been that ride. It had been entirely too brief. It had been torture. He tried to not react to her when she started giggling and squirming so seductively against his back, but he had to shift his muscles a bit. Feeling her nipples brush against his back had caused an instant and equal reaction in him. He'd become completely hard for this woman. He imagined driving her far out into the country and taking her on the back of the motorcycle. Sinking into her softness, palming her breasts, grabbing handfuls of milky-white flesh. His imagination needed a cold shower. She seemed to successfully ignore her physical reaction. He had to do the same. But damn, she had felt good.

He wanted to drop everything and follow her to the Grand Canyon. But he had work to do. He needed to focus on why he was out here. He had to fill the gaps in the family tree, make sure none of the family was lost, alone, or vulnerable to the negative influences of a few vampires. See if he really could track down family from when Margarita Palatine ran away in the early 1900s. He needed to find out how far the lineage went, and who else may be carrying the genetic characteristics that were a predominant feature of the family.

The Palatine family. Calling them a family always made Dante feel like it was some mafia organization instead of what it was, a wolf pack. Today they were more like an old clan of extended family members, family by blood and family by choice. Dante didn't want to overthink it, but the similarities were too close for comfort at times. Strong family ties, a job in the family business if you had the talent or inclination. Questionable legal activities. Well, Dante realized that was mostly him. Julia Palatine, his cousin, ran Truria entirely on the up-and-up. It was a growing business with multiple subsidiaries, a stable financial standing, and prosperous future. And she was growing it into the genetics market to help corner some DNA findings with wolf genes.

Dante's specialty was investigating and taking care of problems. Of course, that usually meant throwing money around more than his muscles and his bite. Typically money and a well-placed threat were all he needed as a means to an end if a situation ever got out of hand.

Their family was older than the Roman Empire. They traced their history back as far as the founders of Rome. From a time of gods and men, before the gods left men to face their own follies on earth. The Palatine's traced their lineage back to Remus and Romulus, the famous twins suckled by a she-wolf, who founded the city that grew into the history-defining empire.

History had parts of the story right. Their mother, Rhea Silvia, had been sentenced to living her life as a vestal virgin after her uncle, Amulius, deposed her father, the king of Alba Longa, an ancient pre-Roman city.

The war god Mars, tempted by Rhea Silvia's beauty, gave her two healthy sons, the twins Remus and Romulus. She was sentenced to death for breaking her vestal vows of celibacy, and the twin boys were also sentenced to death. Thinking that the god Mars would spare his city if the three died from exposure to the elements, Amulius threw all three into the River Tiber

The river god, Tibernius, swept them to safety in the swamps at the foot of the Palatine Hill. Their myth had the twins being suckled by a she-wolf, an animal sacred to Mars, until they were found and raised by a shepherd. Where the tale went wrong was in assuming that Rhea Silvia and the wolf, Lupa, were two different beings.

The shepherd Faustulus and his wife, Acca Laren'tia, raised the two boys. His wife, in some of the stories, was known as "lupa." Another misguided use of language. Acca Laren'tia, Rhea Silvia, and the she-wolf Lupa, were all the same. It was never clear in the myths, but had Mars been attracted to Rhea Silvia because she was a wolf, or had Mars transformed her into a wolf because she was special to him? By changing her identity and marrying the shepherd, Rhea Silvia was able to raise her sons and guide them through their changing natures, increased strength and agility when they entered puberty.

Remus and Romulus grew into fierce warriors. They even reclaimed the city of Alba Longa for their grandfather. When he tried to gift them with the city, they refused in favor of starting their own. They returned to the place where they first found sanctuary as infants, the Palatine Hill. An argument over building the city on the Palatine Hill or the neighboring Aventine Hill resulted in Romulus killing his brother. Some stories claim that Remus fell in an accident climbing the wall his brother had built around the hill, but it had been a bloody wolf fight for dominance. This was also the beginning of the long-lived rivalry between the Aventine family and the Palatines. The rivalry between the two families was well-documented and infamous in its level of brutality. At times the rivalry calmed and the families united, only to split over petty arguments. The family conflict was so famous it was rumored to have inspired Shakespeare.

The Palatine family had experienced a resurgence in power, both financially and with the number of shifting wolves in the family. Midcentury, the lupine gene had seemed to begin fading out. Toward the end of the twentieth century, more children carrying the active lupine gene were being born. New family management practices also contributed to an increase in power. This wasn't leading to a separation in family ties, but a strengthening. And they were cooperating with the Aventines. Julia, a rare female alpha, had recently accepted the Aventine's second alpha as her mate. The joining of two of the families' dominant alphas positively would contribute to a prolonged peace.

Morgan, the Palatine's primary alpha, wanted stronger alliances with other pack families. Families that hid their secrets from the world and each other. Something they did for self-preservation. A recent genetic discovery made hiding from each other seem not to be the best course of action moving forward. Coupled with a renewed threat from a vampire everyone thought dead, Morgan wanted to make sure there were no wolves out there on their own. That was Dante's current job: tracking down wolf shifters, following rumors, locating family, making sure there were no lost branches, no wolves without family support. Any wolf Dante found was to be invited back to the family stronghold in California. If they chose not to go, they were at least provided with whatever they needed, securing them financially and emotionally for the Palatine family. If Dante found wolves not directly related to the Palatines, he was to invite them to ally with the Palatines, or encourage them to re-ally with their larger family pack. The thought being, a lone wolf would have a hard time hiding if they weren't aware they could be identified through their DNA.

Dante's mind drifted back to Geena. He wanted to spend his time with her, not tracking down shifters. He wanted to feel her body with more than just his back. He wished she hadn't been so nervous while holding on and would have run her hands up and down his chest. He ran his hand absentmindedly across his own chest in the way he wanted Geena to have touched him. Just thinking about her ample softness and flesh made Dante hard.

He tried ignoring his erection, letting the blood ease back into his system, leaving him with sore balls. Thoughts of Geena were not going to allow him to relax. Every time he managed to refocus on driving, she would cross his mind, and his manhood would spring to attention again, surging against the front of his jeans. He undid the top of his pants to release the pressure, returning his focus to the road. He already missed her giggle and ability to blush. His hand began to stroke his length through his clothes. His thoughts wandered to her lips and what it would be like to kiss them. He continued to stroke his manhood, freeing it from the confines of his shorts. Fortunately the road was straight and traffic almost nonexistent. Still, this was not a smart choice to be making. With one hand on the steering wheel, he grabbed the only lotion he could find, sunscreen. *Well, it's not like that's gonna get a tan.* He squeezed the cool cream onto his erection. Driving took a bit of extra concentration; this was a hand job he could not devote all his focus to, so it took extra time. He stroked himself repeatedly, and thoughts of Geena helped until he spilled his satisfaction. Probably not the safest way to deal with the boredom of a long drive, he thought as he cleaned up with his shirt. He was going to hunt her down at the Grand

Canyon as soon as possible. He had to admit, his body craved her.

He pulled into the parking lot of the Diné Market. He'd made decent time on the long drive and arrived in Window Rock midafternoon. After finding a clean shirt in the trailer, he crossed the parking lot and grabbed lunch at the fast food place. Back in the Airstream, he sat at the dining table sorting through papers as he bit into his double cheeseburger. He needed to locate the lawyer he had been in communications with. He found the paperwork with the number and punched it into his phone.

The receptionist was professional and to the point. Yes, Mr. Saganitso was in the office and available today. Yes, Mr. Saganitso was well aware of Mr. Palatine's request and had collected the necessary information. The receptionist was also particularly helpful in providing driving instructions from the local McDonalds to the office. Finding the office was easy. Parking for the truck and the thirty-foot trailer was just as easy but probably illegal. Dante was sure he would get a ticket as he left the trailer in a dirt lot behind a neighboring building.

Mr. Saganitso's receptionist did not meet Dante's mental image of her. He had pictured a middle-aged woman with hair in a tight bun, severe features, wearing a no-nonsense gray suit. The young woman who greeted him when he walked through the door, had her long black hair loosely braided. Her features were soft and friendly, and her dress was as casual as Dante's: blue jeans and a T-shirt. When she called into the back office, Dante could not fail to hear her call Mr. Saganitso "dad." When Mr. Saganitso came out of his office, the family resemblance could not be mistaken. Both had the same oval face, deep copper coloring, high, broad cheekbones, and button nose.

Saganitso was a broad middle-aged man of middling height with an easy smile and friendly disposition. Saganitso invited Dante into his office, a room made for work more than as a place to impress clients. Full bookshelves lined the walls, and side tables contained organized stacks of books, files, and notepads. The notepad in from of him on his desk was covered with incoherent handwriting.

"I found one Margarita from the period you had me focus on. She married a Navajo named Joseph Tse-pe. She was Italian and apparently from California, so I followed that lineage. I was able to track down a few descendants of theirs. But there seems to have been a bit of a family feud a generation back with their grandchildren, and"—Saganitso shuffled papers around, flipping through the yellow pad of paper searching his notes—"it sounds like there is a family member no one talks about." He handed across a sheet of paper with a hand-drawn flow chart.

It was a blocky family tree with Joseph1 and Margarita at the top. The branches dropped down away from their names and spread to three male names. The first name, Joseph2, had a note with *WWII* and question mark next to it. The second name, Robert, was circled and connected to the name Alice. A connecting line branched to two girls named Margaret and Carol.

The third name, Peter, was circled with a line connecting to the name Grace and had two branches extending from it. Those branches ended with the name Joseph3 and a question mark. A note next to Joseph3's name indicated that he'd died while in Vietnam. The question mark next to Joseph3 was what Saganitso pointed to. "I couldn't get any clarity on this person. Whatever he or she did, the family could not forgive. Or at least this one can't forgive." He pointed at one of the girl's names under

Robert and Alice. "I spoke with Margaret. She's the one that gave me family history that connected back to where the information you provided ended. She was able to corroborate that Joseph1 left the reservation in the late teens or twenties and came back with an Italian bride, Margarita. According to Margaret, they had already had baby Joseph2 by the time they moved to the area. She rambled on a bit. I was able to build this family tree from her information. She shut down and wasn't willing to talk any more about family matters to me when I tried to get information about this one," he said, tapping on the question mark under Peter's name.

"Here." He handed over a computer printout with an address and phone number. "She lives at an assisted living facility in Farmington. You could make it up there by suppertime. I'm sure she would be willing to talk family with family. It sounded like she didn't have kids of her own. A visit would be good for her.

"Now about that myth you mentioned." Saganitso rummaged through another stack of books and pulled out a thin children's picture book. "This is a watered-down version, but it explains skin-walkers and their legend fairly succinctly. I really didn't find anything more than what you could find on the Internet."

After their meeting Dante thanked Saganitso and his daughter, then drove north to Farmington to find Margaret Tse-pe.

The entrance to the assisted living facility looked more like a hotel lobby. Dante had no trouble convincing the desk clerk that he was a distant cousin to Margaret Tse-pe, tracking down a long lost branch of his family. They called a caregiver to help Dante locate her in the dining hall since he had arrived toward the end of dinner. "Oh, she's always telling everyone she's Italian when we have spaghetti or lasagna."

Dante wasn't sure what to expect. He thought Margaret would be about his grandmother's age, and she was a mean old bat. He hoped Margaret would be easier to talk to than his grandmother.

"Margaret, honey. This young man thinks he's a cousin of yours." The caregiver said as she introduced Margaret to Dante.

Margaret looked up at Dante from her seated position at a dining table. "Don't look like anyone I'm related to." Margaret Tse-pe had salt-and-pepper hair cut short, her features were sharp, and her skin tone was dark like Saganitso's. She appeared to be in her mid- to late sixties, but she could be older. She was closer to his uncle's age than to that of his grandmother. Dante certainly didn't think of his uncle needing to live in assisted living, but then again with extended family everywhere on the Sonoma compound, Uncle Remi was never on his own. Margaret could have been living on her own. Most people her age did, but one illness, one accident could be fatal.

"I'm related to Margarita Palatine. I believe she was your grandmother. My name is Dante Palatine."

Upon hearing the name Margarita Palatine, Margaret's eyes lit up. "Well, sit down, boy. Make room for him. I told you I was Italian." She pronounced it "eye-talyun."

Margaret talked to Dante for several hours. Having a charming, good-looking young man visit her seemed to have put her in a chatty mood. At first she insisted that he tell her about the Palatines in California. She told Dante she knew Margarita had been from California, but had always imagined it was Los Angeles. It hadn't occurred to her that the Palatines would be involved in wine making in northern

California. She was excited to learn she was from a large extended family. Dante had several questions about what she remembered about her grandparents and her uncles. She confirmed that the family was told her Uncle Joseph was killed in World War II. It had been one of the reasons her Uncle Peter's children weren't really part of her family anymore. She wouldn't elaborate on what that meant. Dante could get her to admit there had been two boys, but when Joe had died in Vietnam, they just didn't talk about it. Dante tried to find out what she may have heard of skin-walkers. She called it a silly old legend to frighten children and left it at that.

She did talk about her sister's child. She had one niece. She was a "good girl" but hadn't visited much since her sister, Carol, passed after complications of bypass surgery.

Dante left after giving her his e-mail and promising to write her. It was late, and he hadn't made plans for staying in an RV park for the night. He found a local big-box store and pulled into the back of the parking lot. He didn't go to bed right away. He had a mobile Internet connection and was able to get some much needed work done, including contacting his uncle about Margaret and introducing them via a common e-mail message. He had to locate Margaret's niece. The desk clerk at the nursing home had not been able to give him any information. Even if she did have that information, she was not legally allowed to share it with Dante. He had to track her down on his own. He felt this was going to be an undertaking; Maggie Garcia turned out to be a popular name.

By the time he went to bed, Dante had located three women with the name. He hoped that one of them was the relative he was looking for.

4
———

Geena sat at the dining booth reviewing an area map the campgrounds they'd overnighted at had provided. The check-in clerk indicated parking lots where they could park the RV and take a shuttle into the historic old town area. They wouldn't have to struggle to find parking for the RV in an area that was already tight for cars.

Geena highlighted all the galleries she wanted to visit, while Hannah leaned over the map deciding which restaurant they would have lunch at before leaving. Not only was Santa Fe home to the Georgia O'Keeffe Museum and truly amazing mouthwatering tamales, but also shopping. Brooke had already circled a few shops she wanted to visit. Many of the shops had been closed after dinner when they went out strolling the previous evening. The three agreed to split their time as equally as possible between their interests.

They finished breakfast in the RV while planning their day before unhooking and leaving the campgrounds. By the time they parked and took a shuttle into downtown Santa Fe, Hannah was already talking about finding a street vendor and consuming whatever goodies they had. She had spotted a few set up in front of Park Plaza and was waxing poetically about the food.

This was what this trip had been about: being able to get out into the world and see what there was, eat new foods, walk around old towns, visit museums, shop. One of the perks to a road trip with an open schedule was the ability to change things at a moment's notice. And for Hannah, that meant food now. Geena decided this was already the best trip she had ever taken, and it was pretty fantastic that it was being paid for by Daddy Harris, and made all the better for having gotten to ride on that motorcycle with hot-man Dante. Sigh.

Brooke had razzed her a bit too much over Dante the day before. Geena even tried to call a truce, but Brooke acted as if she didn't know what Geena meant. "A truce is for people who are fighting. We are getting along just fine, sweetie."

Yes, Geena had taken off without telling the others. But in her defense they'd been asleep. At least Hannah had sided with her regarding that. Geena had left a note; it wasn't as if she up and disappeared. Hannah had also come to her defense when it came to understanding why she had taken off. Dante was incredibly good-looking, and he seemed to like Geena. Something Brooke could barely admit. For some reason, Brooke just did not like him. Talking about him offended her deeply. Not so secretly, Geena figured that Brooke was bothered that Dante had preferred her. At least she wanted to think he preferred her and wasn't simply being nice. There was no real reason to believe this, other than he'd bought her doughnuts. And that look—she would never forget that look he gave her. It smoldered.

She remembered riding behind Dante and how it felt to

be pressed against his hard body and to have wrapped her legs around him. Parts of her body quivered just thinking about it. She wished she had really wrapped her legs around him. He had been so warm and strong. She liked to think she would have been wholly wanton and accepting of any moves if he had made any. But in reality, she would have said no. If he had made any advances, she would have been indignant and offended, probably would have even slapped him. Still, thinking about him piqued interests in her body that needed male assistance in satisfying. Preferably assistance from Dante.

Thrilled at the prospect of seeing him again, she had told Hannah and Brooke that he'd said he would also be at the Grand Canyon. Brooke forbade her from spending all her time looking for him once they got there; after all, it would take away from their bridesmaids bonding time. As if Brooke really cared about bonding. Geena didn't share that he'd said he would find her. She hoped he would. Especially since when she tried to get his card from Hannah, her friend said she had given it back. When he had handed her the pink slip on the truck, Hannah had just folded the papers together and handed the lot back when they returned from the ride. Geena was crestfallen. Both Hannah and Brooke agreed, no pouting over men on the trip, so Geena was left to mourn the loss of Dante's number and contact information secretly.

"Here." Hannah handed a warm paper-wrapped churro to Geena. "These are so good," she said as one bite smeared cinnamon and sugar on the side of her face.

"I can't believe you are eating your way around this town." Brooke scoffed when Hannah offered her a bite. "I don't burn calories as instantaneously as you do, and I'm going on day four with no gym. Pass."

Geena could read the judgment in Brooke's look.

"You two plan on an extra lap around the block after eating those, right? I don't think either of you can afford to have your dresses altered this close the wedding if you gain any weight on this trip. I'm going inside." Brooke passed through the store door.

"What's up with Brooke?" Geena asked. Maybe Brooke was missing Ashley at this point as much as Geena was. Had she come, right about now, Ashley and Brooke could be off looking at clothes and not judging Geena and Hannah over their love of food.

Hannah shrugged. "Dunno. I think trying to work at the same time is harder than she thought it would be."

Geena nodded. She wasn't going to let Brooke get to her on this trip, but Brooke was making it difficult. Geena and Hannah lingered in front of the large display window, consuming their treat. The clothes inside were very stylized and fashionable. Geena spotted a blue denim military-style crop jacket, detailed with rows of black soutache braid and brass buttons. She pointed at it enthusiastically for Brooke to look. Brooke picked the garment up, dangling the hanger for them to see. Geena gave a thumbs-up; Hannah nodded her head side to side; Brooke shook her head in a definite no. The next piece she picked up, she nodded a positive vote for—it was a loose flowing velvet cocoon coat. Hannah did the side-to-side nod again, indicating she wasn't sure. Geena shrugged. Holding a finger up, indicating *hold on*, Brooke grabbed another item they couldn't see from their vantage point and disappeared to the back of the store.

Geena and Hannah finished their snack and brushed the sugar and cinnamon off their faces and hands before entering the dress shop. They made their way to the back to locate Brooke when she stepped out from the dressing room. She had put on a sleek body-contouring dress with a row of beaded fringe along the hem and the velvet cocoon. Even with her hair twisted into a messy bun, she looked like a model, tall, slender, blonde. Beautiful. Both Hannah and Geena gushed over how sophisticated and gorgeous she was. The cocoon coat looked fabulous on; Geena had not expected that after seeing it slump on the hanger.

They continued their shopping through several other boutiques. Geena noticed clerks would rush to help Brooke and Hannah but never had anything for her. This was exactly why she had wanted to go gallery hopping and not shopping. She started getting the familiar tugs of feeling like a total poser. Someone was going to call her out on being a wannabe. What was she thinking hanging out with people like Brooke and Hannah? Brooke was gorgeous, magazine-model quality beautiful. Tall, thin but with curves in the right places. Blonde, blue eyes, perfect perky nose. She had been a model in college, working her way through school. She still modeled occasionally and looked smart and professional the rest of the time. Brooke had the kind of figure that made sweatpants look sexy. Geena did give her credit; Brooke ate healthy foods, only gave herself cheat days twice a month, and worked out five days a week. Men responded to her looks. With a blink of her long lashes or a flash of cleavage, men would buy her anything she desired. They were her lapdogs for a smile.

Hannah, also beautiful but in a delicate, old-fashioned way, was small-boned and petite, with sharp, fragile features. Fashion was made for her figure, and men wanted to protect her. They wanted to be gentlemen for her. Around her they held doors open, put their suit coats around her shoulders. Geena wouldn't have been surprised if some date at some point in time had placed his jacket over a puddle for her. No, that wouldn't have happened; they would have simply swept her up into their arms and carried her. Hannah also had the metabolism of a racehorse. She could eat a linebacker under the table, and alcohol didn't touch her. Seriously, Geena had seen her outdrink an entire fraternity in college.

Geena had none of those features, and men did not react to her in any of those ways. She had a heart-shaped face with a little nose and big eyes, yet it always seemed as if no one could see past her large behind or ample belly and breasts. If she were lucky, the rejected friends would come over to talk to her. Occasionally a reasonably good-looking man would be sweet on her, just to see if she would put in a good word for them with her friends. College had pretty much been a string of bad-joke dates. She realized that she at least had dates, but they had mostly been arranged by Hannah's boyfriends, typically to get her out of the way. Only two had ever been interested enough in Geena to become boyfriends and, much to Geena's regret, lovers.

She had no right hanging out and shopping with these two. They had looks, money, and the bodies that clothes were made for. And they didn't really have the same interests. Yet Geena trailed after them from one boutique to the next, while any suggestions from her about museums and galleries were completely ignored. Frequently she wondered why Hannah kept her around. Well, she and Hannah had been friends since middle school, so they had really grown into adulthood together. Brooke and Hannah were cousins and had been roommates at college. Hannah had kept them both as friends. Brooke did her best to make Geena feel like an alien. Just little things she said and did that made it obvious Brooke really thought Geena was completely weird, and not in a good way.

Planning this trip, she and Brooke had gotten along better than ever, but then again, that probably had more to do with Ashley's involvement than anything else. Geena wasn't sure if she really wanted to even try to be friends with Brooke anymore, but for this trip, she would do her best to be friendly.

Geena sighed. She was having a good time, she really was. But moments like these, watching those two try on outfit after outfit, she would just get smacked with doubt. She couldn't help it. They were both so pretty, and things came easily for them.

Being a plus-sized girl in a boutique world never seemed to work for Geena. She liked the styles and uniqueness of boutique designer clothes, but their availability in her size was practically nonexistent. She didn't even mind paying a bit more for stylish clothes that fit and were well-made. Unfortunately, too often when one of the few designers she followed online would announce a new fashion line, her size would be completely sold out by the time she had enough money set aside to purchase the items she liked. Discount and clearance-rack shopping filled in her wardrobe. Even then, her size was quick to sell out. More than once she'd lamented that clothing manufacturers did not realize what sizes sold out first and make more of that one? Hannah never had a problem finding her size and Brooke was a manufacturers' ideal, so she could always find her size, and she never shopped discount. Well, not that she admitted publicly.

Geena attempted to try on one jacket. It looked plenty big, and as a shrug, it only needed to fit her shoulders and arms. After that failure she limited herself to looking at the jewelry.

After several stops and several happy sales commissions,

Brooke and Hannah, with their arms full of shopping, decided it was time for lunch. Geena had two small bags. She had found a set of funky handmade cuff bracelets that featured comic book heroes and rhinestones. She had also found a tourist T-shirt vendor with a Santa Fe shirt in her size.

Accepting that she wasn't going to get any quality time in a museum, Geena looked forward to seeing the sunset at the Grand Canyon; she knew that would fit her perfectly. They had just enough time after lunch to make it. She also looked forward, she prayed, to seeing Dante again. She didn't share that part simply because she didn't need Brooke picking on her for having a crush on a man she'd just met who, as Brooke put it, probably wouldn't remember her name if they did run into him again.

5

In the morning Dante began calling the Maggie Garcias on his list. The second one turned out to be the woman he was looking for. She suggested he come over for a cup of coffee. When he arrived at her house, four kids played basketball in the driveway. She invited Dante into a tidy, comfortable living room and offered him a steaming cup of coffee, explaining that he was lucky to have called this morning. As an elementary school librarian, had Dante called the day before, Maggie would have been at work, and he would have had to wait until after four in the afternoon before she could have returned his phone call.

They chatted about family lineage and how that brought Dante to this part of the country. He described his visit with Margaret Tse-pe the evening before and explained that was how he'd found Maggie. He showed her the family tree that Saganitso had drawn out for him. "Our family is fairly well established in California and has always followed the lineage. We lost track of Margarita's line when she left." They had been looking for Margarita's family for some time. The search became more of a priority when the shifter trait was discovered in DNA tests, but Dante did not share that piece of information.

"And so now you have found some of us. Who in your family had a sudden interest in genealogy for you to track me down?" Maggie asked.

"I wouldn't say a sudden interest in genealogy, I would say it's because they finally gave me the project." Dante flashed one of his toothy grins, not to dazzle but to hint he knew he was being cheeky. "Uncle Remi has been the family recorder for some time. We grew up with the mystery of Margarita. No one knew what had become of her. She basically ran away, and the most information anyone had until recently was that she ran off with an Indian named Joe. Do I have to tell you just how next to impossible that was to track?" Dante chuckled, hoping he wasn't being culturally insulting.

A noticeable uptick in skin-walker reports caught Dante's attention. A shifter out there not knowing what they were could make a person insane, could make a person think they were a monster. And that's when he shifted his focus to the Southwest.

"Our family has a rare genetic anomaly. Margarita's parents had not had it, and as far as anyone knew, Margarita had not either, but her brothers had." Dante leaned forward in his seat. "Was Margarita a carrier? Would she have even been aware if she was? And more importantly, did she pass it along to her children?"

"And so you want to know if I grew up with some rare genetic disorder?" Maggie asked.

"Exactly."

"If I had, then what?"

"You would have known about it when you hit puberty. That's when it manifests. The family that's left in Sonoma is aware this can pose an extreme emotional and mental burden, especially when its unexpected. I'm here for two reasons, to establish a family connection for more Christmas cards, and for providing a support structure if necessary."

He didn't think Margaret or Maggie's mother, Carol, had this anomaly or Margaret would have mentioned something when he'd asked. "Then again, Margaret gave me the impression if she didn't want to deal with something, she just ignored it and refused to talk about it," he said, setting down his empty cup.

"That's pretty much how Aunt Margaret is," Maggie agreed.

Maggie confirmed she did not have an unusual hair growth problem that onset with puberty, and neither did her mother, that she was aware of.

"What about the kids outside?" Dante pointed over his shoulder indicating the group playing ball when he arrived.

Maggie shook her head. "They're mine, but not mine. I raised the unruly group, but I'm not their biological mother. My husband came with a ready-made family. And that was plenty for me."

Dante made a mental note: end of genetic line for Robert and Alice. Joseph2 had died with no offspring. Now just to follow Peter's line. If he could prove the family had died out, then that would mean another source to investigate for the rumors he was also following in the Southwest. Dante preferred to find out what had happened to Peter's sons, hoping they were who he was ultimately looking for.

Unfortunately, Maggie could not expand on the information Dante had regarding her mother's cousins. "I'm sorry. I really don't know much about family heritage and all that. I never paid much attention, never needed to. If it helps, I know my grandparents lived over in Cameron. Not sure if they grew up there or not."

Dante thanked Maggie for the visit, the coffee, and what information she did have. He made a few notes while sitting in his truck before he consulted a map to find his way to Cameron, Arizona.

The first part of his drive along Highway 64 was much more populated than he'd expected. Once outside of Shiprock, the road narrowed and the scenery turned to high desert in all directions. The sparse vegetation and rocky terrain made Dante think of old westerns. Of course this was "The West." Towers of clouds piled high in the sky, making the landscape seem surreal, like an illustration from a children's book. He almost expected to see a cattle drive cross the road at any minute.

Cameron was a small touristy trading post next to the Little Colorado River. He was lucky that an RV campground across the street from the post office and trading post had room for him. Dante set up the trailer, unloaded the bike, and began planning his next step.

Not having to tow the Airstream or the bike around was helpful as Dante drove his truck in and out of dirt roads in the surrounding area. Chatting with one of the clerks at the trading post had proven to be more helpful than anticipated. She directed Dante farther south down the road to a local church, where he might be able to find out some more specific information on the Tse-pe family. He found an old man there who had known a Joe—Joseph3 from the family tree—in the army and was able to identify his brother—the unidentified question mark— as George. Joe had died in Vietnam, and George came back crazy. He thought Joe's wife had a kid or two, but he wasn't sure if they were Joe's or her second husband's. He couldn't remember her name, but he was pretty sure she was from Tuba City. He also thought George was living up closer to Tuba City, off some dirt road in a trailer.

Dante drove down several dirt roads, ending at the wrong trailer home more than once. No one knew who he was looking for. He drove on to the next trailer he could find. One person he encountered knew a George, but he wasn't sure if it was the same George that Dante was looking for. He described him as a crazy old goat, probably more talk than head butt. He hadn't seen George for some time, maybe he died.

Before he got himself seriously lost, Dante decided to try the Tuba City police station to ask a few questions. The young police officer stared numbly at Dante as he explained his situation and described the whole finding-lost-family-lineage issue

"Let me get my sergeant; he might know," the young officer said, disappearing behind a door.

When the sergeant appeared, Dante repeated his story again.

"There was an old guy named George we had problems with a few years ago. Just as you described, a little crazy, a little dangerous. Vietnam vet. Haven't had any problems from him in a long time. He either moved or died."

Dante got information of where he could track down local death records.

"Sorry, we can't help you on the brother's family. Have you tried council records?"

"Yeah, yeah, the lawyer I'm working with has; this was as far as he got. So I'm out here pounding the pavement, trying to dig up some more info. I'm not even sure if George is who I'm looking for. I have the name of his brother who died in Vietnam. Apparently it's some dark family feud or secret, or..." Dante shrugged. "Thanks for your time. One more question. Not related, more a personal hobby. I pick up on local legends and see what I can find out while I'm out talking to people. Ya know, keeps me from getting bogged down and bored." The police sergeant nodded. "Any local stories about skin-walkers?"

"Naw, kid, it's not like they are bigfoot or something where every local has a story." The sergeant shook Dante's hand. "Good luck tracking your family down."

Dante wiped a hand across his tired face. It had been a long day. He hoped he could get county death records online. Maybe he would just call Saganitso back and have him look that information up. He wanted to get to the Grand Canyon by tomorrow, no later than the day after. Geena would already be there, and he didn't know how long it would take him to find her. As it was, he had gotten extremely lucky; there had been a cancelation in the Trailer Village, so he had a spot to park and wouldn't have to travel into the park every day to look for her. He could set up camp right there.

While he sat in his truck contemplating his next move, the young police officer knocked on his passenger door. Dante clicked the lock, and the young man climbed into the truck.

"Look, Sarge would never tell anyone this, but you know how you asked about skin-walkers? It's not something we casually talk to outsiders about but..." The young man looked furtively out the truck's windows. "There used to be a lot of strange wolf sightings, but no official packs are located around here. No one ever found or identified anything officially, but lots of ranchers in the area reported sheep and goat killings that looked like a wolf or big dog. Too messy for a coyote. I remember because my dad lost half a dozen breeding ewes and my grandmother kept saying it was a skin-walker, and how I had better behave or it would get me. There had been one, just one human attack. A lone hiker, throat ripped out. After that, the sightings and rumors sort of dropped away. Like whatever it was, once it killed that hiker, it was finished. That was about fifteen to twenty years ago."

Dante smirked. "Thats exactly the kind of story I'm interested in." He thanked the young officer with a hand shake. Those were the stories that Dante kept track of when looking for lone shifters without family connections, unexplained, and with a hint of local legend. This unknown George, black sheep of the Tse-pe family, and a wolf attack could be a shifter connection. If the man had gone crazy because of his ability to shift, that could explain why other family members were dissociated with him. The drive back to Cameron and the Airstream seemed to take a long time, longer than the distance should allow for. The time gave Dante the chance to clarify his thoughts and action plans.

Back in the camper, he set up his laptop and pulled out his notes. He tossed a couple of frozen pocket sandwiches in the microwave for dinner and made a mental note to buy supplies once he got to the Grand Canyon. He barely had any food left. As it was, breakfast would wipe him out completely.

Dante pounded away at the keyboard. He wanted to make sure he was thorough in his instructions. He typically did not delegate tasks. He was the one to do the work. He was the one delegated to. But there was no reason these documents needed to be found by him. Searching county records and tribal records for birth and death certificates, and marriage certificates was a perfect project for a young legal assistant. He spent several hours writing his notes for

Uncle Remi and Morgan and making a set of tasks and follow-up actions to send to Saganitso. Everything and anything he could delegate over the next few days, he would. He'd already filled in the gap that led to George and found out that Joseph3 may have fathered children. Saganitso and his daughter could find out if George was dead or if anyone knew where he might be living. Cameron and Tuba City could be crossed off that list. They could also find out who Joseph3's wife was, and if she did have any kids, who the father was. All these "clerical" things he didn't need to focus on when there was one warm, sexy, zaftig beauty he wanted to spend all his time focusing on. He had to clear this set of problems from his head so he could focus on his strategy for locating Geena.

6

Last night at the Grand Canyon had been pretty wonderful actually. They had arrived at the campgrounds and set up the RV. Trailer Village was packed, and Geena realized they were fortunate to have gotten a space exactly when they wanted on such short notice. Sunset over the canyon had been spectacular. It was one of the most beautiful things Geena had ever seen in her life. The sun caught on the rock formations, licking them with bright orange fire and casting cooling purple shadows. The clouds building above the canyon caught colors that made them look like a painting. Pinks and purples and yellows danced in the clouds, in contrast to the cool blue of the sky and the fireball of the setting sun. Geena spent more time watching the colors change as night claimed the canyon than she did listening to Hannah and Brooke as they ate dinner at the lodge along the rim. After dinner they found a campfire talk directly behind the campsite around a blazing fire. A park ranger told them about local wildlife. He included a few local legends and myths of the various animals they might encounter while in the park. Geena hadn't realized she could fall in love with a place, but she was pretty sure she just had.

Hannah had not received a single call or text from Tim the entire day. Maybe he was going to relax and let her have her vacation. Brooke didn't complain once about the food or about getting hit on by "another gross trailer park guy." Her snide comments directed at Geena had mostly stopped after their morning of shopping in Santa Fe. Geena relaxed and let the setting sweep her up without thinking about Dante, too much.

With a yawn, Brooke hooked her laptop bag over her shoulder. "I'm out; see y'all later." She descended the stairs and disappeared toward the food court. Geena flopped back on the bed. The three had agreed to split up for the morning. Brooke still had work to finish up, and Hannah planned to do some laundry.

"You gonna get up today?" Hannah asked as she collected the clothes she intended to wash.

"Shhh, I'm sleeping. Don't tell Brooke, but I'm trying to conjure a dream with Dante in it." She could picture him here with her, his laugh in her ears, his arms around her, the canyon expanding out in front of them. That was a dream worth staying in bed for.

"Sweetie, I hope you aren't setting yourself up for disappointment if he doesn't show."

"Of course I am, Hannah. Why do you think I want to dream about him? So I can convince myself that's all he ever was, a dream." Geena sighed dejectedly. "You don't think I was making it all up in my head, him liking me? I mean, big girls get the hot guy sometimes, right?"

"Sweetie." Hannah sat on the edge of the bed. "You're so pretty; why wouldn't he like you? Unless we run into him here, we'll never know. So I say go for it in your dreams and think he likes you until he says otherwise. Just..." Hannah paused. "Just don't make him up to be something more than he is, some guy you met in a trailor park."

Hannah's ringtone reverberated loudly through the front half of the RV. "It's Timmy. I got to get that."

Geena rolled onto her back and closed her eyes, picturing Dante as he smiled wolfishly at her.

"Hey, baby!"

Geena winced as she heard Hannah's greeting.

"You're what? No! No. You are. Wow. No. Wow."

Geena pulled a pillow over her head with misguided hopes of blocking out Hannah's voice. Silence. Either it worked, or the phone call ended.

Geena felt the bed jostle. She flopped the pillow off her face and glared at Hannah.

"Geena, I'm gonna head out. Ah, set yourself an alarm, okay?" Hannah seemed hesitant.

"You all right?" Geena asked.

"Yeah, just a bit distracted. Ten thirty at the food court, okay?"

"Ten thirty at the food court," Geena confirmed. She heard Hannah leave the RV. She closed her eyes and tried to conjure Dante again.

∼

"How's work? Almost done?" Geena asked as she approached Brooke.

Brooke leaned over her closed laptop, smiling into the face of a reasonably handsome, sandy-haired, bearded man. She was engrossed in whatever it was he said. The glare she shot Geena for interrupting made Geena feel like withering. Why did Brooke have to do that? Classic Brooke mode, paying all her attention to the handsome man and daggers to any other woman. Geena shook her head. Brooke did not need to worry about Geena being interested in Mr. Beard. He wasn't Dante.

She looked up, searching for Hannah. She didn't find Hannah right away, but she did notice Mr. Beard's friends behind him. They were all kitted up to go hiking.

Geena's heart sank when she did see Hannah, walking in with a broad figure in a polo shirt and khakis.

Geena painted a fake smile on her face. "Hey, Tim. Surprised to see you here."

Tim was considered an all-American good-looking guy with his perpetual southern tan, short clean-cut blond hair, and pale blue eyes. Tim had a strong football player build, not too tall with wide shoulders. Hannah always seemed exceptionally petite around him. Mostly he looked like a playground bully.

Tim sneered at Geena. At least the disdain was mutual.

Brooke stood quickly, knocked over a closed bottle of water, and made a fuss over some papers. She looked shocked to see Tim. "Oh, hey, Tim. What are you doing here? Oh, um, right. Blake"—she pointed to the man she had just been batting her lashes at—"these are my friends."

Blake stood and extended his hand.

"Hannah and her fiancé Tim."

Blake reached toward Geena after shaking hands with the others. Brooke said nothing. Geena glanced at Brooke, to see her staring wide-eyed at Tim and Hannah.

"I'm Geena; she forgets I exist." Geena shook Blake's hand.

By the time their hands were apart, it seemed that Blake forgot she existed as well. Perfect, this is going to be so much fun. Not.

Brooke explained that Blake and his friends had invited her and her friends to go hiking for the day.

Geena would have had to be stupid not to notice that Hannah was expected to join the hike, but that she was not. Geena was tired of Brooke assuming that just because she was a big girl, she was not interested in participating in physical activities. A hike in the woods around the canyon would have been nice. No, she would not have joined them on a hike down into the canyon, but then again if that were their goal for the day, they would have left much earlier in the morning.

"Well, Hannah, maybe you and Tim could join us?" Brooke turned a brittle smile toward Tim. "You like to hike, right?"

Hannah placed her hand on Tim's arm and turned to him. At that point everyone in the group directed their attention to Tim. It seemed to Geena he was well aware of this and stood a little straighter, took a little longer to answer.

"Well, I didn't really pack appropriately for hiking." He patted Hannah's hand. "I really didn't think this through in my rush to get to my little Hans."

What tripe, and Geena couldn't understand why Hannah ate it up. Hannah smiled up at Tim. This was the type of action Hannah would justify with *you know how he is* while Geena thought *what a patronizing jerk*. But Hannah was in love with him, so Geena would bite her tongue.

Brooke frowned, her disappointment obvious to everyone. Turning to Blake, she said, "Well, I guess it's just me then." She asked Blake's friend if he wanted to spend the day with Geena. When he replied with more than just a no, but included that he was there to camp and hike, Brooke acquiesced and suggested they get started.

Geena had not failed to notice Brooke, once again, had tried to pair her off with some random member of the new group. It annoyed Geena that Brooke was constantly trying to set her up with not-so-attractive guys, and guys with no personality. Brooke did it so that she looked like a caring friend trying to find a partner for Geena. Poor Geena who couldn't get dates on her own. Poor Geena who really needed to hang out with some different people. Poor Geena who was still more than a bit hung up on Dante. Now he was a prime, grade-A cut of alpha male.

Brooke pointed out repeatedly that he was just being nice. "Guys like that aren't interested in women like you, Geena." Brooke had a very limited idea of what kind of man should be interested in Geena.

Geena hadn't shared that lovely leer he had given her at the coffee shop. That wasn't being nice; that was a look of lust. Remembering it made Geena smile. That brief look gave Geena the confidence to insist that she would be fine on her own for the day.

Alone at the Grand Canyon, her day of touristy giggles and obnoxious Instagram group selfies cancelled. Hannah left breakfast with Tim, muttering something about getting her things to take to his hotel. Brooke and the group of campers had departed to stock up on some supplies for the day at the general store. Geena took her time finishing her coffee and people watching. She wasn't in a hurry to get anywhere now that her so-called friends had effectively abandoned her.

She followed the path between the shops and her campsite. This morning had turned into a complete mess, all their plans had changed, and it had included another negative interaction with Brooke. If Geena walked away with anything from this excursion, it was that she and Brooke really were not friends and never had been and never would be. Going forward, she would not participate in activities if Brooke was going to be involved. Hannah wasn't going to be enough of a buffer, especially now that Tim was around. Once those two were married, Geena was confident that Hannah would lose touch with her friends for quite some time.

The plus side of being alone, was that she could commune with nature at her pace. She didn't need to rush through the walk. She didn't need to hurry up and go anywhere. She should have been really hurt and disappointed by her friends, but she decided to control her own reaction and focus on the good.

She squeezed her eyes closed, forcing away the sting of threatening tears. Geena sniffed. Focusing on anything good at the moment was difficult, no matter how hard she tried.

Of course Hannah would go off alone with Tim. He had more control of Hannah this way. Why hadn't Geena realized that was Tim's modus operandi before? He really didn't mix well with Hannah's friends. Except for Brooke. After seeing Brooke's reaction to Tim this morning, Geena wondered if there had been something between the two of them at some point, probably before Hannah and Tim got together. Knowing how many men Brooke dated, it wouldn't be a surprise. But why hide it, unless they both thought it had been one of those "mistake" dates? Geena had been on enough of those in her time.

She hitched the laptop strap back up onto her shoulder and wiped her cheeks dry. Why exactly had she agreed to deliver Brooke's laptop back to the RV? Why couldn't she have said no? Why couldn't she have said she was going to head to the rim and stare into the abyss, literally. Because she was nice, because she needed Brooke to be friendly through the end of this trip. They had seven days left of being stuck together in the RV. It was in Geena's best interest to not antagonize Brooke. Peacemaker was on her for the rest of this trip.

Geena spotted a little girl playing with her dogs in a clearing just off the path. They looked so happy. Geena reminded herself, on her own or not, she was at the Grand Canyon, a place she had always wanted to visit. It was time to put the laptop away and get her butt up to the rim. Her visit to the rim last night had been too brief. But it had set her soul free. She didn't understand why, but just being here had a palpable soothing effect on her. Maybe this was the euphoria people talked about getting from yoga.

Walking back into Trailer Village, she wondered if Dante had arrived yet. She did not see his truck; then again, she wasn't about to cruise the entire RV campgrounds looking for him like a lovesick puppy. She certainly had let the idea ricochet through her brain more than once, but not after experiencing this place. It seemed like a waste of time and the fastest route to crushing disappointment. He'd said he was headed this way. She knew he would be here, and he would find her. She had to let it happen. Besides, he hadn't actually said he had a reservation at Trailer Village. There were other campgrounds and RV parks around the Canyon. It certainly would be nice if he also managed to park here.

Once inside the RV, Geena noticed that Hannah had packed up her things. It looked as if she had taken everything. "Well shoot," she cursed to herself. *If Hannah took everything, that means she'll stay with Tim the entire time, leaving me with Brooke.* From the mess, it appeared that Brooke had also made it back to the RV and grabbed some items for her hike with her new friends. Geena stored the laptop in the under-seat storage to keep it safe. She grabbed a bottle of water. Locking the door behind her, she headed off toward the rim.

She passed by the girl playing with her dogs again. This time something about the group caused Geena to pause. The little girl wore mismatched clothing looking like she dressed herself, a twirly pink skirt over a pair of muddy sweatpants, tucked into tan fleece-lined boots. Her jacket had stripes of various bright colors. The girl's hair was thin and straight and pulled into two little pigtails. She appeared to be almost as wild as the dogs, dogs that looked more like wolf puppies. It had to be that the breed looked wolfish; then the longer she watched, the more she noticed. The dogs weren't wearing collars. The little girl didn't call them by name, she just called them "puppy." One of the animals didn't interact with her. He seemed to skulk around the edge of the clearing. The other two frantically played chase and catch. They seemed to be having a good time. The little girl threw a stick in Geena's direction. When she saw the dog run, it was clear to Geena that was a wolf charging at her. She held her breath and let it out when he grabbed the stick and trotted back to the girl.

"What are your dogs' names?" Geena called out. She glanced around, looking for a parent or older sibling. She didn't see anyone.

"They aren't my dogs; they are wild wolves." The girl emphasized each word.

"If they are wild, maybe you shouldn't be playing with them? Is that safe?" She realized it was a stupid question to ask a five-year-old. Not sure if the girl had any idea just how dangerous those dogs could be, and if they were wolves, they could be very dangerous.

The girl shrugged. "We're just playing." She seemed to think it was entirely logical to be playing with wolves.

"Where's your mom or dad? Do they know you're here?" Geena's concern grew. There really wasn't any sign of anyone around. Maybe the girl came from the campground on the other side of the clearing, but she couldn't see anyone, and she didn't hear anyone.

"I don't know where they went." The girl's brow furrowed. "We were walking... and I"—she paused to look around—"think they went over there." She pointed behind her.

Geena walked into the clearing to be next to the girl. "My name is Geena. What's yours?"

"I'm Mackenzie," she answered.

"Mackenzie, why don't we go find your mom and dad? I know you are having fun with these guys, but I bet your parents are looking for you."

"Okay." Mackenzie rubbed one of the wolves on the head. "Bye, puppies." She took Geena's hand. They walked through the clearing toward the campgrounds.

Mackenzie told Geena that their truck was red and they were sleeping in a yellow tent. They decided to follow the road back up to the entrance and look at the individual campsites along the way. Mackenzie saw nothing that looked familiar.

Geena suggested that they had better find a park ranger, as it was pretty clear that Mackenzie's parents had wandered off while she was playing with the puppies. Geena also wanted to ask about the wolves. Was it normal for there to be juvenile wolves near the campgrounds, and would there be adult wolves nearby? The thought of a pack of wolves made her nervous. She didn't remember the ranger mentioning wolves last night during the campfire talk.

Mackenzie was a sweet little girl. She held Geena's hand the entire time. She never acted nervous or afraid that she might be lost. After all, she knew exactly where she was. Her parents had wandered off. She convinced Geena that a chocolate ice cream cone was in order once they reached the store. Geena completely agreed. A chocolate ice cream cone would taste really good right now.

Headed toward them on the trail carrying shopping bags was a tall man with messy, curly, dark hair. Geena squinted to focus her vision. Her heart skipped a few beats and added in extras. Dante.

She wanted to run and throw her arms around him, but doubt filled her. Maybe she had made it all up in her head. Maybe he really had just been being nice. Either way she couldn't keep from smiling.

"Geena!" he yelled, his face breaking into a broad smile, showing off his perfect white teeth. He put down his bags and pulled her into a big hug, lifting her off the ground and spinning her around. The spin took her breath away. She had never expected a man to pick her up and spin her. Ever. Dante held her close as she slid back down to her feet.

"Hello." He grinned at her. She smiled back at him. He still held her close, his strong arms pulling her into his chest. It hadn't been her imagination; he was interested. She didn't know what to say. She was just happy to be looking at him.

"Hey, Dante." She was made breathless by his presence. She couldn't remember what she had just been doing, but was glad it had put her in his path.

"I just got in. I'm staying over in Trailer Village; are you there?" His voice was as rich as she remembered. "There are a bunch of RVs like the one you're renting, so I wasn't sure if you had gotten here yet."

"Last night, we got here last night." Trying to regain her train of thought, she remembered Mackenzie.

"This is my new friend Mackenzie. Mackenzie, this is my friend Dante. Mackenzie's parents have wandered off, so we are headed up to the lodge to find a ranger and see if they can help us."

"And get a chocolate ice cream cone," Mackenzie added.

"Yes, and to get a chocolate ice cream cone, because we have been walking around for a bit."

"May I join you? I need to put my newly acquired provisions away," he said as he picked up his shopping bags. "I could meet you back over at the food court and get an ice cream cone too?" he asked Mackenzie, and winked at Geena.

Geena felt her cheeks tighten as heat rushed over her face in a blush.

Mackenzie cocked her head to the side and gave Dante a quizzical stare. "What are provisions?"

He leaned down closer to the girl's level. "I went grocery shopping," he whispered.

"Oh." She made a small O shape with her lips.

As they began to go their separate ways, Geena turned back to look at Dante. "Hold on a sec," she told Mackenzie. "Be right back." She headed the few yards to catch up with Dante.

"Hey, Dante, I found her playing with some wolf puppies. They might have just been some kind of shepherd-husky, but I swear they looked like wolves."

"Where?"

Geena described the clearing he would pass on his way to the Trailer Village. "I don't want to freak her parents out if they were just dogs, but I should tell the ranger if they aren't."

"I'll check it out. I agree; that's something the rangers would want to know about."

"Thanks, I'll see you up there?" Geena's face was starting to hurt from grinning so hard.

"Yes, you will." He winked again.

∼

When Dante found them at the lodge's food court, Mackenzie had finished most of her ice cream cone. It appeared that a good portion had smeared itself across her face on its way into her mouth. He wondered why kids' aim for their own mouth was always so bad. It had a charming effect in this case, with the chocolate emphasizing the girl's big brown eyes. She sat at a table, swinging her legs and enjoying her treat. Geena sat across from her watching the backs of two park rangers. One was on the radio.

Dante paused just to watch Geena. She was more beautiful than he had remembered. The soft pink glow of the mate aura surrounded her, that unique shimmering aura that wolf shifters see when they have met their ideal mate. It may have only been a couple of days, but they were long and lonely days without her warm smile. He had been prepared to spend a good deal of time tracking her down once he arrived here. He really hadn't expected to run into her so soon. But this was better, time to be with her and not have to look for her. After what he had just come from, and not finding anything tangible there, maybe fate was helping him locate what he really needed.

"Hello, pretty girls," he said as he approached their table. Geena's eyes sparkled as they met his. It was as if she could only see him. He thought about ditching his responsibilities and just taking her back to the Airstream. He may have only just met her, but he wanted nothing more than to be with her in a carnal manner.

No, he had plenty of time; he didn't want to frighten her off.

"Hey." Geena smiled at him. He noticed her slight Southern accent again. It was such a turn-on. Sitting there smiling, she made it difficult for him to focus.

He sat next to Mackenzie. He felt that she offered a buffer and served as a proper chaperone. Besides, sitting across from her gave him a better excuse to stare at Geena. "Where are your friends Belle and Cinderella?"

Mackenzie perked up. "Your friends have names just like princesses." She seemed amazed.

"No, sweetie." Geena laughed. "He just calls them that because they remind him of those characters. My friends are Hannah and Brooke." She paused, turned to Dante, and rolled her eyes. "And my friends," she said with an exacerbated sigh, "have made other plans, leaving me on my own." She smirked, seeming annoyed by the entire situation. Dante made note to get the details after Mackenzie was securely back with her family. "That's why I just happened to be walking by when missy and I found each other," Geena said, tilting her head to indicate Mackenzie.

Dante liked how Geena phrased things to take the pressure off the little girl. She was currently not afraid of her situation and didn't even consider herself lost. That could change, and she could easily panic. A panicking, frantic child would not be easy to deal with.

The park rangers stepped back to the group at the table. "Looks like your lost parents have been found; apparently once they realized they couldn't find you, they went in search of a park ranger too. You all did the right thing. They should be here in about five minutes."

Geena sat back into her chair, visibly relaxing. Mackenzie nodded and chewed on the edges of her cone.

"Now—" The ranger turned to Dante. "Can you tell me about these dogs she sent you to go look at?"

"They were wolves," Mackenzie chimed in.

"This young lady," the ranger said, nodding to Geena, "said she couldn't tell precisely what they were, and that a friend—I'm assuming that's you—went to go check them out while she came to find us."

"Yeah, that was me," Dante confirmed. "They were just big puppies. Mackenzie was never in any danger, except from excessive drool."

Geena looked at him. Something in how she tilted her head and squinted one eye told Dante she was skeptical. She glowed. As his mate, did that give her other magical talents? Could she read his mind? Dante dismissed it. Geena was a smart woman, and she clearly recognized that he was not telling the truth.

Mackenzie's mother ran in and scooped the little girl up. "I was so worried." She had the same big brown eyes and thin, light brown hair as the little girl. "Thank you so much for finding her," she said to the rangers. They indicated that it was Geena who had located the girl.

"Oh, no problem; she just happened to be where I was walking," Geena explained.

"I played with wolves, Mommy," Mackenzie said as her mother wiped the chocolate from her face.

The mother spun toward the ranger. "Wolves?"

"They were dogs, just regular dogs," Dante interjected.

"Are you sure?"

"Yeah, I found the owners, just dogs."

After shaking hands with Geena and Dante, Mackenzie's mother bundled her off. The rangers thanked Geena and left.

Geena and Dante were alone.

"Just dogs, huh?" Geena asked.

Dante shook his head. Geena had seen right through him. *Good, she'll keep me honest.*

"C'mon, I want to show you something." Dante held out a hand to Geena. She took it, and he pulled her to her feet.

7

Dante held on to Geena's hand as he led her across the street into the general store. Her skin felt so perfect and smooth, and it was just her hand he touched. He stopped just before they reached the store to look at her. He needed to tell her. He wanted her to understand in a way he couldn't fathom himself.

"You all right? What are you going to show me?" Geena blinked her big blue eyes up at him.

"Yeah, look, Geena, I have this driving compulsion to be completely honest with you. You could already tell I was lying about those wolves."

"Oh." Geena dropped his hand as if it burned.

He watched as her face fell from happy amusement to complete dejection.

"I see."

Even the tone of her voice held the threat of tears. Her sadness hit Dante like a sucker punch.

"What is it?" he asked.

"Look, I should go." Geena began to turn away as if she

walked in slow motion, no longer having the energy to move.

Dante stopped her with a hand on her upper arm. "Geena, what did I say?"

She wouldn't look at him. "You want to be completely honest with me. In my world that translates to saying something mean and hurtful under the guise of being truthful and telling it like it is." She looked up at him, her eyes shimmering with unshed tears. "I get it—you want to be sure I understand you're just interested in being friends, and that I need to..."

Dante's mouth was on hers. A zap of electricity shocked his lips as they touched. He pulled back at the zap. Geena blinked; her mouth hung open.

"It's the fastest way I could think of to get you to shut up." Dante tucked a stray hair behind her ear. "I have no intention of friend zoning you. That's why I need to tell you the truth, not to say hurtful things, but so that I don't hurt you."

"You're telling me you aren't always a morally upright citizen who never lies?"

Dante sniggered. "Gods, no." He paused, holding his hand out to her. Dante waited until she slipped her fingers back onto his palm before he continued to lead her into the store.

"What is it you need to be honest about?" She asked.

He couldn't help but notice the small catch in her words. She really had thought he was going say something mean. *Stupid move Palatine.*

"You'll see, it's what I want to show you. Now tell me," Dante said as he started perusing the clothing section. "What happened with the merry all-girls road trip? You seemed a bit..." He paused, checking the sizes on men's shorts before grabbing a handful. "Annoyed, I think is the word."

"No, not annoyed. I'm not being aggravated, disappointed, or perturbed. I am at the Grand glorious Canyon, and friends or not, I plan on enjoying myself." Geena spoke through her teeth. Dante was taken aback slightly by her failed attempt at a calm demeanor regarding a situation that was apparently causing her anger.

"What happened?" Dante asked as he picked up a selection of T-shirts.

"Hannah, the one you call Belle. Well, her controlling jerk-face fiancé apparently could not handle her being off on a trip without him. So he flew in yesterday to sweep her away this morning. I guess he loves her. But still."

"Seriously?"

"Seriously. And Brooke... I think you need to change her name to Cruella. She hooked up with some random J. Crew idea of an outdoorsman and his group. They are off hiking. Frankly, I'm kind of glad to see her backside. I know that sounds so ungrateful. We've never been friends, but we're usually friendly enough. I thought she was just having a bad trip, but she's been flat-out mean to me lately. I have been left to my own devices. I was slapped with the opportunity to take this time to reflect on life, commune with nature, and just soak in the canyon all by myself." She sighed. "I was trying really hard to refocus, and not to feel sorry for myself, when I ran into Mackenzie. Honestly, since finding her and running into you, I haven't thought about them at all."

"So that means, if I want to spend all my time with you, your friends can't object?" He cocked an eyebrow at her. She blushed and looked away. Dante found it so charming that she blushed. She wasn't playing coy, she wasn't playing, there was just a little shyness in her nature.

"No friends around to get mad," she said, grinning.

"Good." He winked at her.

By the time they left the store, Dante had gathered and paid for soap, deodorant, towels, T-shirts, shorts, a pack of underwear, and three pairs of flip-flops.

"What do you need all of this for?" Geena asked as she carried the towels out of the store.

"You were right. They weren't dogs. They are wolves of a sort. I want to show you something." Dante led the way back toward the clearing where she had first seen Mackenzie and the animals.

Dante entered the clearing, indicating with a nod that Geena should follow. He whistled. Two of the wolves' heads popped up from behind a large log. "Hey, guys, I got you stuff." Dante put down the bag with the clothes.

One of the animals took the bag in his jaws and disappeared back behind the log.

"Bring back the garbage," Dante called after him.

Dante smiled nervously at Geena while they waited. He wanted to apologize for making her think he was going to say something jerky. He wanted to pull her into his arms and kiss her.

"What's going on Dante?"

"Give 'em some time, you'll see."

Somewhere between five and ten minutes later a tall, skinny teenager came out from behind the log, pulling a shirt on. He was followed by two more. They all looked exactly the same. Triplets. Tall and lanky, as if they had just hit the first serious growth spurt of their teens. They had shaggy midnight-black hair and the smooth copper skin and high cheekbones of Native Americans.

"Man, we tracked you all the way here," the second youth said.

"I told you there was another wolf," the first one said to him.

The third one held back. He reminded Geena of that third puppy, the one who kept to the edges and wasn't playing. "This isn't who we tracked."

"Sure it is."

"Idiots, you tracked me into the Grand Canyon. Did you even think what would happen if they found wolves in the park?" Dante was very serious.

"Look, here are some towels and soap." Dante took the towels from Geena, handing them to the first boy. "The showers are over there in Trailer Village." He pointed, indicating the way. "Go shower; use deodorant. You stink. Put your stuff in the back of my truck. It's a blue Ford F150 with an orange chopper in the back. Don't touch the bike. I'm towing an Airstream. If anyone asks, tell them you are with me. I'm your cousin, 'cause, well, you are with me until we get you back home." They all nodded. "After you have done all that, come find us along the rim. Then you will call your mother."

"Where on the rim?"

"You're trackers; find me."

"Okay," they muttered. As Dante and Geena turned to go, one of the boys asked, "Hey, man, so who are you?"

"Name's Dante, and we are definitely related."

They walked to the rim in silence. Dante wasn't sure of Geena's reaction. *She's quiet. She's processing. Give her time, you idiot. Maybe I shouldn't have done that. Damn, I'm not thinking straight. I want to do this right for her.* Maybe it was the mate glow that drove him; maybe it was how beautiful she was. Dante had never told, never wanted to tell a woman his secret before. Now, he didn't want to keep anything from Geena. He stroked his thumb back and forth across the back of her hand. It felt soft and perfect in his.

Once at the rim, Dante noticed how Geena's entire demeanor changed. The tempo of her breathing slowed, and her face took on a sense of wonder. She focused on the canyon, the rock formations, and the clouds. He felt that she had forgotten him until she leaned into him for support. This place spoke to her soul. She tugged his hand for him to follow. She climbed over the low wall separating the path from the edge. The actual edge was still another five feet in front of them, but this was close enough to feel as if they were sitting on the edge of the world. She sat on the wall. Dante followed.

"What do you want to do?" Dante asked into her hair. Geena leaned into him again as soon as he sat.

"This," Geena said. The canyon was having a powerful effect on her.

He closed his eyes and breathed in her reaction. Her energy levels changed, and he could sense a change in her spirit. She was at peace. Nothing seemed to bother her; she hadn't even questioned the whole wolves-and-teenage-boy situation.

Dante sat next to her, straddling the low retaining wall. His focus was all on her face. He could see the canyon reflected in her eyes. The sky seemed to enhance their blueness. He wasn't sure if it was the mate glow or the walk that enhanced the pink radiance to her cheeks. He focused on her lips. They were perfect for kissing.

"The clouds, they look like castles in the sky." Geena's voice was barely above a whisper.

Dante agreed, even though he didn't look at the clouds.

"Isn't this the most amazing thing you have ever seen?" Her voice was full of awe.

"Yes." His voice was thick with desire.

She turned to him, her face so close he could almost kiss her. "Dante, you aren't even looking at the canyon."

"No, but I am looking at you."

Geena gazed into his eyes.

"I'm going to kiss you now," he announced. "Properly."

"Oh," was all she said.

He wasn't asking permission; he was stating his purpose.

She closed her eyes as he dipped his head slightly to hers.

Her lips were warm on his. The kiss started off ever so soft before he deepened the pressure and gently licked her lips to open for his tongue. He cupped the back of her head, holding her close, while he tasted the promise of her and offered his own desire. When the kiss ended, he leaned his forehead against hers and breathed in her scent.

Geena pulled away slightly before moving in closer so that Dante's legs surrounded her and his arms could hold her. She sighed and leaned into him. "A perfect first kiss, in such a perfect place."

"Perfect, huh?" Dante's voice was thick in his chest. He had thought so too; it was good to get confirmation. *It's too early to feel this way. It makes sense though. She glows.* Dante knew what that meant. What she meant to him. His mate. He'd just met her, and yet he'd felt different about her ever since that ride on the motorcycle. He reveled in the feel of her leaning into him as they gazed out into the canyon.

After a time of quiet contemplation Geena said, "I've been connecting the dots in my head. Why you gave those clothes to some wolves, but those boys were putting them on. I know I must be dreaming. I have crazy vivid dreams all the time. Those boys, they're..." She paused, gazing out across the canyon. "Why did you out those boys to me? Was that really your secret to share?"

Dante stroked her arm. Outing the boys. It was an interesting way of looking at it. "It's important. I told you I don't want to lie to you, ever. I need you to know who I am. Their secret is my secret."

Geena's breath caught in her chest for a moment. "You really are a nice dream, Dante. I'm not going to be happy when I wake up, and I'm stuck with Brooke and Hannah in the RV. This is so much more interesting. I get the gorgeous werewolf love interest. Great kisser. I bet you are even ridiculously wealthy. Stupid vivid, lucid dream."

Dante let out a breath, relieved. "It's not a dream, Geena. And I think you are the one who is gorgeous, and that definitely was a great kiss. Maybe kissing you some more will prove this is real?" With that, he turned her to face him again for another kiss. One kiss led to another.

The kissing ended when Geena started laughing after hearing an old man walk past and grumble about "God-damned honeymooners kissing in public."

"Werewolf. Really?"

Dante nodded. He placed his hand on top of hers. He knew this was stupid, too early, but he also knew this was right. Do it now, and not when she could accuse him of leading her on and lying to her. Dante pulled his wolf into his hand. He felt the muscles tense, then relax into the different shape. His nails lengthened; his fingers grew shorter. His palm spread thick and wide. Hair grew quickly on the back, covering it all. In a matter of seconds Dante's hand became a large paw with curling black claws, covered in modulated gray fur, mostly dark with brushes of silver. Geena gingerly petted his knuckles. Then he released the form, allowing the paw to transfer back into his hand.

"Like magic," she whispered.

"More like science we don't fully understand," Dante said. "You okay with this? You really aren't reacting much."

"Yeah," Geena sighed. "Werewolf. Of course, this explains everything. A normal guy wouldn't be interested in me. You aren't going to eat me or anything?"

Dante leered at her. "Only if you say please."

Geena gasped at the implications, then smiled, and then laughed.

"Werewolf?"

"Yes and no. Not so much like the legendary werewolf that is pulled to change with the full moon. You won't become like me if I bite you. I can't give it to you like a disease. It's actually something we can now track through DNA. Some genetic human-wolf combo, lupine-sapiens, I don't know exactly. Definitely more human than wolf. Either way I'm an excellent guard, I don't shed, and I don't have fleas." He leaned in to nuzzle her cheek. "And I can be quite loyal."

"How are you at obeying?"

"That depends on who is giving the orders." He chuckled.

"Really, Dante, this is too much." He began nibbling on her ear. "I don't think I care to wake up. But, I do need to find a restroom."

8
―――――

"You're not going to run away, are you? You know, slip out the back?"

"No, I just really have to use the potty." Geena hurried into the facilities. It wasn't obvious even to herself if she was rushing for the bathroom or rushing to get away from Dante.

Slipping out the back was an option, but why would she even consider it? *Right, he can turn his hands into wolf claws. And he's pretty much told you those boys are little werewolf puppies.*

Geena closed and locked the door behind her. She breathed deeply. Good, a single person bathroom with enough room for a freak-out. There really isn't enough room in a bathroom stall to freak out. Cry, yes—she had done that too many times—but genuinely freak out? No.

Geena started walking in a tight circle, stepping high, bringing her knees up to her chest. After a few laps, her hands started flapping as if she couldn't flick something from her fingertips. She began talking to herself. "Pros: He's really hot, and he likes you. Cons: He's too hot. No such thing," she corrected herself. "He's a vagabond. No, he even said this was a job driving the trailer cross-country. All right." She stopped her hand-flapping dance and stared at her reflection. "The wolf thing is freaky, but is it really a con?"

The only way Dante could be physically more perfect in Geena's opinion was if he had blue eyes. That was it. That was the only flaw she could find. Tall, check, curly dark hair, check. High cheekbones and a strong jaw, check. Just enough chest hair to twine fingers in and to tease her nipples.

"Oh my God, I can't believe I just thought that." Her reflection blushed; then she answered herself. "Well, it's true." She grinned. She knew her dreams could be ridiculously realistic, but there was no way Dante was a sleep-deprived delusion. He was real, and she really liked him.

She splashed cold water on her face and looked at her reflection again. "He likes you, and you think he's hot. He hasn't been a jerk to you yet. And he bought you doughnuts. Get over yourself."

She used the facilities, then left the bathroom to find Dante nearby browsing in the gift shop.

She was happy, quite possibly the happiest she had ever been. It was interesting since this was not what she had expected happiness to look or feel like. Once she'd got over her freak-out in the bathroom, she was fine. There was nothing to get in the way of her joy. She had always expected extreme happiness to be loud and involve lots of noise and colored lights, and to be hot, something like a disco. But this was deep and calm. The sounds were soft and muted—wind, birds, mutterings of people in the distance. The light was clear and clean and sharp. The colors were sky and earth. The smell, Dante, feeling warm and protected because of his arms around her. They returned to the rim, and Geena was content to sit next to him like this for hours. She felt no compulsion to get moving. She knew there was more to see, but she wasn't bothered by that. And she wasn't troubled by Dante's secret. Shouldn't she be freaking out more? Who would she tell? And what would happen if she did tell someone? Nothing. They would think she was crazy, and they would be right. She would have to be totally insane to do anything that would send Dante away from her right now.

"Those boys should be here sometime soon, don't you think?" she asked.

"Probably. They think they are trackers; they'll find us." Dante seemed as content to sit and look out at the canyon as she was.

Somewhere between entirely not enough time and a long time later, someone behind them called out, "Hey, Dante."

Geena turned to see the three boys, with wet hair, approaching them.

"So you are the one we were tracking from near our town, right? I mean, you were there the other day, weren't you?"

"I still think it was someone else." The boys jostled each other and were always moving and in each other's way.

"We are good trackers, see, AJ?" one of them said, slapping one of the others in the midsection. "I knew we could do it."

The one called AJ shoved his brother's head. "Idiot, you are the one who was all scared and shit."

"Boys." Dante's voice was sharp, commanding. They stopped messing with each other. "How long have you been tracking someone?"

"Just two days, maybe three."

"It's probably the farthest we've tracked someone so far, and this guy smells like one of us."

"Yeah, we tend to stay close on the res."

"Two days, three days, you've been lupine the entire time? Probably not me, then." Dante shook his head.

"Yeah."

"We're hungry, man."

"What were you doing on the res?"

"Looking for our kind, family connections. But"—Dante scratched the back of his head—"you haven't been tracking me since Window Rock or Farmington, have you?"

"Naw, man, we're from outside Tuba City."

"Definitely not me." Dante pursed his lips with concern. "I wasn't in that area until yesterday. You've been tracking someone else. That means I actually have some work to do while I'm here." He smiled wryly at Geena. "Got to find out who they've been tracking."

Dante pulled out his cell phone and handed it to the closest boy. "Call your mother, tell her where you are and what you did, then let me talk to her." The teen took the phone and focused on dialing. "What are your names?" Dante asked the others.

"I'm Percy. This loser," he said, swatting the boy on the phone in the head, "is Jason."

"I'm AJ."

Geena chuckled.

"What?"

"She cool? She's not one of us."

"Jason, Percy, and AJ? Your mom's big into Greek mythology, right?" Geena asked.

"Yeah, why?"

"Your names, Jason, Perseus, Ajax."

"Who told you my name's Ajax?"

"Greek heroes, you're named for Greek heroes." Geena smiled at their antics.

"Yeah, but you can stick to calling me AJ."

"Jason's the only one who got a normal name."

"Your names are awesome, good, strong, heroic names. Warrior names," Geena said.

"She's cool; she's smart and stuff," Percy declared.

Jason handed the phone to Dante. Taking it, he strolled away from the group.

"Mom was wondering where we went."

"She pissed?"

"Naw, a little disappointed"—Jason made finger quotes in the air around the word—"that we didn't tell her we were gonna take off."

"So who is this guy?"

"If it wasn't him, who were we tracking?"

"Why was he on the res?" The boys finished each other's sentences and talked over each other.

"Are we supposed to know who he is?"

"Who is he?" AJ asked Geena.

"I only met him a few days ago." That felt weird to say. Geena felt like she had known Dante for so much longer than a few hours. The ride, coffee in the morning, and the time today was really all they had had together. He felt so much more important to her than having just met. "He told me he was tracking down some family members, genealogy stuff, that would take him into the reservation in New Mexico. That's all I know. You'll have to ask him."

"If you aren't one of us, and you just met him—"

"How come you already know about us?"

"Because she is with me," Dante stated as he returned to the group. "Okay, your mom is cool with you being here. You will sleep in the back of the truck, and when I leave here, I will take you home." The boys jostled around some more. They were obviously happy to not be punished or sent home immediately. "You will stay in this form while you are here. I will not have some ranger tag your happy ass and ship you to Alaska on my watch."

"All right, but"—Percy sniffed the air—"can we get waffle cones? That smells so good, and I'm starving."

Geena looked up at Dante. "I never did get my ice cream cone earlier."

Geena and Dante strolled behind the three boys after they all got ice cream cones. The boys were in constant motion: jumping over garbage cans, climbing on low walls, climbing over each other. She felt that their mother must be exhausted keeping herd on them, and no wonder she was letting them stay with Dante a few days. They snacked through lunch as they casually walked from one end of the village rim trail to the other end. She couldn't help but wonder if this was what it would be like to have kids: being amused by their antics, buying them food, and always either being far ahead of them or trailing behind. She looked over at Dante and smiled to herself. Or would that be puppies?

9

Geena's phone buzzed with a text from Hannah. *Did I see u with Dante?*

Yep :)

Dinner?

Time? Place?

Food court. Lodge. 6ish.

Hear from Brooke?

"Who are you texting?" Dante asked smoothly against her ear. They rode the shuttle bus along the Village Loop. After lunch Geena, Dante, and the triplets had decided to venture to the canyon information center and museum, taking advantage of the free transportation system around the park.

"Oh, sorry." Geena smiled at him and held up her phone, showing Dante the screen. "Hannah is coordinating dinner. She saw us today, but I don't remember seeing her."

"Me either. Then again, between you and that view back there, I haven't seen much of anything else."

"Yeah, the canyon is amazing," Geena agreed.

Dante leaned closer to her ear. "I meant your fabulous ass."

"Oh." Geena felt her cheeks tighten and heat with a blush.

The phone buzzed again, distracting her from Dante's flirting.

No Brooke yet. You?

Geena texted the other woman. A feeling of guilt for not checking in all day quickly washed over her. It dissipated just as fast. She needed to stop wasting energy on Brooke and a friendship that was never going to happen. Geena knew they weren't friends, but somewhere in the back of her mind she had thought that maybe this trip might change that. The idea they would possibly bond didn't survive the first thirty-six hours of being confined in the RV together. And this morning, seeing how Hannah deferred to Tim, had Geena thinking that they had also outgrown each other. She would always have a special place in her heart for Hannah, but maybe they were not cut out to be lifelong besties. Geena could tell their friendship was not going to survive Hannah's marriage.

Her so-called friends hadn't bothered to check in with her all day. As far as either of them knew, or cared, she was all alone. Why was she bothering to check on Brooke? She needed new friends.

Nada here.

But her day had been filled with new friends thanks to little Mackenzie, Dante, and the boys. She turned back to Dante. "Hannah wants to meet for dinner in about thirty minutes; we should be there around then anyway."

"It's probably time to feed the ravenous horde again," Dante said, referring to the triplets. "I think I can share you for a meal."

Lunch had been a walking buffet—anyplace that sold food or drinks of any kind had been patronized.

"Not enough time to clean up. Pfftt on them. They ditched me. They get me in all my stinky glory."

"You don't stink." Dante tapped the side of his nose. "This isn't just for decoration; it works really well."

Geena quickly ducked her head against her shoulder to check if she actually did smell. She took a quick sniff. "Oh jeez! I'm sorry. I smell like a goat."

"No, you don't. I like the way you smell; it's sexy."

She blushed again, tucking her head into his chest to hide. The entire afternoon had been like this: constant flirting, innocent caresses, stealing kisses. Geena was really quite pleased that Hannah and Brooke had decided to be jerks and ditch her. The phone in her hand buzzed again.

Ah, jerk number one. She read the text from Brooke.

At North Rim for the night, maybe tomorrow.

"Grrr." Geena growled as she clicked off the screen. Dante cocked an eyebrow at her sound.

"She took off to the North Rim. She is such a hypocrite." Geena shook her head; she talked through clenched teeth. "For the past two days she has given me nothing but grief for getting on the back of your bike." She raised her voice into a mocking squeak. "'It's dangerous, Geena. Fat girls don't understand. You don't know what you're doing.'" She added a hand flutter to her chest. "'I know how to deal with men. I never do anything dangerous or stupid.'" Geena's voice returned to its normal pitch. "Oh cuss words, cuss words, cuss words."

Dante chuckled at her use of *cuss words* instead of actual profanity.

"I'm gone for a lousy twenty minutes, and she treats me like an infant. I'm big, not stupid," she grumbled.

Dante kissed her knuckles. "Lousy? Possibly the best twenty minutes, ever. I met you."

Geena's rant was completely deflated. "Yeah," she sighed, getting lost in the depths of his eyes. They looked more gold than hazel at the moment. He put his arm around her and leaned her back against his chest.

They rode the rest of the way back to the lodge with Dante quietly holding Geena. She wanted to be angry with Brooke. She was. But she would rather think about having met Dante. And how he said he would find her at the Grand Canyon, and he had. She wanted to focus on how it felt to lean against his chest and move with him as he breathed. But her mind would not let go of her aggravation with Brooke.

Brooke had always been slightly passive-aggressive toward Geena. It was always in a very narcissistic "I'm doing it for your own good" way. A way that, if Geena complained about it, made her look to be the bad guy and Brooke to be the hero acting in Geena's best interests. She hadn't expected Brooke to be so hostile. Who was she kidding? The more wedding activities they did, the nastier Brooke got.

The time they had gone shopping for bridesmaids' dresses was still fresh in Geena's mind. All the styles Hannah had selected would look good on Hannah. No one else in the group looked good in styles that were meant to flatter someone who was fine-boned, delicate, and petite. Then Brooke took over and did the same thing. She selected dresses that would only look good on herself, lots of formfitting and mermaid styles. The problem was neither Geena nor Ashley looked good in those styles. Brooke, supportive of how the styles looked on Ashley, had been positively rude when it came to commenting on how the dresses looked on Geena. "Good God, you look like a pork sausage," had been one comment on a particular formfitting dress. The other comments ran the gamut from looking pregnant to making Geena's butt look even bigger. "I mean, your butt is big; we just don't need to emphasize it so much." Probably the most hurtful comments were about how much weight Geena might be able to lose, and they should just buy the dress a size or two smaller as impetus.

In the end, the salesperson had come to Geena's rescue after finding her in tears in the dressing room. She convinced Hannah that with such different body types, maybe they could try on dress styles that would flatter each one individually, then coordinate the dresses by being all in the same color and have similar lengths, necklines, or sleeve styles.

Geena wanted this road trip to be fun and epic, and maybe give Brooke a chance to not be so mean. Of course having a road-trip romance with the hot Italian guy definitely qualified for the epic description. Not just any hot guy, Geena reminded herself, a hot werewolf.

She was still more than a bit amazed that she was the one having the romance. *Please let this be a romance,* she silently prayed. Brooke running off with a guy she just met was really pretty typical based on tales Hannah had told. Brooke usually got the guy whenever they went out. Geena wasn't used to getting a guy, let alone "the guy."

"The guy" was always the most good-looking, most charismatic male they would meet. He usually had an entourage of friends and a few girls following him around. Blake would have qualified for "the guy" status if it weren't for Dante. Dante was just too gorgeous with his curly hair and movie-star quality cheekbones. Even Hannah, who was good about not looking at other men, had said Dante was hot. No, Dante was clearly "the guy" on this trip.

She closed her eyes and focused on what it felt like to lean on him, with his arm draped across her shoulders. She offered up another silent prayer. *Let this be epic and not an epic screwup.*

Geena's phone buzzed, bringing her out of her reverie.

ETA? Hannah again.

Tim was probably getting twitchy. He had a bad habit of arranging a time, then showing up for the event early. He would even go ahead and order for himself and Hannah so that when Geena showed up on time, they would already be eating. This always put Geena in a defensive mood. They put her in the position of looking like she was late and rude, when in fact they were rude by not waiting.

Geena sat up and looked out the windows to see if she could figure out where they were. The shuttle pulled up to their stop.

Here. She texted as they disembarked.

Ok getting food meet you inside. Geena's gut quickly twisted and corrected itself.

Geena told Dante and the boys to go ahead and get their food; she needed to use the facilities to freshen up a bit. They would all meet back at the tables with Hannah.

Freshening up had been a paltry excuse and she knew it. Geena ran a cool, damp paper towel under her arms and between her breasts. Everyone else in the lodge had also spent their day hiking and camping. Her personal sweaty smell was no worse than anyone else. Besides, Dante had said she smelled sexy.

She looked at herself in the mirror. *Cheap excuse, girl.* She had to face facts: she was hiding from any potential jibes from dinner with Tim, and worse yet, from Hannah who would supposedly agree with Tim out of concern for Geena's health. Geena knew she had a healthy balanced diet. But when others judged everything about you based on the size of your butt, and your butt was large, it seemed commentary on what she ate was fair game. She had to gird her loins to make it through a meal encounter with Tim.

Dante and food should be the terrifying combination. His opinion mattered, but Dante hadn't given her any reason to think he would say anything. *Dante bought you doughnuts. He's not Brooke, and he's not Tim. He hasn't said anything yet, and he's not gonna.* "Pull up your big girl panties and get out there," she told her reflection.

Geena straightened her shirt and headed into the food line. She saw Dante ahead of her at the register. Based on the pile of food he had on his tray and how much each of the triplets had, she knew she had nothing to worry about.

∽

Dante paid for dinner. Spotting Geena behind them in the cafeteria line, he intended on putting his tray down before coming back to pay for her meal.

Entering the maze of tables, he found Geena's friend Hannah. Dante gave a quick whistle to get the attention of the triplets. "Over this way, guys." He indicated with a nod the direction he wanted them to head.

The quieter of the boys, AJ, asked if they could have their own table "away from boring hipster talk."

"Sure. Don't go too far, and don't do anything that would embarrass your mother." Dante kept an eye on them as they slid into a booth.

Geena had said Hannah's fiancé had shown up this morning, but Hannah sat on her own, with no indication of a fiancé anywhere. She adjusted her plate and utensils as if waiting for someone. Understanding from Geena's description that the fiancé had overprotective issues, Dante slid his tray onto the table opposite and away from Hannah.

"Hannah, right? I recognize you from the other day, even though we never properly met." Dante extended his hand.

Hannah's handshake was curt. He noticed she removed her hand quickly.

"I remember you, Dante. I'm glad you found Geena. I felt a little guilty leaving her with Brooke. I didn't realize Brooke was going to abandon her too." Hannah's smile wavered.

"Frankly I am glad you and Brooke took off. I didn't have to compete with anyone for her attention." Dante smirked. Pleased to have Geena to himself, he questioned the loyalty of her friends. Well, friend. From what Geena had said, she and Brooke were acquaintances at best. Geena deserved better from the one that was her friend.

"So you?" Hannah wagged her finger back and forth, indicating that he and Geena were together.

Dante nodded.

"Really?" Hannah melted into a smile. "I mean, that's good. She likes you. You're gonna be nice to my friend, right? This isn't some game at her expense?"

Dante pulled out his chair. She had the nerve to ask if he was going to be nice to Geena? He should be asking her if she was planning on being nice to her own friend. "No games. I—"

The shove to Dante's back pushed him into the tables, knocking them askew. Dante jerked forward, falling across his tray and tipping his chair over. Hannah cried out. Drink and food spilled everywhere.

"What the...?" Dante turned to see what or who had slammed into his back. He caught a glimpse of a fist flying toward his face. He folded back. The punch glanced off his brow, making contact with enough force to break the thin skin above his right eye. Blood trickled down his face.

Hannah gasped. "Timmy, no!"

The next punch Dante caught with his hand. The assailant, Tim, groaned as Dante squeezed his fist. Dante heard knuckles pop as he continued squeezing. Tim's face turned red with anger and effort. He pulled his fist from Dante's grasp. Tim stepped back and then rushed Dante.

With a step and a twist, Dante had Tim turned around facing away, pulling his arm up into a half nelson. Two quick kicks to the backs of his legs and Tim was on his knees yelling, "Get off me, you son of a bitch! Keep away from my fiancée, you asshole."

Dante held the struggling Tim. "Dude, you need to calm the fuck down."

"Get off me," Tim barked.

"Not until you rein it in," Dante growled.

"Okay, fellas, what's going on here?"

Dante looked up at two approaching park rangers.

"Sir, I need you to let him go," one of the rangers directed Dante.

Dante released Tim, raised his hands in front of his chest, and stepped back.

Tim lunged at Dante. He was caught around the waist by one of the rangers. Tim twisted and complained as the rangers subdued him.

"We're gonna have to take you in."

Dante nodded in agreement.

∼

A crowd gathered around the area of tables that Geena headed toward. Initially she could not see why. Her stomach sank when she saw Hannah standing in front of scattered tables, overturned chairs, and food spilled everywhere. She groaned when she saw Tim. He had his hands behind his back and was yelling at one of the park rangers. "He attacked me; arrest him, not me. Tell him, Hannah. I'm the victim here."

Then her gaze found Dante. Blood streamed down the side of his face; food smeared the front of his shirt. He stood calmly still as a park ranger handcuffed him with zip ties. "Are you all right?" she asked, approaching him, her voice cracked with worry. "What happened?"

The ranger tightened the restraints. Dante winced. "I'll tell you later. This is going to take some time to clear up. Stay here and eat your dinner, okay?"

Geena nodded.

"Make sure the boys eat enough; get them seconds if they are still hungry. Take care of you and them. Then come get me."

The ranger tapped Dante on the shoulder, indicating it was time for him to move. Dante turned back toward Geena. "Bring me a cheeseburger when you come to pick me up. I'm gonna be starving." He let the ranger guide him out the door. Turning back, he added, "Make it a double, with bacon. And fries."

Geena smiled weakly and shook her head. Tim yelled for Hannah to follow, and at the rangers about violating his rights.

"He didn't hit that loser."

"Did you see his moves?"

"He gonna be okay?"

Geena joined Jason, Percy, and AJ at their table. "Yeah, sure, I'm sure it will all be all right. You heard him, we need to eat, then I'll go see what's going on and bail him out if that's what needs to happen." She suddenly didn't feel hungry, all her previous anxiety over tonight's dinner turned to concern. *What happened? Why was he bleeding?* She left her tray on the table and returned to the scene of the mess. She began picking up the chairs that had gotten knocked over and pushed the tables back into alignment.

"You don't need to do that, miss." Two service workers had shown up with cleaning supplies and a mop cart. "Thank you, miss; we'll finish."

"Thank you. Sorry about all this."

"No problem, miss."

Geena sat. She really didn't feel like eating now but did so anyway. She spent most of her time watching the boys. She noticed that as scattered as they seemed in all other activities, they were very focused on their eating.

By the time Geena made it to the ranger station to pick up Dante, it was clear that everything had been sorted out, settled. Two narrow pieces of medical tape held the skin together across the corner of his brow. He stood talking to Hannah. They both looked serious and Hannah a little sad. Hannah shook his hand when Tim appeared from a back hallway. He stormed past them, growling, and continued out the front door. Hannah turned and saw Geena. "I've got to go. We are leaving tonight. Tim is being ejected from the park, and I'm going home with him. I'm sorry, Geena. Here's the RV key. I'll call you in a few days." She pressed the small brass key into Geena's hand before giving her a quick hug and then turned to Dante. "Thanks again. I'm... I'm sorry." She rushed out after Tim.

Geena stood holding paper to-go containers with Dante's dinner. Looking at him, she felt inadequate, stupid, unsure. Brooke had said he could be dangerous. Had he somehow instigated the attack? Was getting jumped by her best friend's fiancé a deal breaker? Dante stepped up to her, took the to-go box with one hand, and wrapped the other arm around her, bringing her in for a deep kiss. His lips were warm and soft, melting away her uncertainty. Clarifying her thoughts that this man couldn't be anything but one of the good guys.

"You all right?" she asked tentatively, touching above his eye.

"Lucky shot. Just don't tell Morgan that loser ever landed a punch on me."

"Who?"

"My cousin." Dante stroked her hair; it was damp. "Raining?"

"Just a bit. It must have started during dinner. Oh, I put the boys in the rental. I left them watching a movie."

Dante led her out to the porch, sat on a bench, and began eating. Between bites, he explained how Tim jumped him at the table. Fortunately an older couple had seen the entire incident and followed them to the ranger station to provide witness for him. Tim had struck first in an unprovoked attack. "Talking to your girlfriend's friend is not adequate provocation in the opinion of the rangers. Since my eye was cut and bleeding, the rangers accepted that as proof that he attacked first. They didn't arrest anyone, and I told them I would not file assault charges if Tim left the park. So Hannah decided to leave with him."

Geena couldn't help but notice that Dante had called her his girlfriend. "He's lucky he didn't get arrested," Geena commented. "Why is Hannah leaving?"

Dante nodded. "It doesn't sound like he's giving her much of a choice. Pressing charges isn't worth it. It wouldn't teach a guy like that any lessons. He's lucky this is federal land and that cafeteria was full of people. Next time, private property, no witnesses, I won't be so reserved." He wagged his eyebrows at her.

He put the last few french fries in his mouth and chewed. "Hannah seems like a nice girl. What is she doing with a whiny bastard like him?"

Dante placed the empty wrappers in the garbage. He wrapped a protective arm around Geena, and they walked to the nearest shuttle stop. The rain had eased back to a fine mist, but it was too wet and dark to walk back to Trailer Village.

"I don't get what she sees in him either," Geena began. "They first started dating in college. Having an in to frat parties was a good thing, and as the BFF to the date, I was always allowed to tag along. Otherwise I would have had no way into those parties. Not that they were really as great as everyone made them out to be." Geena was relieved to finally be able to tell someone how she really felt about Tim. "They broke up for a little while after graduation but got back together about three years ago. I don't understand what she sees in him. He's a vain, entitled, self-righteous jerk. I don't understand how Hannah puts up with his jealousy and control issues. I mean, jeez, he couldn't even let her have this trip without interfering."

She knocked on the RV door. When no one answered, Geena used her key to unlock the door. Stepping inside, she and Dante found the three boys gently snoring in the main bed. The movie flickered blue light against the walls.

"They look like a puppy pile," she commented on their overlapping limbs. "I hate to wake them."

"You said Brooke is off at the North Rim for the night, right? So why don't we leave them here," Dante suggested. "I can stay with these guys, and you can have the Airstream for the night."

Geena nodded in consent.

"Besides, I haven't given you a tour of that thing."

Geena collected the clothes and toiletries she would need for sleeping elsewhere for the night.

"Did I tell you my cousin Morgan completely restored and renovated this?" Dante asked as he unlocked the Airstream door.

Once inside the dark camper, Dante reached around Geena for the light switch. He paused, stepping in close. "We could always leave the lights off." His voice was low and husky as he nuzzled the side of her neck.

Geena's heart skipped a beat before it began racing in anticipation. "Dante." She rested her hand against his chest. It felt solid under her fingers. She wasn't sure if she should say yes or slow down. This was moving too fast in calendar time. In emotional speed, she felt she had known him for weeks, months, forever. Not just hours.

"You're right." He flipped on the lights. "It's better with the lights on."

A double row of inset lighting ran the entire length of the camper along the ceiling. He stole a quick kiss as he took the tote bag with her things and placed it on the table. His shopping bags from earlier in the morning still sat there, half unpacked.

They stood just inside the door, in the kitchen area. All the appliances were new and stainless steel. The counter was light, blond-colored wood, and the walls were white. Behind Dante was a diner-style booth. The table was the same type of wood, and the seats were upholstered in a silvery-gray fabric. Overall the effect was classic modern, with minimalist lines that were somehow contemporary and retro all at the same time.

Just beyond the kitchen, the living room took up the

entire width of the trailer. A large sepia-colored leather couch dominated the space. It was accompanied by a matching side chair, a low cabinet across the opposite wall, and a large flat-screen television.

"This is my favorite part." Dante indicated the end wall where a bank of cabinetry started floor to ceiling, then stairstepped down, extending about half of the width of the camper. An accordion folding door completed the back wall. Dante grinned widely as he folded back the door, revealing the bathroom. Geena hadn't realized that a luxury bathroom could fit into a trailer. Standard functional bathroom features tucked in behind the cabinets. A Jacuzzi bathtub large enough for two people dominated the rest of the bathroom. Large enough for both her and Dante.

"Come sit here." Dante guided her to the tub and positioned her on the edge. He then stepped over to the television. Gently he pulled the TV away from the wall. It was mounted on a swing arm. Once the mount was perpendicular to the wall, he began to pivot the TV. After he completed moving the device, he joined Geena at the tub.

"You're right. I can see why this is your favorite part." With the bathroom wall fully open and tucked into an alcove in the cabinets, and with the television repositioned as it was, it was possible to watch TV from the bathtub.

Leaning forward, Dante opened a cabinet door. "Bath salts are in here." He leaned back and twisted the water on. "Now you can relax and watch a movie before you go to bed." He kissed her gently on the temple. Geena trailed her fingers under the rushing water. It was hot. A bath was going to feel grand.

"I didn't think dogs liked baths." The quip was out of her mouth before she had time to think. Dante turned sharply to face her. The prickly sharp chill of fear washed over

Geena in an instant; had she uttered a deal breaker? Dante began laughing. He roared from deep in his belly.

Dante opened a drawer loaded with DVDs. "What would you like to watch, pretty girl?"

"How about a nice relaxing monster movie," Geena replied.

"I knew there was a reason I liked you, Geena Davies, and it's not just that hot ass and beautiful face of yours."

Geena smiled, blushing a bit. She wasn't sure if she would ever get used to having him call her pretty and beautiful, or saying he liked her butt.

"How about monsters and giant robots?"

"Even better. So..." She paused. She wanted to be sassy and sexy and invite him to stay. She felt uncertain about what words to use. She watched Dante pull the sofa into a large flat bed. He placed, then inflated an air mattress on top. The muscles in his arms bunched and pulsed as if they were showing off just for her, flexing on their own.

She had never slept with a man on the first date. Casual sex wasn't her style; she was never comfortable with situations like that. But now, was today a first date or a second date? How many hours determined date length? They had been together since midmorning. Geena quickly calculated that to be at least eight hours and three meals if the doughnuts counted as breakfast—certainly that should qualify for more than one date. She didn't care. Any previous dating rules she may have had for herself no longer applied. She felt wanton. Dante had just admitted to liking her. They had spent most of their time together touching and stealing kisses, if not actually making out. So why was she being stymied now for words to express her own desire for the man?

"Um, there's room for two in this tub."

"Yes, there is." Dante grinned wolfishly at her. He had been gathering clothes and held a fat book in his hands. "I won't be joining you tonight."

Geena was crestfallen. Her luck at hitting on men had always been bad. Dante must have seen the change in her expression. Putting his things down, he crossed to her and cupped her face in his hands. "Make no mistake, I want to stay and scrub your back, but..."

"But?" She searched his face.

"But you have had a long and stress-filled day, and I am exhausted. Besides, we both know you aren't the type of girl to jump into bed with someone you just met."

"You don't want me?" It was getting difficult to not physically curl up into a ball and hide; mentally she could already feel her ego folding into itself. Even though they had spent the entire day kissing, even though he had said he wanted to stay, this felt like a complete rejection. She had put herself out there expecting a yes, and she got a no. She got a lot of nos in her life.

Dante pulled her into a kiss. It was long and deep. His lips were hard and seeking against her mouth. His tongue plunged between her lips. When he broke the kiss, Geena felt breathless and confused.

"Oh, I want you. I'm trying to be gentlemanly and noble here. I don't want you to regret wanting me." He smoothed her hair and stroked the side of her face. "Enjoy your bath. I'll see you in the morning."

10

Morning. Bright sunlight streamed through the RV windows. When Geena woke up, she had slept on her arm and couldn't move it. She was in the big bed in the rental RV, and not in the Airstream. *Well, looks like Dante had indeed been a beautiful dream.* She decided the fantasy of Dante was better than anything this morning could offer, so she tried to roll over and go back to sleep.

She was frozen. She could only move her eyes. She couldn't call out for help. The malicious shadowy presence lurked beyond her vision. The shadow drifted closer. She felt its weight on the bed. She wanted to scream.

Geena thrashed awake.

It was dark. Rain made a reassuring constant pattering on the Airstream's hull. She gulped for air and then tried to calm her breathing, focusing on the in and out. She lay staring at the trailer's ceiling, her legs tangled in blankets. Stupid sleep paralysis dream. She knew once they started, she would have a run of them over the course of several weeks. Two nights down, how many more to go? At least this time no repeat false waking dreams. Just the one.

To prove to herself this wasn't a dream, she got up to use the toilet. If it had been a dream, she would wake up just as she started to urinate so that she wouldn't wet the bed. It worked; this was not a dream. And that meant Dante wasn't a dream. Smiling to herself, she crawled back onto the air mattress, grabbed the pillow that most smelled like Dante, and fell back asleep. Her dreams for the rest of the night featured a silver-gray wolf. Whenever some malevolent shadow appeared in a dream, she was protected by the wolf. Even though protected in her dreams, she spent the rest of the night waking frequently, worried there would be another sleep paralysis and false-waking incident.

The smell of freshly brewed coffee woke Geena. She instantly knew this wasn't a false waking. She cracked her eyes open slowly. Lights were on. The soft, steady tapping beat let Geena know it still rained. Dante stood at the kitchenette counter facing away from her. His damp hair curled at the base of his neck, his back bare. Geena marveled at his broad shoulders that tapered to narrow hips. Low-riding jeans hugged his perfect butt. When he moved, she could see the shifting of muscles under his bare skin. He turned to her. His chest was covered in even black hair that tapered to a line defining his perfectly formed abdominal muscles, and continued past his belly button, disappearing into the waistband of his jeans. She realized she stared at the front of his jeans when he spoke.

"Good morning, pretty girl."

She groaned and sat up, running her hand over her face and into her hair. Dante was almost too chipper for her this morning.

"You didn't warn me you would be in your sexy underwear." Dante approached the edge of the bed.

Geena wore men's dark blue boxer briefs and a tight

white tank top. It was the kind of quip Brooke would say, indicating how unattractive Geena's choice of sleepwear was. "Dante, don't."

"Don't what? Tell you that you are undeniably sexy right now?"

"Don't pick on me." She didn't want to deal with passive-aggressive jabs from him. He was supposed to be her epic romance.

"No picking. You look amazing right now. Very sexy, all warm and rumpled. And in my bed. You know what's missing from this picture?"

"Hmmm?" She blinked up at him, working on waking up. He had just called her sexy. Warmth radiated from deep within, making her happy.

"Me. I'm not in that bed with you." He sat in front of her on the edge of the mattress and rotated to hand her the mug of coffee.

She shook her head no. Her brain still reeled from Dante calling her sexy. She didn't want coffee right now. She wanted him.

"You think I'm sexy?" She leaned into his back and stroked the skin along his shoulder. She agreed that he was missing from the bed with her. Sitting on the edge drinking coffee didn't count, not when she needed him to touch her.

"That might not be safe," he said, his voice dropping into a low rumble.

Geena purposefully pressed her breasts into his back and along his upper arm. She slowed the petting to a lighter, more tickling touch. She planted wet, sucking kisses along the back of his arm, each one progressing to more of a bite, her teeth scraping and teasing along his flesh.

"Not fair, woman." He leaned forward, depositing the coffee mug on a counter before turning to face her. A low growl escaped his lips as he leaned in. He kissed the side of her neck, nibbling the soft flesh from neck to shoulder. She scooted away from him to the center of the bed. He crawled in after her. He was on his hands and knees in front of her, kissing the soft flesh under her ear.

"What happened to being noble?" she asked between breathless gasps. Placing her hands on his broad, square chest, she gently pushed him back. She ran her fingers through his chest hair, teasing his bronze nipples with soft circular motions, allowing the hairs to tickle her fingertips. "Do I know you well enough for this yet?"

She looked into his eyes. They glowed gold.

With one hand he gathered her wrists and pulled them above her head, laying her back against the pillows. "That was last night, and last night was a very long time ago. What do you say now?" he asked as he continued to kiss along her collarbone. "Yes?"

"Yes." Her answer was breathy with excitement.

He practically growled as his lips claimed hers. He continued to hold her hands above her head; then he slid his other hand up the soft flesh of her thigh and beneath the edge of her shorts. He grabbed a large handful of her bottom and began kneading as he continued to explore her mouth.

Dante made her feel sexy, desired. She wanted Dante to touch all of her, and she wanted to touch all of him. He wasn't playing fair holding her hands away from him like that. She began to squirm with pleasure, lifting into his chest and rubbing her bare legs against his jean covered ones.

He pushed his knee against her core. She rocked her hips against it, the jeans and his hard thigh making a delightful friction against her sex. He rocked his hips against her thigh, the bulge behind the zipper growing larger with each stroke.

They pulsed and rocked against each other in rhythm. Geena sucked on Dante's tongue as he plunged it into her mouth. His free hand moved from grabbing her butt, and slipped under her shirt. His hand cupped the outer edge of her ample breast, his thumb caressing over the nipple, teasing it to a hard point. Geena moved her leg from between his and bucked Dante between her thighs. He thrust his denim-clad hips against hers. Geena curled her leg around his knee and arched into him. There were too many clothes between them, and he prevented her from using her hands. She wanted to feel his skin against hers. She needed him inside of her. He released her hands and moved his mouth to her breast, gently biting at the hard point of her nipple through her shirt. She laced her fingers in his hair, tangling them in his curls. They ground into each other as if by sheer will and action their clothes would disappear.

There was a pounding on the camper's door. They ignored it and continued to thrust against each other through their clothes. The pounding on the door continued.

Dante broke their kiss. "Go away!" he growled. He returned his attention to Geena, palming her breast, and prepared to pull her shirt up to expose the soft white flesh to his eyes.

"C'mon, man, we're hungry," one of the boys yelled with more pounding on the door.

Dante gazed down at Geena. She panted with excitement, her lips full and red from kissing, her cheeks flush. He turned his head toward the door to yell at the boys. "Hold on!" To Geena, he said, "Don't go anywhere."

He left Geena in the bed and padded over to the door.

He adjusted himself. His excitement was in danger of extending past his waistband, so he confirmed all erect anatomy was angled to the side and tucked in before opening the door.

"We're hungry. There wasn't anything to eat in the other RV, and we don't have any money."

Reaching behind him, he grabbed his wallet that had been left on the table. "Here, go get some breakfast," Dante said as he opened his wallet. "Crap, I'm out of cash."

The only breakfast food Geena remembered seeing put away last night after Dante left had required cooking.

Dante looked at her. She saw disappointment in his eyes. "Wait here," he said and closed the door. He stepped back to Geena and leaned onto the bed. "Breakfast?"

"All right." She sighed, running her hand down his chest.

He captured her hand and kissed her fingers. "Get dressed, temptress."

Once Geena was safely sequestered in the bathroom, she heard Dante let the boys in. They made loud ooh and ah sounds over the large-screen TV and gaming system, the reconstruction and sophisticated remodeling not even noticed.

"This will last one meal with this lot," Dante said, nodding toward the large mass of scrambled eggs and bacon he'd cooked. "So what should we do with them today?"

"We can't go hiking; it's too wet," Geena said.

"Sure we could, but then we would get all wet, and everyone would need a clean, dry change of clothes, and that is something they don't have. I guess our first stop is back at the store and get them some more clothes. What had you planned on doing?"

"Hannah and Brooke had talked about maybe doing that

mule ride down into the canyon. But that's out, especially today. Sitting on top of a wet, smelly mule is just not appealing. We thought about driving up to the North Rim." Geena flipped through a brochure she had picked up earlier. "I'm not seeing that sky bridge in here. I thought that might be cool."

"The Skywalk isn't in the park; it's another four hours up the road. It's a day trip if you want to go."

"Naw, I'm kind of enjoying not driving for a day or two, besides…" Geena peered over at the boys as they yelled and jumped around playing a video game. "I don't want to be stuck in a car with them for hours. The 'are we there yets' might be fit to kill me."

Dante laughed. Geena smiled. This was nice, hanging out with Dante, no agenda, and not worrying about one either. The triplets were loud, but she could handle that.

"Maybe we can just leave them in here playing video games while I sneak you back to your RV?" Dante wiggled his eyebrows at her. Geena felt the blush explode across her face.

"Brooke might come back." She cleared her throat.

"Damn Brooke. You hear from her this morning?"

"Not yet. You know, part of the point of the road trip was to be flexible. Not stuck to a travel schedule. I didn't really mean for it to be this flexible, with all of us just headed off so completely on our own." Geena sighed. "I guess I will know if we are on schedule to go back if Brooke lets me know where she is."

"How soon do you need to head home?" Dante asked.

"We have reservations for five nights, two down, three to go." It was too soon. Geena didn't want to think about having to leave Dante in only four more days. "And then two or three to get back home."

11

Geena hated eating alone in public. She always felt people were judging her. Mostly because too often they were. In college mealtimes hadn't always coincided with the times her friends had been available, and she would frequently find herself in one of the commissaries alone. They say children can be cruel; well, if those children don't learn any manners, they grow up into cruel young adults. Geena always tried to ignore the barbs and the comments. She found if she could lose herself in a book or wear headphones, she could just phase the rude comments out. She'd grown a thicker skin as she grew up, but the fear that someone would feel the need to comment harshly on her for eating in public alone lingered.

There were plenty of things she liked to do on her own. Being a single woman pushing thirty, without a lot of dating opportunities when her friends were either queens of dating or in committed relationships, she found herself on her own more than she cared to admit. She could take herself out to a concert or a movie or even a convention trade show without any pangs of self-consciousness, but not eating. If she ate out on her own, she more often than not would order takeout or drive-through and just eat in her car.

Waiting for Dante at the food court in the lodge was as bothersome as if she were any place else. She knew he was trying to be nice and not make her wait any longer for lunch when he suggested they meet up there, and that she should just go ahead and eat since she had told him she was getting hungry. She agreed. It made sense.

It made sense until she sat down at the table, alone. She didn't have a book to hide behind, and she didn't have any headphones. It was just her and the loud voices in her head. She imagined she could hear everyone who looked at her. The voices ranged from pitying her for being on her own, "Oh poor dear is here all alone, bless her heart," to judgments on her food choices.

Her biggest problem was that she was hungry and had gotten herself a substantial lunch. Now she had a hard time eating it. She considered her options, if she waited for Dante her food would get cold.

"Damned if I do, damned if I don't," she muttered and began to eat.

The rain had brought cooler weather, and cooler weather always made her crave the warm comfort of potatoes. Mashed potatoes were not available during lunch today, so she chose a baked potato. She loaded it up with everything they had: barbecued chicken, sautéed onions, mushrooms, cheese, sour cream, and real bacon bits. It was a bit over-the-top, but then again, it was delicious.

She'd put a forkful of food into her mouth when Dante sat across from her. She was embarrassed to have been caught eating such a substantial portion. Too many years of being conditioned to think boys shouldn't see you eat more than a few bites.

Dante smiled. "That looks good." His eyes sparkled, and his grin seemed more wolfish than usual. She swallowed her bite. "It is," she said and wiped her mouth.

He tapped the table with both hands. "I'm gonna go grab something; be right back." He came around the table, kissed her on the cheek, and headed over to the cafeteria line.

That was one fine backside walking away from her. He was one fine man. She shook her head. He hadn't made one comment about her eating, not one. He commented on the food, but not that she was eating it. He was almost too good to be true, but he was true, and he was better than just good.

In the few hours she had known him, he had been nothing but kind and generous. He didn't need to buy those boys clothes or even take care of them. He hadn't known them, but he had known what they were, and maybe that was kind of the same thing. And he actually liked her. He wasn't being nice as a way to get to her friends. Been there, done that far too many times not to know the difference. Besides, this morning he hadn't been trying to get to anyone but her. She smiled to herself thinking about it, his body pressed against hers. And this time face-to-face and not on the back of a motorcycle. Damn he was sexy.

She slowly took bites of her potato; she didn't want to finish before Dante returned with his lunch.

He came back with something similar but bigger. He also had a side salad and a bowl of soup. "It just looked so good, I had to get one," he said as he placed his tray down and slid into the chair across from her. He began eating enthusiastically while constantly grinning at her.

"What?" she finally asked.

"You're just so beautiful," he said between bites. "And I've got you all to myself this afternoon."

"What do you mean?"

"You haven't asked where the boys are. Aren't you curious?"

Geena gasped, covering her mouth with her fingers. She instantly felt guilty; she enjoyed being near Dante and had gotten so stuck in her own head over food that she hadn't noticed they hadn't come back with him. Maybe she'd just thought he left them playing video games. But no, she knew better. She hadn't thought about them at all.

Dante chuckled at her discomfort. "It's okay. I distracted you with my wily ways and dazzling smile," he joked, but there was truth in that statement. Dante did distract her.

"That group we ran into earlier at the rim..." Dante took another large bite of his baked potato. "The boys knew some of the kids, and it turns out it was a field trip from a church from their town. One of the chaperones knows their mother, so some artful pleading on their behalf, a little bribery from me, and the boys have joined their little camping trip for the night."

"Wait, what? You bribed some church group to take the boys? How?" Geena wasn't sure if she should be laughing or mad at Dante for paying someone to take the boys he was supposed to be minding.

"Yeah, I agreed to cover the costs of the s'mores and some other stuff for tonight's cookout. That's what took so long—they needed to buy some supplies, and I was paying." He looked at her, slightly chagrined. "Besides, it wasn't just a completely random church group. It's a group of kids they know, and that one woman knows their mother. We get them back in the morning, when the group heads home. Look, they know who they are with, and..." His smile widened. "And it's just you and me, no distractions this time." He winked.

Geena couldn't help it; she blushed and hid her eyes

behind her hand. She wanted Dante, no doubt in her mind, and here he blatantly claimed to have freed himself of responsibilities to be with her. So they could be together, physically.

"I'm being presumptuous." She felt his fingers caress her skin as he reached for her other hand. "I didn't mean to embarrass you. I just thought..." His eyebrows knit together in concern.

Geena lowered her hand to cover the lower half of her face. She was still bright red with blushing. She peered up at him through her lashes. "I didn't say no." She gave a breathy giggle. "I just, kind of"—she lowered her hand—"I'm still kind of shocked that you like me."

"You keep saying things like that, Geena. Why shouldn't I like you? You are..." He rolled his eyes up, making a production of his thinking. "Sweet and kind, generous, and so very beautiful. And I really shouldn't tell you what your kisses do to me; we are in public."

"Dante." Her blush refreshed its bright pink glow.

On the walk back to Trailer Village butterflies rioted in Geena's lower abdomen. She wrapped her arms around Dante's arm, and she leaned into him as they walked. She felt so brazen, with plans to have sex in the middle of the afternoon, like everyone they passed knew what they were going to do. As if she had a neon sign on her forehead that flashed: *Going to have sex now.* How could Dante be so calm about it, so confident? He didn't have a flashing sign on his head. No, he kept his head up and his focus on the path ahead of them.

Once inside the Airstream, Geena didn't know what to do. Her nerves got the best of her. She began fussing in the kitchen area, cleaning dishes left over from breakfast, suddenly overtaken with shyness.

Dante grabbed her hands. "Come here." He led her to the couch. "You don't have to do anything if you don't want to. I would like to hold you." He sat in the corner of the couch and brought her down, sitting in front of him. He wrapped his arms around her. She twisted so she could lie back, leaning into his chest. He was warm against her back. His arms surrounded her, and she felt protected, as if she was something precious. He reached past her to grab the TV remote. He hit play on the movie in the DVD player. "Now you can just relax, watch the movie, and I can hold you."

The movie had been an excuse, but Dante was right, it would give her time to relax.

She wanted to be here with him, but her nerves had wound her up past the point of excitement and anticipation.

Dante pressed his lips to her hair and nuzzled against her ear.

Geena sighed. This felt so comfortable, so natural. This felt so right, just as sitting with Dante at the rim had. This wasn't loud and bright; this was soothing. This was new for her. Dante just wanted to hold her; he wasn't in a hurry to get anything over. Her last boyfriend had always made being intimate feel like a chore that he had to hurry up and be done with. He had never been willing to sit and hold her like this. He actually had never been responsive to her wants or needs. Of course, that was also why they hadn't been together for terribly long. This feeling of just being together with Dante was enough to make her heart explode.

She was falling for Dante, and she knew it. He was everything right, everything she could have ever wanted in a man. He was kind and took on responsibilities. He didn't comment on her weight. He thought she was pretty, without any "only ifs" attached. He was tall. He was so painfully handsome. And—this was the clincher—he liked her. Not one of her friends, but her.

She sighed deeply, content. The sigh caused her chest to lift dramatically. Dante shifted his hold so he could cup her breast. Geena lifted her chest again, this time on purpose, pressing into his hand.

The nuzzling by her ear turned into kisses along her neck. "I want you, Geena." The whisper in her ear was low and thick with desire. The sound sent a chill down her spine. Dante shifted out from behind her. He rolled so that she was lying on the couch and he was over her. "Will you let me make love to you?"

Geena couldn't speak, the words stuck in her throat, so she just nodded. Dante claimed her lips in a fierce kiss. He pressed against her mouth, playing his lips against hers. He worked her lower lip and ran his tongue in a caress across the front of her teeth. Geena fumbled with his shirt, her hands searching for the hem. Once she found it, she pulled his shirt up, exposing his chest. Her hands found purchase on his flat pecs, burying her fingers in his chest hairs. She ran her fingers over his chest and down his sides, around and up his back. She marveled at the feel of his lips crushing hers, the taste of him, the feel of his hard muscles under his smooth, hot skin.

Dante pulled the shirt over his head and off, then lowered himself to her, removing any space between them. Geena made a soft grunt of discomfort, and Dante shifted one leg and fell off the couch. Geena rolled over to look at him on the floor. He laughed at his mishap. He reached up and grabbed her arm, pulling her to him.

"Come here." He smiled at her, and there was something more in his grin; it was devious and hid promises of passion.

"I'll squish you," she teased.

"Oh, I hope so." He exerted pressure on her arm again, and this time Geena followed, so she rolled off the couch and onto his chest.

Geena noticed he didn't flinch when she landed on him. She should have knocked the air completely out of him. He pulled her down and continued kissing her. Her teeth nipped at his mouth, and he consumed her lips. Their tongues intertwined as his hands stroked up and down her arms and across her back. Dante let out a satisfied groan. It sounded like a growl.

Geena pulled back from his kisses and pressed up away from Dante. "I am squishing you." She pushed herself up so that she sat on her knees, hovering above his hips she didn't put any pressure on him.

"And it feels so nice; come squish me more." He grabbed her hips and dragged her down so that she rested on the tops of his thighs.

"I'm going to hurt you if I'm up here. I'm too heavy." Neither of her previous lovers ever let her be on top. The last one had straight out said she was too big.

"You are not too heavy, and you are not going to squash me flat like a bug." He grabbed one of her hands, rubbed it over his chest, then had her hand pat at him. "See, I'm solid. A soft little girl like you isn't going to dent me. I'm more likely to bruise you, and your softness, than the other way round. Now come back down here and kiss me." Geena obliged, too enamored with him to argue. It felt good to be on top, like she was the one in control.

Dante's hands traveled up her back. His hot touch left tantalizing trails against her skin. Geena sat back up on her haunches. Dante grabbed and stroked her thighs.

"Your eyes, they're glowing," Geena said, tracing her finger along his cheek.

"That's because I have intense need right now." Dante reached for her shirt and, agonizingly slowly, unbuttoned each button from the bottom. "How many of these damned things does one shirt need?"

Geena giggled. "As many as it takes." The shirt spread to expose her pale belly. She felt her stomach clench. This was the moment of reckoning in her mind. He had already indicated that he liked her squish, but would he feel the same the second he saw her marshmallow middle?

Dante spread his hand across the soft flesh. His long fingers looked dark against her translucent skin. "Like porcelain," he breathed.

The next button he undid exposed the bottoms of her breasts. She was grateful that she wore the sexiest bra she had packed, a bright pink and yellow floral print. Dante teased his finger along the lower edge of the silky fabric.

Geena bit her lower lip and closed her eyes and relaxed into his caress. He was still touching her. He wasn't coiling away in distaste from her body. He continued teasing her with his fingers.

His next attempt at undoing a button was foiled by a strategically placed safety pin. He tugged at the fabric, but it stayed connected over Geena's breasts. "What kind of freak modesty shirt are you wearing? It's protecting your virtue all on its own."

"Oh, sorry." She looked down, fumbling with the pin. "It keeps the gapposis closed. Manufacturers never put a button right in the middle where it's really needed." She attached the safety pin to the hem of her shirt and undid the last top button. Her shirt hung to the side, exposing her bra-clad breasts.

Dante's expression changed from one of mild amusement to that of a kid in a candy shop. Every time she looked at him, he had a smile on his face, even if it was just a small one. Now it was broad, and his teeth gleamed. She watched him lick his canines. It was a very predatory smile. It was a smile only for her.

Dante sat up, cupping the back of her head to hold her to him. He attacked her mouth like a starving man. He took her air and bruised her lips. He laced his fingers into her hair. His other hand snaked behind her back and fingered the catch on her bra. When the last hook unfastened, his hand moved, slipping up between the fabric and her skin.

Geena sucked in her breath, pulling air from Dante as his lips continued to consume hers. His skin on hers felt noticeably hotter than normal, as if his body heat had risen under a fever. His hand cupped and massaged her breast. His other hand moved down her back and grabbed her butt, massaging in a similar fashion. He began kissing down her neck to her collarbone. He gently nipped and scraped the flesh along the top of her breasts with his teeth, kissing down the center of her chest along her breastbone. Geena leaned into his kisses. Her shirt had slipped off her shoulders and draped across her back, catching on her elbows.

"Dante! Dante!" There was loud pounding on the camper door.

Dante groaned in frustration. "I'm going to kill them."

There was more pounding. "C'mon, man, I need your help."

"The universe doesn't want me to get your shirt all the way off, I swear," Dante growled. Geena giggled nervously as she scooted back out of the way so Dante could get up. She quickly refastened her bra and began buttoning up her shirt.

One of the triplets stood at the door when Dante flung it open in aggravation.

"What? Which one are you?"

"AJ. Look, some kids got lost; we need your help," AJ explained as he climbed into the Airstream.

"Who's lost? Where are your brothers?" Geena asked while putting on her shoes.

AJ explained that half the group had taken off on a hike into the backcountry area. It seemed like all of a sudden three girls were missing. No one could find them.

"How long have they been missing?"

"Over an hour now, but it's going to start getting dark soon. And they are afraid it's going to start raining again."

"Hasn't anyone tried to call them?"

"Not everyone has a cell phone, man. We have to go look for them," AJ insisted.

Dante pulled on his shirt. He and Geena followed AJ back to the group's camping site. Along the way AJ continued to explain that Percy and Jason had taken off after the girls, thinking they could track them. But they had been gone for a long time, so he came to get Dante to help.

At the campsite the remaining teenagers sat around in small groups, murmuring about the missing kids. Dante approached one adult in particular. Geena figured this must be the one that knew the boys, the one Dante had essentially bribed for some alone time with her.

Geena listened carefully.

"About forty-five minutes out, we noticed a few girls had gone missing. We looked for them as a group, but then decided for two of us to stay behind and look for the girls while everyone else came back to camp and notify park rangers." The woman nervously looked around at the remaining group of teens. "On the way back one of the triplets had become rather agitated and ran off on his own to go look for the girls. The other two boys argued, and one of them took off after their brother. This one," she indicated AJ, "said that his friend could help, so he came back with us.

"He said you were some sort of expert tracker, that you could help find them?" The look on her face was full of concern. "We've already alerted the rangers, and they have sent people out there. But I've got five missing kids, and two chaperones out there. I don't know if sending more people into the backwoods is really going to be of any help. Besides, it's going to get dark soon."

Dante nodded. "I can help; this isn't a problem at all. Like you said, it's going to start getting dark. Let's get everyone back to camp before that becomes a problem."

He turned to Geena. "I want you to stay here and wait with the group."

"Not happening. I'm going with you."

Dante's expression became stern. "Geena, it might not be safe."

They walked away from the group, and Dante lowered his voice. "I'm going to have to change for this, and we'll be running. I don't want you to get lost too."

"If it's a bunch of girls, you don't need to go scaring them any more than they probably already are. I can be helpful. I'm following you."

Geena looked at him. His brow creased, and he looked like he wanted to bark "no" at her. He blinked, long and slow, and took a deep breath. "Okay."

"AJ, I need you to come with me," Dante directed.

"Like you could stop me, man."

AJ began jogging away from the camp, heading south away from the rim. Dante was right behind him. Following at a much slower pace was Geena. Once they were well away from other campsites, Geena saw Dante change. It was like watching a superhero reveal his super costume. As Dante continued to run, he removed his shirt, unbuttoned his jeans, then leaped forward. When he landed, he was a large silver wolf. The fur along his back was a pale almost white, and it became a dark gray along his underside and the tip of his tail. As soon as he landed, he began running in earnest. AJ attempted a similar change. Unfortunately, he wasn't as practiced or as strong of a wolf, and Geena was left with the vision of his naked, skinny butt running away from her burned into her brain. Geena gathered their discarded clothes and continued after them.

Geena had thought the land south of the Grand Canyon was flat. The drive in had been level and even. She hadn't really put any thought into the fact that road construction had built it up to be level. The land was not flat, with plenty of hills and steep drops in the woods. She slipped in the wet mud climbing up one hill, and had fallen on her backside more than once on steep down slopes she had not expected. AJ doubled back on his run to make sure Geena still followed on the right trail as Dante continued running ahead. Geena would occasionally catch up with the two wolves as they paused to sniff the surrounding ground and try to catch a scent on the breeze before running off in another direction.

At the top of a steep rise, Geena paused. She heard voices. Below her there was a small clearing. She could see the missing teenagers. Three girls and one of the triplets sat on a fallen log. Just to one edge of the clearing she saw the other boy; he was in his wolf form. He appeared to have been hurt and was lying as if he were unconscious. Geena covered her mouth. She hoped he was just knocked out, but she couldn't tell from here. She couldn't see the kids' faces, only the tops of their heads, but the triplet on the log was looking at his brother. He had an arm around one of the girl's shoulders. That must be Percy, and that arm around the girl explained why he had taken off after her.

The reason the four teenagers weren't moving was that a few feet away from them, stalking them, was a thin brown wolf. It was an old male with graying around the muzzle and a mangy-looking mane of fur around its neck. It also looked hungry and dangerously skinny. Geena could make out ribs. Every time one of the kids moved, the wolf would growl and feign a lunge. The wolf paced stiffly between the kids and the trees. All of a sudden he made twitchy motions. First it looked over his shoulder; then it growled more fiercely, louder. Geena could hear the girls gasp and huddle closer together. The old wolf swung around, glaring into the forest. Geena began scanning the surrounding area to see if she could see who or what he had heard. She caught a glimpse of a silvery movement in the trees, followed by a smaller blur. Dante and AJ.

Geena placed the clothes she had diligently carried on the ground, carefully so as not to make a sound. She scanned her surroundings. She was about twenty feet above the site on a bluff. To her left, the ground sloped down in a steep embankment, but not so steep the teenagers wouldn't be able to climb up. She watched. The old wolf spent more time focusing away from the group of kids, trying to find what was in the woods behind him. She crept slowly down the embankment, about halfway, and inched closer to the clearing. The old wolf started barking and howling. The sound was eerie. Geena froze. She didn't want the wolf to see her or smell her. She certainly didn't want to be attacked by the beast. It may not have looked rabid, but the drool dripping from its jaws was foul. She was convinced it had to be toxic. Geena began scooting her way closer when she realized the wolf was just barking into the woods. She hoped the sounds it made would cover any of her noises.

She held position when it began moving, skulking around the site. Mostly its focus was on the areas just past the trees, opposite from Geena's location. Occasionally it spun and growled at the kids again. They were terrified. Geena could see their faces now, and one of the girls had been crying.

Geena heard a loud growl and a crash from the woods. The old wolf spun and darted into the trees. Geena didn't pause; she quickly called the teenagers to come over to her.

"Run," Geena whispered as loud as she dared. "This way." She waved them up to her.

The kids all scrambled up the hill. Percy, in the back, pushed the girls in front of him. Geena led them to the top of the bluff. "All right, is this all of you; no one else is left?"

"My brother," Percy said.

"Dante and AJ are back there. They'll find him. We need to leave," Geena insisted.

"I'm not going anywhere without Jason." He turned and ran back down the hill. Geena decided to not wait for him; Dante and AJ were there. Besides, he was a wolf, so he could handle himself. She hoped.

Geena led the girls at a running pace back toward the campgrounds. She heard voices ahead, voices that were calling names. She directed the girls to run in that direction. After several hundred yards they found a park ranger and one of the chaperones from the camping trip. The ranger had water, and they were able to give the girls drinks. They radioed the other searchers, and everyone headed back to the group's campsite.

The girls were welcomed back to their group with hugs and sighs of relief. The tall girl who had been next to Percy on the log refused to talk until everyone came back, meaning she wasn't doing anything until Percy was back. Geena understood completely. She didn't want to go anywhere until Dante and the boys were back either.

About fifteen minutes later Dante, AJ, Percy, and a limping Jason walked into camp. The tall girl ran and hugged Percy. Geena grinned at Dante, thinking she would like to do the same thing but too shy to actually do it. She watched Dante as he pulled one of the rangers to the side. Their heads were lowered together as Dante talked intensely. Dante pointed in the general direction, and then the ranger began pointing. The ranger stepped aside and radioed to others. It seemed obvious to her this was regarding the wolf back in the woods. Dante and that ranger nodded, then parted ways.

Dante approached Geena as she stood near a different group of rangers and the teenagers they had just found. As he began to put his arms around her, she blocked him. "I am covered in muck; you don't want to touch me."

Dante moved as if he was deterred. Walking behind her, he leaned into her ear and whispered, "I most definitely want to touch you. Do you seriously think a little mud is going to scare me off?" He wrapped his arms around her and pulled her back against him. She rested her chin on his powerful forearms crossed over the top of her chest.

"Why is Jason limping? Is he all right?"

"Faking it. Providing some verisimilitude."

Geena turned to face Dante. They were already speaking in hushed tones, almost whispering. But she lowered her voice further. "What will they find when they go out where you told them we were?"

"An old, dead wolf." Dante's tone was serious, somber. He wasn't pleased with what he had to tell Geena. He had said he never wanted to lie to her, so she wasn't surprised he wasn't going to hide what had happened from her.

"And just how did the wolf die?" She braced herself. Dante was confessing just how dangerous he was to her. She wanted to know. She felt that if she wanted to handle his good side, she was going to have to handle his bad side. Right now his bad felt pretty scary.

"Hopefully, they will find it died of natural causes."

"All right, um, would another wolf be considered natural causes?" She swallowed. A lump was forming in her throat; she hadn't realized just how nervous this discussion was making her. She could fall hard for Dante. He was everything she could have dreamed of in a lover: skill, looks, personality. Could she accept the darker side of his life? *He's a wolf, and not just figuratively but literally. A wolf, a large, dangerous, predatory hunting animal.*

"In this case no, there's nothing to suggest anything attacked it. More like a traumatic fall."

Geena looked into his eyes. She couldn't hide the concern on her face. Concern but not fear. She wasn't afraid of him, even if he had just killed that animal.

"We can talk about this all you want and need to, you can ask me anything, but let's get this sorted out here, okay?" Dante kept his voice soothing and calm.

Geena nodded. She had lots of questions but needed to figure out how to ask them. She also had to ask herself some hard questions, all revolving around Dante. Did she want him just for a thrill ride? Could her heart and her head agree on and accept a common position regarding their opinion of Dante? What was her head's opinion of him? She certainly knew how her body reacted to him, and she was afraid of where her heart was heading.

The three girls and the triplets were still separated from

the main part of the group, telling their story to two of the park rangers. The girls sat side by side, with Percy on the end. The tall girl, Emily, held Percy's hand tightly.

"I don't think his mother is going to thank me for that," Dante said, nodding toward the two holding hands.

"I think it's his brothers who are going to be more upset." Geena looked back over her shoulder at Dante.

They stood there, Dante holding Geena, as they listened to the girls' story.

"I thought I heard a baby," one of them started.

"Me too."

"Probably just a stupid cat. Or a fox."

"Yeah."

"We tried to listen to figure out where the baby was. Then we couldn't see the group anymore, so we ran to catch up."

"I think we ran in the wrong direction." Two girls nodded in agreement.

"We got turned around, and then we couldn't agree on which way was back to the canyon."

"That's when Percy and Jason found us."

"Yeah, we were headed back to the camp when that wolf showed up," Percy said.

Jason continued. "It was growling with all its teeth exposed, and began forcing us backward. We thought about running."

"But figured that might make it attack," Percy said.

"We just kept inching back away from it, hoping it would back down. Next thing we knew, we're in that old campsite," Emily added.

"Then Jason was just gone."

"I tried to sneak off to find a big branch or something to hit it with. It was just a scruffy old dog, that was more growl than bite. Frail too. I thought I could knock it out so we could all escape. That's when I tripped on a stupid root and fell down this stupid hill, twisting my stupid ankle. I tried not to make any noise so the dog wouldn't attack me."

"It felt like we were being trapped by that wolf."

"Totally did."

"But it didn't do anything, just growled at us and bared his teeth."

"But it would lunge at us if anyone tried to stand up." The girl who had been crying earlier started to cry again.

Emily rubbed her friend on the shoulder. "It was just terrorizing us, and we don't know why."

"Another wolf came in out of nowhere. It just ran in from the woods and slammed into the side of that demon dog."

"I thought it was a coyote; it was smaller and skinnier."

"The mean dog grabbed the smaller animal by the neck, shook it, and threw it across that clearing."

"It just lay there," one of the girls said. "We thought it might be dead. Percy wanted to go pick it up, but the wolf really lunged at him then. Emily wouldn't let him try anymore."

"We were there forever; then the wolf went mental. It just started to growl and bark at something in the trees behind it. That's when she showed up, and we all ran." The girl pointed at Geena.

Geena joined the conversation at this point. She corroborated everyone's story that she tried to get Percy to leave with them, but he insisted on going back and finding Jason. And then everyone was back at the group's campsite. Geena described how AJ had come to find Dante, because he knew Dante found people.

"What does she mean that you find people?" one of the rangers turned to ask Dante.

"I'm an investigator for my family's company. I typically find people through different means. The boys are my cousins. Their mother put them in my care, so yeah, they go missing, I'm going to go find them," Dante explained.

"I understand you found the boys shortly after these young ladies fled."

Dante nodded. "I had AJ with me, and we had gone to the far side of the clearing. We threw rocks and branches to make noise, wanting to distract that wolf."

"Yeah, and it worked," AJ added. Dante glanced at him, not a glare, but Geena noticed it was enough to quiet him.

"The wolf ran off in one direction, and we saw Geena and the girls go off the other way. We started to head after them when Percy came back; then we spent a few minutes looking around and found Jason lying on the ground not sure what do with his twisted ankle."

"You just said their mother put them in your care; weren't they part of this group?"

"Not originally. The boys ran into some of their friends earlier, and we found out this group was here, and"—Dante singled out the woman he had spoken to earlier—"it turns out that she also knows their mother and was willing to let them join them for the night.

"No one expected anything like this to happen. I seriously doubt their mother is going to blame anyone but me for any wrongdoing."

The park rangers began closing up their notes. They let the kids head back to the rest of the group. They stood conferring with each other, occasionally looking back at Dante and Geena.

"I don't think we're done here," Dante said, kissing her

hair. "You know earlier, it was just about to get really interesting when we were interrupted."

Geena felt her cheeks tighten as a blush creeped across her face. "We weren't done, were we?"

"I hadn't even gotten started."

"We can always pick up where we left off, when they are finished with us here." She smiled, remembering Dante's frustration with her state of dress.

"True."

"I don't think we're going to have any more questions for you, miss." The shorter of the two rangers nodded to Geena. Redirecting his attention to Dante, he said, "But we are going to have a few more questions for you."

Dante grabbed Geena's hand and placed his keys in her palm. "Why don't you head back and get cleaned up. You can take a hot bath while I finish up here." He winked at her.

"Don't be too long; we need to pick up where we left off. And I'll need you to scrub my back." She returned the wink. Dante kissed her lightly before turning his attention back to the rangers.

Geena felt like whistling on her way back to the Airstream. All sense of doubt was gone. She was clear in her head where she stood regarding Dante. At least where she stood regarding his body and the rest of tonight. She felt like singing but restrained herself. She figured belting out, *Hello, world! I'm gonna get laid,* in her best Broadway voice would be highly frowned upon. Her best Broadway voice would make people's ears bleed. Being loud and having her voice carry wasn't the problem—being in tune, that was the problem.

12

Dante couldn't find Geena. She hadn't returned to the Airstream. He went to her rental—maybe she had decided to grab a change of clothes. She had gotten terribly muddy on the trek into the woods looking for those kids. He smiled to himself remembering how her ass wiggled covered in mud. She really had no idea what effect she had on him. He desperately wanted to show her. They had the entire night together, and he did not plan on sleeping much.

She wasn't at the rental. He turned and headed to the bathhouses. Maybe she thought she was too muddy to bathe in the Jacuzzi tub. When he got there, he yelled into the bathhouse to see if anyone was in there. He had no qualms about walking in to find Geena, but he didn't need to cause trouble by walking in on anyone else.

"You need something?" a middle-aged woman asked, giving him a side eye.

"Yeah, I'm looking for my girlfriend; she isn't at the camper. Would you see if she's in there? Her name is Geena."

She was gone barely a minute. No one was inside.

Dante headed back to his trailer—still no Geena. He didn't want to worry, but he had a gut feeling something was not right. He returned to the trail. How would Geena have come back from the group's campsite? He backtracked, following the path he expected that she would have taken. In an area among a thickening of trees, he noticed an increase in dried mud on the trail. Mud that could have fallen off Geena's jeans.

Dante slowed down and opened his wolf senses. Geena had definitely come this way; he could smell her lavender shampoo.

A few feet away he caught site of changes in the ground—something had been dragged from the path, forming two furrows in the mud. Like feet being dragged. He followed this a few yards before finding the keys he had given to Geena. Then deep footprints. Whatever was being dragged had been picked up and was being carried.

He carefully followed, not making noises as he stepped. He wanted to run, but he had no idea how far in front of him the abductor and Geena were. He had no idea how much danger she was in. Who would take Geena, and why? She had no enemies that he could think of. Brooke was jealous. She was a classic frienemy—enemy in friend's clothing—but she wasn't the type to do something physically malicious. No, her weapons were words and the wounds she inflicted manipulated Geena's self-esteem. Besides, he didn't think Brooke would have been able to pick Geena up.

This was someone who was strong. And based on the size of those footprints, not particularly large but strong. This pointed to another wolf, another family? Was this who the boys had tracked? The odds were more in favor of someone trying to get to him. But he had been playing nice lately. He started to get angry with himself. He hadn't been careful. He had been so focused on Geena that he wouldn't have noticed if the Gauls and the Huns had been knocking on his doors. Maybe he had stirred something up on the reservation, and it was now catching up with him.

Dante groaned. This didn't smell right. It wasn't vampires. Vampires hadn't moved into the Southwest, at least not so far as Dante had found. Based on the latest intelligence, Lazarus manipulated and recruited in traditional vampire haunts. Besides, part of this entire trip was to find family alliances, and to see if Lazarus had begun building forces within the wolf community. Dante hadn't noticed any activities that could be traced back to the vampires. It was too light out for a vampire. And it didn't smell like any of the vampires' bodyguards, daywalkers. This smelled like unwashed, unhealthy human, old dog, and Geena.

His focus split on his tracking and on figuring out who had Geena. He needed to concentrate. *I can find a motive later. Right now I need to find Geena, keep her with me, keep her safe.* He smirked when he realized he needed to protect his mate above all else. *My mate.* When had he started thinking of her as his? At what point after that first smile did he even think of her not being his? She glowed, and he didn't fight it.

It was time to change. Hard dirt and ground cover hid footprints. As wolf, he could use his nose better. He removed his clothes, loosely folded them, then shifted. Energy surged through his body. His skin prickled with electricity. A large silver and gray wolf shook his fur into place, then began sniffing the immediate area. *Yes, Geena had come through here; so had that old wolf.* He paused. That old wolf was supposed to be dead. He would not make that mistake twice. Dante rushed through the woods. He slowed when he approached a campsite. It belonged to the old wolf—his smell was strong here. The smell of the campfire and what the old man was burning masked Geena's scent.

At first he didn't see Geena, but he could sense she was close, as if his heart could feel hers. There was an old man wrapped in a wolfskin. *That wolf is a shifter.* Carefully Dante crouched down and crawled to stay downwind. He didn't know how keen the old man's wolf senses would be. Dante observed the antics of the old man, listening to catch as much of the mutterings as possible. Based on his words, the old man seemed to think he was a skin-walker. Dante made a connection to the triplets when he heard the old man muttering about bone powder and boys. Legends said corpse powder had to be made from powder of the bones of infants, and that the most powerful bone powder came from multiples: twins, triplets. Those boys were entirely too old. Maybe he was reaching. Dante crawled around the sight, just beyond the edge of the trees. The old man was sure to sense him, but Dante had to locate Geena, had to see if she was all right.

∽

Geena woke up. It was smoky, and she couldn't move. There was that evil shadowy presence she could sense, just beyond her vision. *All right, this is another stupid paralysis dream. If I go back to sleep, then I can get the stupid false wakings over with and get back to sleep.* Smoke drifted past her face. She coughed. She froze—her thoughts, her breathing, everything stopped. *That's not normal.* She usually couldn't smell in her dreams. She typically didn't cough in her sleep paralysis dreams either.

Where was she? Was this a dream? She wasn't in a bed. Whatever she was on was hard and cold. She lay on the ground. She realized she could just barely move her fingers as she scraped up fingernails full of mud. She tried to roll over, but she couldn't lift her arms. She managed to lift her shoulder. Barely. She blacked out.

This had to be a dream. She could hardly move. Maybe the paralysis this time wasn't as complete because the setting was different. The smell of sour smoke filled her nostrils. She shouldn't be able to smell if this was a dream. Fear rolled in, and her gut clenched. Her brain tried to hyperventilate. Her body wasn't breathing fast enough. She felt like she was suffocating. Geena squeezed her eyes shut and forced herself to focus on her breathing: in through the nose, out through the mouth, in through the nose, out through the mouth. Another cloud of smoke rolled over her, and she coughed.

This level of panic was much worse than that of her most vivid and terrifying sleep paralysis nightmare. She tried to focus on her breathing again. Her heart boomed in her ears. Her rising blood pressure triggered a headache. She tried to consciously slow her racing heart and lower her blood pressure. The pain started to build as a stabbing pressure just above her temples. This accentuated the pulsing throb of pain on the back of her head. She tried to reach up and touch her head, but her arm wouldn't leave the ground, as if gravity was heavier here. She wasn't asleep. As far as she could tell she wasn't restrained, but she couldn't figure out why she couldn't move.

Opening her eyes, she tried to look around. Her head could only move like it was sunk in thick ooze. She looked up into trees. She watched smoke winding its way up into the sky. Moving her eyes made her dizzy. She closed them and tried to listen to what was going on around her.

Geena woke up again. She was in the same location,

same position. Same panicky feeling. Lucid dreams, with frighteningly real detail. She kept waking up, and couldn't shift her body, so she knew this couldn't be real, definitely sleep paralysis, now in the false waking phase. She drifted back to sleep.

The next time she woke, a face too close to focus on hissed foul breath at her. She still couldn't really move, but it wasn't the same sensation as a sleep paralysis dream. This was worse than any nightmare she had ever experienced. This was real.

"No." She groaned and tried to turn away from the foul stench of rotting teeth and bad breath.

"Stupid cow," the face hissed, then disappeared. She felt a hard kick in her shoulder. When she looked up again, she could just make out low branches of trees, lit by a flickering campfire, against a black sky. She could hear the *crackle* and *snap* of the fire and smell the wood smoke. Geena was used to incredibly vivid dreams. As much as she wanted this to be a nightmare, this was real. She could smell the smoke. She tried to roll over, to get off the back of her head. The pain throbbed a pulse that matched her heartbeat. She must have been hit pretty hard, enough to knock her out. But the rest of this... She was too groggy to finish the thought. She tried to focus again. On ground, on back, near a campfire. *Where am I? How did I get here? How long have I been here?* She tried to vocalize her questions, but all she managed was a slurry groaning sound.

"Shut. Up." She was kicked again; she felt it sharp in her leg. It was the same voice that had called her a cow. *Who?*

The face appeared in her vision again, this time not as close. This time she could focus on the features. The face belonged to an elderly Native American man. He might once have had sharp features, but old age and many broken noses had given him a soft, weathered appearance. His skin was like tree bark. He snarled at Geena, exposing more gaps than teeth, and the teeth he had were stained dark and pitted.

"You took those kids away from me. Those stupid girls got lost. They were just in the way." He moved, continuing to mutter. "Need those boys."

Geena gained enough strength to turn her head toward the fire. The old man had a fur pelt wrapped around his waist, and very little else on. Skin hung from his bones. Skinny legs extended from underneath the fur wrap, and long, thin arms that appeared more like branches with gnarled knots for elbows grew from a wide barrel chest. He had been a big man once, but age had changed that. Geena could make out the edges of ribs and his spine. He muttered and threw things into the fire. He kept repeating certain words. Some she could understand: three, bones, boys, dust, stupid. Other noises might have been words, but she didn't understand the language he spoke.

"Who was the other *yee naaldloshii*, woman?" Again, his face was too close. She wanted to cringe away from him.

"Is he after their bones? They are too old. But three. Three is better than two." This time Geena noticed his eyes —they were gold, and they glowed the way Dante's did when he was aroused.

Please make that mean intense emotions and not... ew. She tried to speak, "Yanalooli" was all her tongue could manage.

"Yee naaldlooshii, you stupid cow. Skin-walker. Who is the other skin-walker? Is he after those boys?" He kicked her again before moving off. Most of what he said made no sense to Geena. He would be in her face one minute, then off again. Muttering about skin-walking and boy bones.

The fog in her brain began to clarify on one thought:

Dante. She was supposed to be getting naked with Dante. Not lying here, wherever here was, in the mud, with some scary, smelly old man. She began to wonder if Dante would have noticed if she was gone by now. How long had it been? In dreams, she understood time dilated and moved differently than reality, but in this groggy reality, how long had she been knocked out? And each time she had passed out, how long had she stayed out? Was Dante even done talking to the park rangers? She began to drift off again.

Geena's attention snapped into sharp clarity. *Was this guy the other wolf?* Skin-walker... she wondered if he was Navajo or another tribe. She knew enough to recognize the general myth but not the specifics. Were skin-walkers and werewolves different animals? Or were they the same thing with different names. Too many questions were picking up speed in Geena's head, and she didn't have any answers.

Another thought slowly came into focus. Hadn't Dante said they would find a dead wolf? So if this guy was that wolf, he wasn't dead. Just then the old man's mutterings turned more into snarls and growls. He started moving more rapidly around his campsite, the speed emphasizing a limp, and stiff movements. Geena couldn't track him. Her head still hurt, and her body still didn't respond to her attempts at moving. His legs shuffled past her vision, back and forth. Something was causing him great agitation. Between snarls, he began to cackle. He sounded maniacal, crazed.

∽

Dante spotted Geena when the old man crouched over her and hissed in her face. She appeared to be nonresponsive. He wanted to strike immediately, but his analytical brain was still in control. He needed more information. He focused on Geena. The old man kept muttering the same thing repeatedly; Dante wasn't going to learn anything new from him. He focused on her chest, watching for the slightest lift indicating that she was alive, breathing.

Her chest lifted, and Dante let out the breath he was holding. The more he watched, the more movement he saw. Slight as it was, she seemed to be fighting to move her arms. When she did move, it was practically imperceptible, and she seemed to give up and relax, as if she put great effort into her attempts. Maybe corpse powder really worked, or more likely the old man was using a modern drug to the same effect. Geena probably had been given Rohypnol. The thought of the old man giving Geena a roofie caused Dante to lose control.

A snarl escaped his lips.

The old man heard him and went to Geena. Dante had to get him away from her. He stalked into the clearing of the campsite. The old man shifted into the wolf Dante had fought. The wolf was slow and old, but he had been powerful once. Only dominant wolves could command a change with that much ease and speed. He was cunning, having convinced Dante that he was dead earlier.

Dante had made a concerted effort to make it look like the old wolf had fallen from a ridge, leaving no teeth marks or traces of there being another wolf in the park. Now no such considerations were made. The old wolf threatened and hurt his mate. He was out for blood.

Dante leaped into the campsite, well away from Geena, trying to draw the other wolf away from her. He stood his ground. If the old wolf wanted a fight, he would have to come to Dante. The old wolf slowly inched its way forward, passing just above Geena's head. His claws were dangerously close to her face as he stepped over her chest. The hind paws didn't bother to step over her. One landed just below her breasts. She had to have felt the weight of it, but she didn't react, didn't curl up under the pressure. Dante's vision turned red as he watched the other wolf step on her belly.

The desire to bury his fangs into that neck raged through Dante. Yet, he still did not approach. He needed the old shifter to move away from Geena, since it was clear she was unable to move away from the wolf.

With a fierce snarl and growl, the old man finally lunged. Their fight was all claws and teeth. Dante kept trying to roll and move them farther away from the prostrate woman. He slammed the other wolf against a tree, then turned to see blood spread across Geena's abdomen. This unlocked a new level of fury within him that he hadn't known he possessed. The wolves collided and scrabbled together again. As much as he tried, Dante could not completely direct the fight away from his defenseless mate.

Bodies thudded together. Dirt spray hit her on the side of the face. Dante kept himself between Geena and the old man. Finally, she must have produced enough adrenaline to allow her to roll onto her side away from the fight. Dante's leg pressed into her shoulder.

After another impact of his leg against her back, the wolves scrabbled away from her. The other animal kept rolling and pressing back into the same area. The smaller animal slammed into her and then rolled over her legs.

Dante's growls became fiercer if that was possible. The wolves locked together, teeth in fur. All the colors of fur ran together, browns into grays. They became one snarling monster of claws and teeth, unable to distinguish one wolf from the other.

The wolves rolled away from Geena again. Then they both slammed into her midsection. Geena cried out as the air left her body in a rush.

Distracted by her noise of distress, Dante turned his attention to his mate. She was covered in dirt spray and small scratches. The old wolf slammed into Dante. They rolled together down Geena's legs. They separated, and the smaller animal crouched low and panted heavily. Other noises coming from the old wolf were more pitiful whines of pain. He fought like he had spent his entire life fighting, but this fight was taking its toll on him.

Rushing back to stand guard over Geena, Dante changed his approach to the fight from forced offensive to protective, defensive. The soft movement of her breathing ruffled the fur on his chest. He analyzed his next move.

He knew he should find out who this guy was, but Dante no longer cared. He wanted to end this fight and remove the threat. His burning need was to protect Geena, hold her, feel her breathing in his arms.

The other animal dared to skulk closer. Dante lunged one last time. More claws, more teeth. Blood and fur, torn and flying. His jaws found purchase behind the other animal's head. One, two, three shakes with all his fury, and he snapped the neck in his grasp.

Dante tossed the limp body aside and pounced to Geena. A moan escaped her lips. He whined and began licking her face, his tongue covering her eyes and cheeks. Dante shifted and sat back, pulling her into his lap. Safe and in his arms at last, Geena opened her eyes and looked up at him. It was apparent she was having a hard time focusing. Alternatively, he applied pressure to the cut on her stomach and stroked her face.

Geena made a slurred noise in an attempt to speak.

"Oh, sweetheart." He kissed her forehead, then held her to his naked chest.

Geena made more garbled, barely audible sounds.

"You're okay; you're safe. I'm going to put you down for just a few moments. You won't be out of my sight, okay?"

Geena managed a nod, a practically imperceptible movement of her head. He needed to get her back to the trailer so he could tend to her. She needed to sleep this drug out of her system. He could carry her, but he didn't have any clothes on. Not that it mattered to him, but if they encountered any hikers, it would look bad: an unconscious, bleeding woman and a naked man.

Placing Geena down carefully, he explained he would be right back. He wasn't sure how much she actually understood. She was doped up pretty well. Quickly shifting, Dante ran at high speed back to where he had left his clothes. He wished he could teleport or magically conjure clothes. He amused himself—wishing for superhero powers when he had shape-shifting abilities was pretty pitiful. Once dressed, he ran as fast as possible in human form back to Geena. She was asleep, probably hadn't even noticed he had been gone.

Once again, his strong arms were around her, lifting her from the ground. Geena looked up. Dante gave her a worried smile. Holding her close, with her head resting against his shoulder, Dante's heart pounded heavily in his chest. She was so precious and delicate.

Dante carried her back to his trailer, cradled and safe. He didn't want to let go but laid her down on the couch so he could tend her wounds. The front of her shirt was torn and soaked in blood. Expecting the worst, he lifted the ripped fabric from her abdomen. The bleeding had stopped. That was a good sign. He removed the shirt and then helped her off with her pants, still caked in mud from her earlier slide down a hill. He stepped into the bathroom and rifled through the cabinets, finding what he needed. Occasionally he swore.

"Sweetheart, this is going to sting."

Geena gasped as he poured cold hydrogen peroxide on her stomach. Dante cursed again as she moaned in pain. He gingerly cleaned the scrape. It wasn't deep; it hadn't gone past the layers of skin. It easily could have been so much worse. So much worse. After he bandaged her midsection, he passed a damp cloth over her face. A breath he hadn't realized he had been holding left his body as relief flooded in. There weren't any other injuries he could see. The small scrapes seemed to wipe away with the dirt.

She seemed to be losing the fight with what consciousness she had. Her mumbles became quieter, more incoherent. Dante pulled a clean T-shirt over her head. He smiled as she let out a contented-sounding sigh and sank into the chair to fall asleep.

Dante quickly made the foldout bed and gently transferred Geena from the chair. He wanted to curl around her and hold her safe in his arms. But he knew now that he had her cleaned up and settled, he needed to take care of that wolf. Couldn't leave evidence of that nature here in a park that didn't have a registered wolf population. Walking back to the old shifter's campsite, he made his plan on how to dispose of the dead animal. This part of his job he never looked forward to. Not that he was a professional hit man, or even a professional cleanup guy. It was just that sometimes he needed to attend to matters that the family didn't need made public. Fortunately wolves tended to stay wolves once they were dead. The real problems were when wolves transformed before they died. If remote police stations ever compared notes on who found random dead bodies, Dante's name would show up far too often.

Walking through the forest with a shovel would have looked too suspicious, not that he had one anyway. He had a spade for tending campfires, and that's what he used. After spending some time searching as a wolf, he located desiccated coyote remains. He returned with the dead wolf and buried it under the dead coyote. Other animals would mix the bones and confuse the remains if it ever became an issue.

Back at the old man's campsite, Dante found a few dead squirrels, randomly collected herbs, and wild plants. Okay, the old man might have been a shaman. He had seemed to think he was a skin-walker. This may have been the person Dante had been looking for in regards to the increased whispers he had found regarding a skin-walker/wolf shapeshifter. Before burying the animal, he cut a sample of fur and skin. Once back in California he would have it analyzed for DNA. Of course a spit sample would have been an easier test, but harder to collect from an unwilling participant. What was he thinking? As if he had test tubes with him. *Here, crazy old man, spit, and I'll see if you're a long lost cousin.* That reminded him. He should get the triplets tested. He made a mental note to order kits in the next day or two and have them sent to the boys' home.

Geena was sound asleep when he returned to the trailer. He didn't want to chance being away from her any longer. Sliding the accordion door closed he took a quick shower, hoping not to disturb her. He smiled when he stepped from the bathroom and heard her soft sleeping breathing sounds. Not exactly snoring, Geena made cute, gentle noises. He needed to hold her, to feel her against his skin, but he didn't want to scare her, especially if something had happened that would make her not want to be touched. He wouldn't know how traumatized she was until the morning, and that was if she would tell him. The side chair pivoted, so he lay back and rested his feet on the bed. He slept lightly, wanting to be available if she needed him for anything.

13

Geena woke up. She gasped in a frightened breath. She pushed herself up in a panic. Everything was dark. She didn't know where she was.

Warm arms surrounded her. "It's okay. It's okay. I'm right here. You're safe." Dante's voice crooned in her ear. He stroked her hair and gently rocked her back and forth.

Geena tried to catch her breath. Panic washed over her as she remembered past events. She pushed against Dante. "I'm gonna throw up." She scrambled off the bed and rushed to the bathroom.

Dante held her hair back as she wretched into the toilet. She sat on the edge of the tub panting. Dante carefully handed her a cup of water and began wiping her brow with a damp cloth.

Geena felt a mountain of panic rise in her throat again. She wretched until nothing more came up.

Dante was there with cool water, a cool washcloth, and strong, warm, supporting arms. Geena didn't want to move. She let Dante support her as he gently stroked her hair. Her head throbbed, but his touch was gentle and soothing.

Geena relaxed against his warmth. All the concerns she'd had earlier in the day, all her questions about this man were answered. Would she be able to mentally deal with his wolf, and all the power and violence that it brought with it? Unequivocally yes. She knew in her heart that he would do whatever was necessary to keep her safe. And that his wolf, while large and frightening, would only fight to protect.

That even meant that here, on the edge of the tub next to the toilet with Dante was safe, especially if she was going to throw up again. When she felt as if she could fall asleep where she sat, she motioned to Dante to help her up. He guided her back to the bed and tucked her in after she placed her head on the pillow. He sat on the edge of the bed and soothingly petted her back until she fell asleep.

When Geena woke up again, it was light out. The scent of Dante lingered on her pillow. Awake and safe. She remembered everything that had happened. Everything. Groaning, she slowly sat up. *Oh God. I threw up in front of Dante.* Of everything she'd endured, vomiting in his presence seemed to be the worst thing possible. She rubbed her face and looked around the trailer. There was a tented note with her name next to a tall glass of water on the dinette table. Next to the water were two blue gel tablets. There was also a single large white daisy lying on the table. She downed the water and took one of the gel tablets.

Beautiful Geena,

Sleep as long as you need to. Go back to bed if you want. Drink plenty of water. Eat if you are hungry. I will come back to check on you. I've gone to collect the boys. I wonder if I'll be able to extract Percy's hand from that little girl's? I think I've had more than enough hiking, so how does sitting at the rim all day sound?

Be back soon.

Dante

She smiled and held the note to her chest. Not a love note, but her first note from Dante. Dante wanting to spend time with her, even after she had thrown up in front of him. Her mouth tasted gross. She needed her toothbrush. She found her pants. They were covered in mud. She didn't see her shirt anywhere, but she remembered that it had been ripped and bloody. She needed clean clothes and to brush her teeth.

She found another piece of paper and a pen. She scribbled a quick note and left it next to the flower:

Bathhouse, back soon.

-G

She looked for Dante and the boys on her short walk over to her RV. Inside she grabbed bathing supplies and fresh clothes. She noted that Brooke had not returned yet. Geena checked her phone. Had she missed a call or text from her while things were happening yesterday? Nothing. She was surprised to see the time. It was early afternoon. She had slept in longer than she realized. Geena quickly texted.

Hey Brooke please check in.

Expecting an instantaneous reply, when nothing came, Geena figured that Brooke was running low on battery. She hoped Brooke would let her know what was going on, not that Geena counted on it. Taking off with people she had just met while on vacation apparently was a bad habit of Brooke's. Total hypocrite. Geena no longer cared that Brooke had taken off. However, they were obliged to leave the campgrounds in a few days and return the RV.

Geena needed to know if Brooke was driving back with her, or if Brooke had decided to return home on her own. Something Geena didn't expect her to do, not without her laptop. After all, she needed that for work. But Geena would not put it past Brooke to leave her to drive cross-country on her own. Geena quickly checked the under-seat storage to confirm the presence of the computer. Yep, it was still there.

Geena made her way to the bathhouses. Both her RV and the Airstream had showers, but the bathhouse offered privacy. Something she would not have in either camper if anyone returned while she bathed. She stood for a long time under the hot shower. The water felt good on her sore body. She knew better than to touch the wall, but she needed to lean against it for support. She was mentally exhausted and physically beat. The terror of the evening before had not completely left her body. The cool tile of the shower wall felt good against her forehead. She focused her breathing. *No throwing up, no throwing up* became her mantra for about five minutes. Fortunately, she did not have to empty her stomach again. She found her center and stood to finish her shower. She carefully cleaned her scrapes and rebandaged them. They weren't deep, but they needed to be carefully cleaned since muddy claws had made them. There was no sign of Dante yet when she stopped by the Airstream on her way back to the rental.

She strolled back to the RV, contemplating if she should look for him. He had said he would come back for her. When had he written the note? How long would it take to collect the boys from their overnight with the church group?

Geena admired a vintage trailer camp setup; they had definitely understood the concept of "glamping." She squeaked. They had a table with a vaseful of large white daisies. Distracted by the flowers, Geena hadn't noticed the person sitting on her rental's step.

"Where the hell have you been?" Brooke barked.

Startled, Geena dropped her bundle of dirty clothes and towels.

"Oh, you scared me." Geena let out a nervous giggle.

"Well? Where have you been? I looked for you at the lodge and the stores. Nothing. I don't have a key."

"Did you text me? Did I miss it?" Geena fumbled for her phone to see if she'd missed a text from Brooke.

Brooke knit her eyebrows together in annoyance. "No, I didn't text you. My phone's dead. I just expected you to be here." She dramatically flourished her hand out for the key. Geena handed it over.

"Look, I'm tired, I've got a headache, and I've been in these same clothes for three days now. Hiking is disgusting." Brooke waved her hands around. She turned and opened the door to the RV. She stepped up, turning in the door to look down on Geena. "I'm going to go to the bathhouse, and then I'm coming back here to take a nap. You think you can be quiet? Or maybe you should leave for the afternoon. I need to be alone."

"I'm just going to put these things away, then spend the day at the rim," Geena explained, keeping her voice neutral. She was still too raw from last night to want to engage in a fight. Brooke was trying to start something. Geena let it go again. Like she always did.

Brooke let her step into the camper. "You look like a drowned rat, by the way. Fix your hair."

Geena glared at Brooke's back before quickly tossing her dirty clothes into the bag she had for them. She dragged a brush through her damp hair, grabbed two hair bands, and placed her toiletries caddy away.

"Um, text me when you wake up. Maybe we can have dinner together?" Geena wasn't exactly sure why she was being nice, other than that's just how she always was. Maybe Brooke needed someone to be nice to her, and her attitude would change. Then again, maybe not.

Brooke harrumphed. Geena stepped out of the RV. Maybe she should feel bad for Brooke. After all, Brooke had had a bad time. Geena didn't even want to sympathize with her. Brooke's attitude made it hard to be cordial. Parts of this trip could not be over soon enough.

Shaking her head to clear it of Brooke's negativity, Geena headed back to the Airstream. Happily, the triplets sat in camp chairs under the awning by the front door. The door opened, and Dante looked out. In one long step he was out of the trailer and wrapping his arms around Geena. Carefully he brushed a stray hair from her brow and stroked his fingers down her face. "You okay? I didn't want you going anywhere without me."

"I'm all right. I just went to the bathhouse and the rental for clean clothes."

"You should have waited." Dante searched her face as if he could read what she needed from him there. He stroked her arms, visually made sure all of her was intact. He cupped her face and searched her eyes. "Are you okay?" he asked again, slowly, deliberately. His forehead creased with worry.

"I'm all right, really I am." Geena placed her hand over his and leaned into his palm. She felt comfort and, dare she even think it, love in that caress.

The boys made unappreciative noises of the moment the two of them shared, breaking the mood.

"Oh hey, Brooke is back. She's taking a nap. I told her to text me for dinner plans."

"Sure." Dante nodded.

"Other than that, I'm all yours for today."

Dante grinned at her. She didn't think she would ever get used to that smile directed at her. She took a few minutes to braid her hair into long pigtails. Dante insisted she eat an apple before they headed out to the rim.

Sitting on the low wall at the canyon rim, Geena felt calm. The events the night before should have traumatized her to her core. She reflected that it probably had, and she would experience post-traumatic flashbacks in a few days or weeks. But at this moment, sitting on the rim, looking out into the canyon with Dante by her side, she felt at peace.

"I need to ask you..." Dante swallowed. Geena could hear the worry in his voice. "Did he hurt you? Did he..." His voice dropped off as if he were afraid of what she would tell him.

Geena tenderly rubbed over the bandage on her stomach. "Just this. I think he beaned me in the head, and he drooled on me." She wrinkled up her nose at the memory of the spittle rolling down her cheek and the stench of his breath. "His breath..." She shivered. "Positively toxic. I think it killed brain cells. Ugh." She turned to face Dante. "He didn't touch me like that. He scared the crap out of me, and I'm sure I will need therapy for years because of it. But, no." She shook her head. "He didn't touch me." She rested her hand on Dante's chest and felt the air leave him slowly, as if he had been holding it against bad news.

"I'd kill him all over again if he had." His voice was low and calm, and a little bit frightening in its intensity. Yet that protective ferocity in his voice made her feel safe, secure.

"So did he die of natural causes?"

"If you call a broken neck natural, then yes. He was a danger to those kids. He died because he hurt you."

"What will the rangers find?"

"They won't find anything other than an old campsite, if they are looking for anything. I took care of it last night."

"Do you know who he was? He called you a skin-walker. I think that's what he thought he was."

"I don't know who he was. I have some ideas. I wasn't done tracking those family members down on the reservation. I'm going to have to get back to that when I take the boys home. I have a tissue sample that I need to send to the lab. Hopefully that will provide some answers."

Geena leaned against him. He was dangerous, deadly even. She never felt safer in her life.

"Dante?"

"Hmm hmm?" His lips were against her hair.

"Why me?"

"Last night?" His voice was full of concern, and he tightened his arms around her as if he could protect her from past events.

"No, not that. Why did you pick me?" She turned to peer at him. His curly dark hair twisted in the breeze. She pulled the sunglasses from his face so she could see his hazel eyes. They were more green, in their calm, peaceful state.

"I think I should ask you that." He stroked her cheek. "I think you picked me."

"How? You could have any woman you want, but you're here with me."

"Yeah," he nodded, "and I want you. The first time I saw you, you glowed. Like a host of angels had spotlights trained on you. So I paid attention. But then I think you picked me when you said you wanted me to take you for a ride." He raised his eyebrows, emphasizing the double entendre.

"I meant on your bike." Her cheeks tightened, she knew she blushed.

"At first you meant the bike. When you wrapped your arms around me"—His eyes went out of focus, before returning to gaze into hers—"that was it—you claimed me. I didn't have a choice."

"You're teasing me. You said I glowed?"

"Your every smile is a tease. How could I not oblige you? Yep, a soft pink shimmer. That glow told me you were special, and it was right, and you picked me. It would have been stupid not to accept. I'm many things, but I do like to think that I am not stupid. So, Geena, why did you pick me?"

Geena had to think. She had picked him for his instant sex appeal, but she was still here because he made her feel safe and he liked her. "Reciprocal attraction."

"What?"

"I like you because you like me," she explained.

Dante cocked an eyebrow at her.

"Don't underestimate the power of knowing someone is actually attracted to you. I mean no, I'm not only going to be attracted to someone just because they like me. But, well... You are so gorgeous." She laid a hand across his cheek, letting his beard stubble tickle her palm. She sighed. This wasn't easy without sounding foolish. "I asked for a ride because it's a pretty bike, and you are tall and good-looking. I wanted to see if you bothered to ask Brooke and Hannah, who always get the guys..." Geena paused. "I wanted to see if you would be nice to me too. Even if it was just to impress my friends." Geena took a drink from her water bottle, a move to hide her embarrassment.

"You looked at me differently. You made me feel like"—she paused, thinking—"like a piece of steak and you were the big bad wolf going to eat me up. It was thrilling, a little bit frightening, and a whole lot of sexy."

Dante grinned. "I didn't think I had been that obvious." He leaned into her, nipping at her ear. His voice dropped, low and thick with desire. "I am the big bad wolf, and you do look like a thick, juicy steak to me." He licked slowly, tantalizingly, tracing up the skin of her neck with the tip of his tongue.

She felt every part of her body respond to him. Butterflies quivered between her legs. Her nipples hardened. Her breathing grew ragged. "Not fair," she managed in a whispery voice.

Dante grabbed her hand and placed it on his hardening crotch. Her eyes widened in shock. He hadn't done anything so blatant before. She hadn't touched him below the belt before—rubbing on her thigh didn't count. "Tell me about it. I'm sure my balls are inventing a new shade of blue as we speak." Geena couldn't help it; she giggled.

"Hey, are we gonna ride the bus up to the Hermit Trailhead or not?" Geena looked back over her shoulder. She thought it was the triplet AJ. He was the more sullen of the three. Then again, it could be Percy. He had been rather moody since his new girlfriend had to leave earlier. Dante moved away from Geena, giving her room to stand up and himself some time to let body parts subside.

"Yeah, yeah, yeah. Just needed some time to take it all in," he said as he approached the boys. They had found a soda can and had been playing soccer with it since just after lunch, giving Dante and Geena some time to sit and talk.

Geena held Dante's hand on their walk along the trail to the bus stop. If this was the only way she was going to be able to touch him, she was going to hold his hand as much as she could.

14

Geena stretched and yawned. The fire hypnotized her with its dance. She sat as close to Dante as the camp chair would allow, bundled up in a blanket. They had spent a wonderful afternoon riding the canyon shuttle to points away from the village. Visiting the Hermit Trailhead had been a long bus ride away, but she'd had a perfect view with a window seat on the ride there. The views of the canyon were glorious from the different location. Different rock formations caught the light and played with shadows. On the trip back her view of Dante had been just as perfect. She spent the entire time holding his hand and playing with his long, tapering fingers while the ride lulled Dante to sleep.

She remembered looking at his perfect face, his angular jaw covered in a day's beard growth, and thinking, *Well, I finally get to have him sleep next to me.* Of course, it wasn't the way she had been hoping for. The reality was, with Brooke back and having the three boys, they weren't going to get another chance to be intimate. She just didn't see it happening.

Dante had made it clear that he was also disappointed they weren't going to have time for being alone.

She yawned again. It was late; she was well-fed and warm. Dante had grilled steaks, sweet potatoes, and asparagus for dinner. It made Geena happy to know he could cook—or at least he could make breakfast and knew his way around a grill, and that counted.

"I'm going to have to go to bed soon," she said, trying to hide the regret in her voice for having to leave. She stifled another yawn.

"I wish you could stay, but..." Dante looked over his shoulder at the trailer. "I have guests." They could hear Jason, Percy, and AJ inside the Airstream playing video games on the large-screen TV.

"You have responsibilities." Geena sighed.

"Speaking of responsibilities. I'm going to have to take them home soon and get back to work."

"And I have to take the rental back to Atlanta."

"Geena, I..." He paused.

"Nope, nope, nope, stop right there." She held up her hands. "It's late, and we are both tired. You aren't allowed to dump me tonight. We can talk about it tomorrow." She stood up.

"I'm not going to dump you." He smiled up at her as she leaned over him for a kiss.

"Oh good, 'cause I think I like you."

"You think you like me?" He emphasized the *think*, cocking an eyebrow at her.

"Sometimes." She smiled and gave him a quick kiss on the lips.

"Good." Dante stood and wrapped his arms around her. "'Cause I know I like you."

They kissed again, and this time Dante's lips lingered on

hers. He pulled at her lower lip with his mouth and pressed against her until she opened for him to slip his tongue in. Geena tried to pull him closer. She did not want to let go. She didn't want to think about parting ways, even if it was for the night. She wanted to feel as much of Dante as she could. When the kiss ended, Dante rested his forehead against hers.

"Yeah, I like you." He sighed.

Dante draped his jacket across Geena's shoulders. The night had gotten chilly, and her jacket wasn't thick enough. She shivered more from nervous energy and emotion than from the chill. "Come on, pretty girl, let me walk you home." Dante placed his large, warm hand in hers and led her back to the rental.

Dante stood with his hands in his pockets as she stepped inside and closed the door behind her. Brooke was not in. Geena had expected her to be asleep. Brooke had declined to join them for dinner, claiming she was just too tired and was going to stay in and watch a DVD or read, or maybe just go back to sleep.

Geena wrapped Dante's jacket around herself and breathed in his smell. It was a warm, manly smell with a hint of aftershave and wood smoke from this evening's fire. He'd said she could hold on to it for the night. She might even sleep in it, to help ward off bad dreams or another bout of sleep paralysis.

Geena was brushing her teeth when she heard an unidentifiable buzzing sound. After searching for about five minutes, she found that the sound was coming from Dante's phone. He left it in his pocket before he gave the jacket to her. He may have said she could hold on to the jacket, but she was pretty sure he didn't intend for her to have his phone for the night.

She pulled jeans on over her sleep shorts, put the jacket back on, and walked the short distance back to the Airstream.

Less than five minutes ago she had been happy. Convinced she was falling in love, and that Dante felt the same. Now she stood in shock. Tears welled up in her eyes before she was fully certain of what she was looking at.

Dante was leaning back against the Airstream, with Brooke pressed against him in a romantic clinch. His hands grasped at her shoulders. Her hands cupped his face as they passionately kissed. Brooke had been right. He had wanted her and not Geena. Geena stared numbly from just beyond the corner of the neighboring RV. She could see them, but they wouldn't be able to see her—she was beyond the reach of the fire's light, and they were in its spotlight. The fire that so recently she had been snuggled up to Dante in front of.

Brooke pulled away. Dante's gaze intense on her face.

Geena took off his jacket and just dropped it where she stood. Her mind numb, she turned and walked back to the RV. She didn't want to think about what she'd just seen. She was in shock. Tears streamed down her face. Angrily she wiped them away. As if on autopilot she made her way back inside the rental and climbed into the big bed. She didn't care if it wasn't her night in it. She didn't feel anything. Why would Brooke have done that if she knew Geena liked Dante? Clearly girlfriend code didn't mean a thing to her. Why would Dante have done that? He had just said he liked her.

Geena tried to not think about it, she forced her brain to go blank. She wouldn't let Brooke know she had seen them. She didn't know what she would do the next day. She had asked Dante to not dump her tonight. *Oh my God! He was going to tell me he preferred Brooke, and I stopped him.* Geena buried her face and her grief into her pillow. She was so distraught, she didn't notice when Brooke returned. She wouldn't have been able to tell if it had been only five minutes or an hour. Geena felt like her heart wasn't just breaking; she felt as if her entire existence shattered around her.

15

This time when Geena woke, she was all too aware that this was not a dream. When she had gone to bed the night before, she had been hurt and angry; now she was confused. The RV shimmied and shook underneath her. It should not be moving. It should be hooked up in its place in Trailer Village. It should be stationary. It should be where Dante was.

She rolled out of bed and found her balance in the moving vehicle. Brooke sat in the driver's seat, guiding the RV down the freeway. The patchy morning light glared through the clouds, and the squint on Brooke's face indicated it was directly in her eyes as they headed east. Geena's head hurt, she was pretty sure her face was splotchy and red, and her eyes felt swollen from all the crying.

"What the hell, Brooke?" Geena asked, her voice groggy with sleep.

"We needed to get out of there. I unhooked us and left before dawn. The Grand Canyon was a fucked-up idea and not safe for either of us." Brooke's voice had a hitch in it, as if she had been crying too.

"What do you mean, not safe? We were perfectly safe. Dante—"

"Dante!" Brooke's screech cut her off. "He's who we both needed to get away from. Geena." She paused. "Sit down, sugar. I don't know how to tell you this without hurting you." Geena pivoted herself into the passenger seat. "Dante, he tried to attack me last night."

Geena sat silently. She had decided as she finally fell asleep last night that she was going to find out exactly what it was she had witnessed. She should listen to Brooke's side of the story. But she also wanted to get Dante's side of things. She wanted to be a fair judge. Now she couldn't.

Brooke described how she went to join them around the fire pit. Instead of finding Geena, she found Dante. Alone.

"He said mean, hateful things about you. What did you do with him? Please don't tell me you slept with him. The things he said were just cruel and crude. He told me he was just biding his time with you until I came back. I'm sorry, Geena. He asked me how to get rid of you for the night so I could stay with him." She described how when she tried to leave, he'd grabbed her and pushed her against the trailer. She described how he'd tried to kiss and fondle her. "I wouldn't go with him because you liked him so much. He was scary, Geena. When I said no, he tried to hurt me and force me into the trailer." Her eyes stayed focused on the road ahead. Geena closed her own.

"I'm so sorry, sugar. I know you liked him. But he was just using you. He was not a good man to have a crush on. Please tell me he didn't hit you or anything."

A tear ran down Geena's cheek. Behind her eyelids, she reviewed everything she'd seen the night before. Replaying it like a movie—or a bad dream—Dante had been the one against the trailer. Yes, they were kissing, but... But nothing.

Geena saw them kiss. Why was Brooke asking if he'd hit her? Geena inhaled, her breath an uneven, ragged sigh.

"I... I..." She couldn't think to form words. She wanted, she needed to talk to Dante. All of Brooke's recent actions did not support this protective, friendly attitude. But she had known Brooke for years. Yes, she had been annoyed with her during most of this trip, but would that really make Brooke lie to her? Why would Dante...?

Geena wanted to call Dante and talk to him. His voice would soothe her. And if he had something bad to tell her, she was already on her way away from him. But she couldn't call; she didn't have his phone number. She didn't even know if he had found his jacket where she had dropped it. Once they met at the Grand Canyon, they hadn't been apart for more than a few minutes at any time. Since she was always in his company, she had forgotten to ask for his phone information. So nothing. She could probably look him up or trace him through the company he said his cousin ran. But she didn't have the full name of his cousin, only Morgan. Not helpful. How many Morgans were out there working construction?

"I hate men." Brooke slammed the steering wheel. "I hate them. I'm going to become a nun or a lesbian. I swear."

Geena sat in silence, crying. She'd thought she had cried it all out last night, but it seemed her tear ducts were capable of producing infinite tears.

"Dante isn't one of the good ones. I wish you had more experience with men. He just took advantage of you, sugar. You need to learn to not be taken so much with a pretty face and a nice set of abs. I should have stuck with my original feeling the first time we met him, that he was dangerous."

"I don't think I can hear this right now. I need to process." Geena pivoted out of the passenger seat into the

Dangerous | 173

back of the RV. The cabin swayed too much for her to be able to get dressed, so she just sat on the bed. A particularly large bump in the road jostled the RV, causing her to lose balance. She allowed gravity to take her and fell onto the mattress. Burrowing her face into the nearest pillow, Geena sobbed.

She cried because she was convinced she would never see Dante again. She cried because she saw Dante kissing Brooke. She cried because she actually didn't believe Brooke. She cried because she didn't know what to believe. She cried because she was pretty sure she fell in love with him and her heart was breaking. She cried until she had no more tears, and her breathing became so hard she gave herself the dry heaves. The reaction in her system produced nothing but a coughing fit. Once that subsided, Geena lay on her side staring into nothing. Occasionally a dust mote would win her focus, but those couldn't keep her attention for long. She didn't think. She didn't cry. She was numb.

Looking back, her best estimate was that she was semi-comatose like that for about two or three hours. Brooke pulled the RV off the freeway and parked it. Geena was aware only because the movement stopped.

"Geena, you should probably get dressed. I'm going in. I'll grab you a sausage biscuit."

While Brooke was in the restaurant, Geena put on a pair of sweatpants and a T-shirt. The first shirt she grabbed was of the Grand Canyon. Maybe Brooke had been right, maybe this had been one big, bad idea. She grabbed her Santa Fe shirt instead.

Brooke set the paper bag of fast food down on the table when she returned. In the other hand she carried two large Cokes in a gray cardboard drink carrier. Geena rifled through the bag and found the biscuit breakfast sandwiches. She handed one to Brooke and began picking at the crust of the one she had opened for herself.

Dante was dangerous, she had witnessed that firsthand, but he had also been so kind and gentle with her. She had a hard time balancing Brooke's account with the man she'd come to know. Again she reminded herself she had barely known him.

"I'm sorry about Dante," Brooke began.

"I don't want to talk about Dante," Geena snapped. She put her hand up with the fingers spread, indicating stop. "I... I'm still... I'm not ready. I'm sorry." She took a small bite of her food; it was dry and flavorless. She took a drink; it barely registered as being wet in her mouth.

"Can you drive a bit more? I don't even think I can focus properly to drive safely."

"Sure thing." Brooke acted nicer than she had the entire past week. Geena just knew she could no longer trust Brooke. She didn't like the feeling growing in her gut. There was something wrong with Brooke's story, and Geena could not figure it out. She had always sworn she would not be one of those women to choose the man over her friends, to not be lured by devil penis magic. Then again, Brooke had never really been her friend, and she'd never had a chance to find out if Dante had magic in his pants.

After a tense, silent lunch Geena joined Brooke in the cab section of the camper. "Talk to me. What happened back there?" Geena asked. "Start with Blake, what happened with Blake and his friends?"

Brooke regaled Geena with her lacking adventure with Blake. She had collected a few items from the RV before they took off hiking. They saw the vans that ran the North Canyon shuttle, and after talking to one of the drivers, they were able to make reservations for the next scheduled trip north. "It was all so exciting, nothing planned, just winging it. We had enough supplies to do it." Of course, it wasn't nearly as much fun when they got there.

"The North Rim lodge and everything was still closed for the season. And being at a higher elevation, it was so cold. I hadn't anticipated actually camping outside. I thought there was a hotel up there. So, I decided this was the best time to make my move on Blake and get him to share his sleeping bag. He was very receptive, as most men are. Even if he was a bit slow on the uptake." Brooke slurped her drink before continuing.

"It was all romantic, we had a great cookout, and we watched the rain over the South Rim. Blake was getting cozy. And then nothing happened. I was ready to come back, but apparently they had planned for two nights at the North Rim. More hiking, taking pictures, looking at rocks. Rocks are rocks. And the canyon is just a freaking hole in the ground. More rocks. I don't get what those guys were all excited about. One day was plenty. But Blake was more friendly. It was all going so well until some stupid tourist campers from Germany showed up. Then Blake got all weird and cold and shit. There was this one tall girl. I even think her name was Heidi. Are all girls from Germany named Heidi?"

"Just the models, I think," Geena managed. So Brooke got turned down again.

"Well, Heidi and her friends, all women, joined us. Fortunately they had tents. Or unfortunately. I don't know. Blake and Heidi went off in her little tent and made noises like breeding gofers most of the night."

Geena scoffed. "Gofers. Well then I guess that's a little piece of Blake you probably didn't want," she said wiggling her pinkie.

Brooke started laughing. She wiggled her pinkie also. "Trouser worm more like it."

The laugh did Brooke good, and her mood, which had darkened as she described her failed hookup with Blake, lightened considerably. "I ended up sharing a tent with a girl named Amalia; she was nice enough. The next morning we got up, and instead of hiking off with everyone else, I sat and waited for the shuttle back to the South Rim. I think I slept better on the ride back than I did the previous two nights.

"I was overtired and cross by the time I got back to the RV, and the stupid thing was locked, and I didn't have a key."

"You could have called or texted me," Geena offered.

"My phone was dead. I just wanted to lie down in a bed. I wanted to get warm. And Hannah wasn't around, and you had taken off on your own." Brooke waved her hands around.

"It was only later when we ran into each other that I found out you were holing up in Dante's camper, having a fine old time. You know you could have left me a note or something."

"I'm sorry. I should have realized you didn't have a key when Hannah gave me one."

"About that, Geena." The two women looked at each other. Brooke turned her attention back to the road after the eye contact. "What did you see in him anyway? There is something wrong with him."

Geena frowned at Brooke.

"I mean, he attacked Tim and then got them thrown out of the park. What was that all about?"

"He di—" Geena cut herself off. Her brain had just downshifted and sped up. "How did you know about that?" she asked slowly, drawing the words out as her brain clicked gears together. Brooke hadn't been there. Geena hadn't told her anything, and Hannah knew exactly what had happened.

"Oh, Hannah told me. When I got back to the RV and it was locked, I called looking for y'all and reached Hannah. Geena, she told me he jumped poor Tim for no reason. Then, when Tim fought back in self-defense, because Dante is all appearances and no real action, Tim managed to clip him. And so since he fought back and can actually fight, Tim is the one who got into trouble with the park rangers. Dante threatened to sue the park, so they had to ask Tim to leave."

Geena listened to Brooke and bit her tongue. Hadn't she already said her phone was dead? Brooke's story was full of holes. Tim's-point-of-view holes. Of course Tim would think he had been the victim in that exchange.

"Yeah, I didn't see it happen. And Hannah really didn't talk to me afterward, so I don't really know what happened," Geena lied. She knew exactly what had happened. But she needed to process all the lies coming from Brooke. Did Brooke think Geena would so easily believe her because Dante wasn't around? Of course she would, there was no one to contradict her. What else had Brooke been lying about all this time?

Brooke hadn't talked to Hannah. She had to have talked to Tim. Hannah had thanked Dante for not pressing charges; she had seen the whole thing and knew what had happened and who had started all of it. But why had Brooke talked to Tim? Maybe he'd answered Hannah's phone. Then why not just say she had talked to Tim? Talking to Tim wasn't a crime; it was unpleasant, but not a crime. And why hadn't Brooke called Geena once she knew Hannah wasn't in the park? Had her phone been working or not?

Geena knew Brooke was lying to her about the call, so then she was certain Brooke was lying to her about last night. It didn't make sense for Dante to try to get her into the trailer. The triplets had been in there. Brooke didn't know about them; she wouldn't know to account for them in her lie. The pain in Geena's chest throbbed. There was only so much she could put up with in abuse from Brooke: the not so friendly jabs, knowing her size embarrassed Brooke. Brooke had always been vain. Geena just hadn't thought she would be so vindictive. Geena wasn't allowed to be happy. Geena wasn't allowed the good-looking lover.

Geena had to play nice, at least for the rest of the trip. Geena didn't want to play nice, but she was too tired and too emotionally beat-up to fight back. She reached under the seat and pulled out the thick campers guide the rental company had included with the RV. She began flipping through it, looking for a place for the night.

"We are making really good time. How about we park at that place in Amarillo again?" she suggested.

"It's gonna be a long drive today, but I'm with you. We need to get home and get this behind us."

And I need to get away from you and your toxic lies.

What she didn't tell Brooke was that she was hoping the guy who ran the place remembered Dante, and might be convinced to give her his phone number or something so she could find him.

Unfortunately, the clerk at the RV park wasn't any help. He remembered Dante, but he couldn't give her anything. He couldn't even confirm Dante's name, just agreed there was a fella there a few days back with a blue pickup and an Airstream.

Geena and Brooke barely spoke on the return trip. Geena's animosity grew more each day, reflecting Brooke's.

They decided that driving for more than twelve hours a day was too much and broke the return leg of their trip into two days. The second day they shared driving. Switching between driving and napping. That night it started raining.

On the third day, it rained the entire drive back into Atlanta. Geena felt this was appropriate as she had a hard time not crying. She found herself crying on and off all morning. They decided to clean out and unpack the RV at the rental center. By the time the RV was returned to the required condition, the keys turned in to the rental agency early, and Geena dropped Brooke off at her home, it was well past dinnertime.

16

Geena drove on mental automatic through the rain back to her condo. When she pulled into her car park, she fell limp against the steering wheel in defeat. She had forgotten to pick up something for dinner, and all she had planned on was some fast-food drive-through.

She sat in her car staring blankly ahead, not focusing on anything, trying to decide if she needed to back up and get food, or just give up and go inside.

The motion detector lights over her back door came on. A large, dark shape moved. Geena gasped. She switched her headlights back on to see more clearly. It had been lying across the stoop, and now it rose. A large wet wolf sat waiting for her. She turned the car off and slowly, tentatively got out of the car, and approached the animal. "Dante?"

He continued moving up, morphing from his wolf form to stand in front of her. Dante cupped his hands around the back of her head and pulled her to him. The kiss was long and deep. Geena felt as if Dante was trying to pour himself into her and consume her all at the same time.

"You're here," Geena whispered.

"I found you."

Geena started crying again, this time tears of joy. "You found me."

She looked down at his chest, realizing his state of undress on her doorstep. "You're naked, and wet."

She unlocked the door and switched on the lights. Without looking back to ensure that he followed her inside, she quickly walked through her kitchen to the living room to grab a throw blanket for Dante to wrap himself in.

"Here." She handed him the blanket and focused with some concentration on his face. It wasn't until he finished wrapping himself up that she let her gaze drift over him. He was more handsome than she had remembered, strong and tall. She moved into his embrace. He wrapped his arms around her and kissed the top of her head.

Dante was here, in her kitchen. He had found her.

"I thought I would never see you again." There was a hitch in her voice.

"No such luck, pretty girl." He stroked her damp hair.

Leaning against his bare chest, she realized she was still in her coat, and it had to be wet and uncomfortable to hug. She reluctantly left his arms.

"Where are your clothes? How long were you out there in the rain? And why were you a wolf?"

Dante explained that his clothes were in his truck, and the truck was over in guest parking. He realized that waiting around as a man would raise suspicions, but a large dog, less so. He also realized after a few hours waiting out front, that she wouldn't use the front door for regular in and out, so he'd come around back. He had been waiting in the rain about six hours.

"I... I... You're here. I can't believe it. Why are you here?"

Geena could not believe her good fortune. Why would Dante come find her across the country?

"Geena." Dante touched her face gently and pulled her back into his embrace. "I'm here because when you left, I was gutted. I was terrified something had happened to you again. Then I figured something did happen to cause you to leave without saying goodbye. I'm here because I realized I couldn't lose you. I'm here because I'm in love with you."

She looked up at him, blinking fresh tears from her eyes. He gently wiped them from her cheek with his thumb. "You love me?" she asked, not quite sure she'd heard him correctly.

"Yes, I love you." Dante nodded.

She reached up and pulled him down for a kiss. He released his hold on the blanket and wrapped both arms around her, deepening the kiss. Geena's exhausted brain understood enough to know that was a good thing.

"We need to get you some clothes." She sighed. "It's too wet. You're too naked, and I'm too tired to go back out and get them. I'm sure I have some sweats you can wear. If that's all right?"

Dante followed her up the stairs to the second floor. Rummaging through her dresser, trying not to let her self-esteem be too terribly damaged when she realized none of her pants would stay up on him or be long enough. Geena located a pair of gray drawstring sweats and a pink shirt that wouldn't fit him like some crop-top tent. She purposefully averted her eyes from his perfect body. Why would someone so perfect be here with her?

She sat on the edge of her bed waiting for Dante to change. She was so tired she felt like she was deflating. Dante stepped from the bathroom. He was even gorgeous in her clown clothes. The pants were wide and reached his leg midcalf. The shirt was wide and looked like a minidress.

"You look exhausted."

"I'm tired and cold and hungry and—" Geena sniffed. She didn't want to cry again, but after the frustration and the emotional beating of the past few days, she felt like she would collapse. "And you found me." She could manage being a human-shaped lump, and that was about it. Had Dante said he was in love with her? She already couldn't remember properly.

Dante sat next to her, stroked her hair and her back. "We're together now. It will all work out. Why don't you take a hot shower, and I will find something to make for dinner, okay?" He looked ridiculous in her clothes. but she didn't care; all that mattered was she saw concern on his face, and he was here.

"All right."

Clean and in dry, comfortable clothes, Geena padded downstairs to find Dante and dinner.

"How?" Geena asked as she lifted a forkful of food from her bowl.

"Those boys said they were good trackers. And they are."

"I thought they meant using their noses and looking for footprints."

They sat together on the couch in the living room. The TV was on, but neither of them paid it any attention. Geena's feet rested on Dante's lap. Geena took another bite of her dinner; it was warm and felt like comfort food. Dante had made macaroni and cheese, with canned tuna and green beans. It wasn't fancy, but it worked. Geena was happy he was able to find anything in her kitchen. She had cleaned it out of fresh food before the trip, leaving only condiments and a few beers in the refrigerator. She knew there was nothing that would quickly make a meal in the freezer.

"At first that's what I thought too, but no. They pay attention to little details. They know how to ask questions. And, they know how to access files over the Internet that companies don't want them to have access to."

"Like hackers?"

Dante nodded. "Like hackers. They got the license plate from that RV you were renting. They probably rifled through the rental agreement when you left them in there to watch movies," he said, taking her empty bowl and placing it in the sink.

"They found your address for me. I dropped them off at their mother's and then drove straight through to get here," he said, gathering her into his arms as he sat back down on the couch. He pulled her close to his chest with his arms around her shoulders. They watched TV for maybe twenty minutes until Geena passed out from exhaustion.

17

The aluminum case had a black plastic handle. The handle was warm in her hand. That was significant, but Geena couldn't remember why. She also couldn't figure out why she was in a train station, or why her head was leaning on a pink counter, or why the counter lifted and fell as if it were breathing. The case and handle lost all color. Geena adjusted her grip, and the handle throbbed and thickened in her grasp. That was good. It meant the case wanted her holding it. Dante's large hand covered hers on the handle, and he guided her hand, sliding up and down the length. He sighed. She came fully awake.

Dream transitions were always disconcerting, determining where and how the dream morphed into reality. Her face wasn't resting on a counter—it was Dante's chest, and his breathing was growing more rapid. She froze for a second in recognition that the handle was not a piece of plastic belonging to a metal case but, in fact, Dante's engorged manhood.

Once reality and recognition had cleared her brain, she continued stroking him through the sweatpants. His cock pulsed and jumped as more blood filled and expanded its girth. She began nuzzling his chest, searching for the nipple closest to her. He felt smooth and warm through the T-shirt fabric. Her nose scraped the hardening nub. She extended her neck to reach it with her mouth.

Dante drew in a sharp breath as she teased the peak with her teeth. He left off guiding her hand and reached for her breast. He palmed her through her shirt, massaging her soft flesh with his large hand. They continued to tease each other before Dante shifted to a sitting position. He pulled the pink shirt he had been wearing off, pulled off the sweats, and reached over and removed Geena's sleep pants. Dante lay back and grabbed Geena by the hips, pulling her over to straddle him. They stared at one another, lost in each other's gaze. He guided her down along his length.

Geena closed her eyes at the feeling of containing him. Her body shivered, then relaxed as warmth spread throughout her entire being.

Dante hissed his pleasure at finally being buried in her softness. His hands slowly caressed up her thighs and around her ample hips before beginning the slow, stroking descent down her legs again.

Geena didn't move, just reveled in the feeling of him within and his hands on her. She placed her own hands on top of his. He grabbed her waist and thrust up into her hard.

She began to slowly rock back and forth, easing along his length and stroking herself against the crisp hairs and soft balls she pressed against. When she opened her eyes again, Dante's gaze was on her face. Geena noticed his eyes glowed vibrant gold.

Dante reached under her shirt to caress her breasts. He buried his hands under their weight as he smoothed his palms around her ribs and soft middle. Again he thrust into her, causing her to overbalance in his direction. At this angle she had to hold herself up on her hands, but it allowed her to rock her hips more extremely, moving up and down a greater distance of his length. He curled up and latched on to one of her breasts with his mouth. His hands dug into the flesh of her hips. His tongue twirled and teased her nipple through the thin nightshirt. When he sucked on her hard, she gasped in excitement. He continued to thrust harder and faster.

Geena matched Dante's pace with her hips. Erotic pressure built with each thrust. Geena couldn't help but to make small, satisfying groans each time Dante plowed into her. He added his own growls to her chorus of pleasure.

Waves of pulsing joy washed over Geena as she seized in orgasmic delight. She froze as all movement in her body was limited to the cacophony of muscle spasms as she gripped and released Dante with her sex. Lights flashed in her head as she clamped her eyes shut. All the air rushed out of her lungs in a deep, satisfied moan. When she opened her eyes, the smile of joy she saw on Dante's face made her heart pound with love. Then his expression changed as he continued to thrust, his satisfied smiled melting to an expression of uncontrolled physical release. His jaw dropped, and his lips puckered out a groan as he exploded into her. Geena continued to pump her hips as she milked him of his orgasm.

Dante dug his fingers into her hips to hold her still. His breathing was ragged, as if he could take no more pleasurable torture. He found her hand with his and brought it to his lips to kiss her palm. Smoothly he grabbed her leg and rolled her onto her back. He moved with her, holding himself above her on one elbow, looking down at her. Dante stroked the side of her face, his eyes searching hers.

"I love you," she whispered.

"What have you done to me, Geena?"

"What do you mean? I think we did that to each other." She smiled. She liked his face this close. She liked the feel of him caressing her.

"I can't think of anything but you, and I don't ever want to leave this bed. You are my mate." He lowered to her, claiming her lips for a kiss.

Geena draped her leg over his, feeling the firm muscles, hair, and skin of his leg with her own for the first time.

Dante stroked her face, following his hand with his gaze, and he continued the caress across her shoulder and down her arm. He gathered her hand in his and brought it back to his lips. This time he kissed her fingertips one at a time. Slowly his tongue licked along the length of her middle finger, sucking it into his mouth. He laved the space between her first two fingers, caressing each with the sides of his tongue.

Geena watched his face as he caused thrilling sensations low in her abdomen with well placed licks on her hand. She reached up and gently moved a curl from his forehead, following around the side of his face to his ear with her fingertips. She couldn't believe her luck. Dante was here, in her bed. He had found her, tracked her down. And he had just rocked her world with the most fantastic wake-up sex she had ever had.

He pressed his hips against her, and she felt his manhood begin to enlarge again. She reached down with a hand and found she could just stroke the tip. It was firm, yet velvety soft.

Dante opened his eyes, and Geena felt she could get lost in that gaze forever.

"Sweetheart, tell me I didn't just mess up."

Geena closed her eyes, he couldn't be saying what she thought. Her gut clenched. His words sounded as if he had regret, but his actions said he enjoyed what they had shared. "What do you mean?"

"I'm not going anywhere if anything happens. Okay?"

"All right Dante, but what are you talking about?"

Dante spread his hand out across her stomach. "Forgot a condom."

Geena shook her head. She ran her hand over his. "We're fine, I'm covered."

"Hmmm, good," Dante nuzzled her neck. "I want to see you, Geena."

It was a simple enough request, but it made Geena realize they had never before been fully nude together, and they had spent all their attention of the last few minutes locked in each other's gaze. She felt a momentary stab of doubt.

"You sure you want to see me? I'm... I'm not..." She hesitated.

"You're not what, Geena?"

"I'm fat." Her voice was barely above a whisper.

"Oh baby, I don't care about that. So what? You are beautiful. You are soft. You are warm. You feel so good in my arms." He kissed her cheek. "I have hair; that doesn't mean I'm hair. There is more of you to hold, but that doesn't take away from your good nature, kind heart, or sexy ass. You have no idea what that ass of yours does to me, do you? And these"—he palmed one of her breasts—"are like magnets for my hands. I'm in love with you. All of you. That means size, shape, brain, smile, and your giggle, your smell, your sense of humor and kindness, and your kisses." He kissed her. His lips lingered just above hers, teasing them ever so softly.

"So," she said, gathering her self-assurance around her. "You show me yours, and I'll show you mine?"

Dante chuckled.

"Deal. I'll go first." He twisted to sit up, and as he did, Geena grabbed the top bedsheet, covering herself. "Hey, I thought..."

"You first." She giggled.

"Fine, this is my ass," he said as he stood up. He slapped his own butt.

Geena giggled and rolled away from him, uncovering her backside. "This is mine."

Dante laughed, realizing what her game was. He grabbed his shirt from the floor and held it in front of his crotch, hiding his sex from her when he turned to face her. He propped a foot on the bed and wiggled his toes. "These are my toes."

Geena pulled up the sheet, exposing her wiggling toes.

"Arms." His arm rippled and bulged as he flexed his large bicep.

Geena exposed her soft arms and wiggled her fingers.

Dante twisted in a classic bodybuilder pose to flex his pectoral muscles.

Geena removed her shirt and lowered the sheet just enough to expose the tops of her breasts, but not entirely. She enjoyed the show Dante gave her of his body. He was built like a Roman god—large muscled arms and chest, tapering narrow abs, his long thighs thick with powerful muscles. His backside was square and muscled and firm. His front was covered appropriately in a fine dusting of dark hair, perfect enough to tease her fingertips and provide necessary friction in erotic places. The shirt he held in front of himself covered up just enough to tease but not so much to not see the thickening mass of hairs.

Dangerous | 191

He leaned closer, his free hand tracing circles around one of his nipples. "Nipple." He licked his lips in anticipation.

Geena bit her lip. She had to strategically shift the sheet to expose just the pink flesh of one of her nipples while concealing the rest of the breast. She blinked flirtatiously upon completing this limited exposure.

"Temptress," he growled. He paused, clearly thinking about his next move. He put his leg back up on the bed. "I get the whole leg all the way to the hip this time," he demanded.

Geena obliged, exposing one pale, tan-line free leg from toes to hip.

"Middle." Dante pointed to his perfectly formed abs.

Geena pursed her lips and tentatively moved the sheet away from her tummy. This was literally her soft underbelly, her personal weakness. The gash from the wolf fight was still a collection of angry red lines slashed at an angle across her middle. Usually, with her midsection visible she felt more exposed than if she had been completely naked. But with Dante and this exposing game they played, she felt comfortable. Of course, knowing that Dante had seen her before when he doctored the deep scratch, and still wanted to see her, helped.

Dante smiled wolfishly at her as he tossed aside the T-shirt. His manhood was aroused but not fully erect. It emerged from a thicket of dark curls.

Geena blushed. "I, ah..." Dante was gorgeous. Seeing him in all his glory was almost as thrilling as the orgasm he had given her. "I don't have one of those." She giggled as she tried to roll herself back up in the sheet.

"Oh no you don't, tease." Dante jumped on the bed and pulled the sheet from her, exposing all of her to his gaze for the first time. He paused and took her in with his eyes, his expression changing from playfulness to passion. His cock pulsed longer and more erect as he looked at her. He lowered himself to her slowly. Geena's heart pounded. For a long moment she felt that he might change his mind. Feeling his erect manhood on her hip altered that fear. He desired her. His physical reaction could not be missed.

He pressed the length of his body against her and claimed her lips with his. He entered her smoothly and quickly. This coupling was slower, more rhythmic. They rocked their hips together, tongues twining, hands grasping at any body part they could find. Geena's legs wrapped around Dante's as he continued to thrust into her. For a second time that morning Geena groaned as an orgasm claimed her body. This one didn't build as the previous one had—this time she went from everything feeling so good to everything seizing in uncontrolled sexual explosions without preamble. Dante didn't stop his pattern of in-and-out thrusts. He continued until he gave one last hard push and held himself deep within her. He collapsed against her chest, his spent manhood still encased in her warm folds.

"I'm never letting you out of this bed," he murmured against her breasts as he pet her with soft caresses.

"I don't think I'll be able to walk anyway if you keep this up."

"Maybe after a nap. I think you've done me in."

They fell back to sleep entwined in each other's limbs.

When they woke, they made love again. Dante's plan to never leave the bed would have happened if they hadn't realized they were hungry and there was practically no food in the condo.

"Where's your truck?" Geena asked while she got dressed. Dante explained through the shower where he had parked, and that the truck was unlocked and the clothes would be in the cab.

Once both were dressed, Geena drove to a nearby strip mall with an IHOP, a grocery, and a big-box store.

Geena smiled as the waitress delivered their food.

"I love you, but what I saw really hurt, Dante. I know Brooke lied to me, 'cause what I saw and what she said just don't add up."

"What did you see?" Dante asked as he took a bite.

Geena shook her head. "Uh-uh. I'll tell you what I saw after you tell me what happened. I need to know you aren't changing things to fit my story."

"Fair enough." Dante carefully placed his fork down with a sigh. "I was about to tell you I developed some serious feelings for you when you shut me down."

"I thought you were gonna break up with me," Geena confessed.

"I know; you told me. Instead, I walked you home. Brooke was sitting next to the fire when I got back. I told her you had gone back to your RV. She said she wanted to talk to me alone. I figured she was going to read me the riot act for hooking up with you. She started unbuttoning her shirt and telling me that I no longer had to settle for you. She used some unsavory descriptive terms. Let's just say she did not like it when I told her I preferred your shapely ass and she needed to leave. She's screechy and very unladylike when she gets mad. I had to physically restrain her from going into the Airstream. That's when she got me pinned to the side of the camper and..." Dante paused. "I didn't kiss her back, I swear it. I was trying not to hurt her, but she landed pretty hard when I pushed her off me. She kept saying I would change my mind if I would kiss her."

Dante took a sip of coffee. Geena watched his face. He looked pained.

"She stormed off in a huff. I stayed outside watching the fire and trying to figure out how I should tell you what had happened. I found my jacket on the ground when I headed over to see you the next morning, but you were already gone." Dante blinked, clearing his eyes as he looked at Geena. "I was terrified something had happened to you again. Then I realized Brooke had probably told you something and the two of you left.

"Those boys stepped up with all kinds of help when they realized I needed to find you. Now, will you tell me what you saw?"

Geena nodded. "I saw you and Brooke kissing. I thought you really were trying to break up with me 'cause she was back."

"God no, Geena, I..."

Geena shook her head and held up her hand to stop Dante. "By the next morning, I realized I needed to talk to you and not jump to conclusions. But Brooke had us unhooked and on the road. She told me you tried to attack her and get her into your trailer. I think that's when I started to realize something was wrong and she was lying. It took me a while to figure it out. There was no reason for you to get her into the trailer. She still doesn't know about the boys."

"Geena, I've never lied to you. You know my secrets. Why would I do what she said?"

"I don't know. I was confused and hurt. And then we were gone. I never got the chance to find out from you what had happened." Geena sighed. "But you're here."

"I'm here, and I love you." Dante shifted from his side of

the booth so that he could sit next to Geena. "You said Brooke has been lying about all kinds of little things lately."

"Yeah, I'm pretty sure she always lies. But recently they've been easy to catch, stupid lies too. Things that just don't add up." Geena chuckled to herself. "She was probably outraged that you like me, and couldn't accept it."

"Well, it's something she's just going to have to get used to. You know I never would have gotten between you and your friend on purpose."

"Yeah, I do. And Brooke's not my friend. I'll be cordial enough to her through this wedding of Hannah's, but then I am officially done." Geena rested her head against his shoulder. "You love me?"

"I think I have from your first smile, pretty girl." He kissed her on the forehead.

They picked up a change of clothes for Dante at the big-box store. He didn't buy too much, as he expressed a preference to take Geena shopping later for properly fitting clothes, as he described them. He did purchase enough necessities and sundries to get him through the next few days. Dante told her he planned to go back to bed and not need clothes for at least two more days. This made Geena blush and giggle nervously.

They strolled through the aisles of the grocery store. Geena added food she would need for her week. Dante made sure they had plenty of quick, frozen meals. He seemed serious regarding his plan of not leaving the bed for several days except for food.

"Things we need to discuss"—Geena swallowed hard, discussions on responsibility were always so awkward—"especially if we really are going to spend days in bed."

"You said you're covered. So pill?"

Geena nodded. "But what about the rest? You know," she paused, "health, diseases, that kind of stuff."

"This is easy," he started. "My body temperature is slightly more elevated than yours. I'm not running a fever. Let's call it an ethnic trait. We think it serves in a similar capacity to a fever, in that it burns off disease. I don't get sick. And if I do, there's something about transitioning that heals most anything."

"That's convenient."

"Sometimes." He nodded. "I can't tell you how many tattoos I got before I finally gave up."

"What?"

"Yeah, hours and hours and hundreds of dollars of ink, and poof, one shift and it's all gone. Ari—Arianna, my sister—is constantly repiercing her ears. On the upside, little things like that heal quickly when we stay in this form."

"So, no disease then."

"Nope. Your turn. And it doesn't matter. You can't give me anything."

"Well, until you I was a born-again virgin." Dante tilted his head, looking sideways at her. "It's been a long time, a really long time. There were only two before anyway."

Dante continued to stare at her in disbelief.

"What?" Geena shrugged at him.

"You are so beautiful. I wonder at the idiocy of some men. I guess I expected you to tell me..." He paused in his thought, then shook his head. "I don't know."

"Guys aren't exactly lining up for me, Dante, not like they do for Brooke, or Hannah even."

"They're all idiots. You are gorgeous." Dante grabbed her in for a kiss.

"No kissing in the chip aisle," she teased, then tossed a few bags of chips into the cart. "Anyway, I do the whole annual health checkup, and after the last boyfriend I got the full workup. I am clean. So, yeah, I have nothing to give you anyway."

"You give me love," Dante said as he stole another quick kiss.

Geena found it satisfying and comfortable to be doing such domestic activities as grocery shopping. Dante insisted on paying for everything. When they returned to her home, he put groceries away. He claimed it gave him a better opportunity to learn where everything was.

"I'm going to have to go pick up the Airstream and drive it back to California at some point," he said as he placed items into the refrigerator.

"Oh yeah, where is it?"

"I left it in Arizona with the triplets' mother. I'm going to have to spend some time finding out how much she knows and seeing if the boys want to go to California or not. They have to learn how to control themselves."

"How long can you stay?" Sadness crept into Geena's voice. She didn't want to think about Dante leaving so soon. She sat at her kitchen table watching Dante explore her small kitchen.

"About a week, maybe a bit more." Dante turned and saw Geena. He crossed to her and wrapped his arms around her. "Wild horses won't keep me from coming back to you. When I'm in California, I'll talk to Morgan. He'll give me leave from work, or maybe I can figure out how to work from here."

"You will come back?"

"Of course. I love you." He thumbed a stray tear from her cheek. "I don't do long-distance relationships. So until I can convince you to come to California with me, I have to be here with you."

Geena was deliriously happy for the next two days. As planned, they barely left her bed. If they weren't making love, they were talking, learning everything about each other. The more Geena learned, the deeper in love she fell with Dante. Monday morning came entirely too soon.

Geena quietly got dressed, cursing having to return to work. She longingly looked down at Dante's sleeping face. His mussed hair and relaxed features reminded her of a sleeping child. His beard growth and occasional loud snore corrected that vision. Maybe she was seeing her children in his face. She would like that. She placed the key into his hand and kissed him tenderly on the cheek. "Work," she whispered, then reluctantly left.

The drive from her condo into the industrial park in Stone Mountain may have been a reverse commute, but with Monday morning traffic and Dante back at home in her bed, it was far too long and entirely too far away. Geena pulled into the parking lot and was momentarily confused. Where were the other cars? The lot should have been full. She wasn't early. She pulled out her phone to confirm that it indeed was Monday. Then she started to laugh. She laughed at herself until tears smeared her makeup. With the stress of the trip and the distraction of Dante, she had completely forgotten that this site had been shut down just over two weeks ago. She didn't have a job. "Stupid, stupid, stupid." She cursed herself as she turned her car around and joined the commute headed into Decatur.

Dante was dressed and making coffee. "You're home early. Couldn't stand to be away from me a minute longer?"

Geena dropped her purse on the kitchen table and slumped into a chair. "I don't have a job."

"What? What happened? Did you get laid off?" Dante's voice sounded concerned.

"Yeah, I got laid off"—she held up her hand to keep Dante from speaking—"before the trip. The plant shut down, everyone was laid off. I think days in bed with you have befuddled my brain. I have to start looking for a job, I guess." She sighed.

"You don't have to work. I can take care of you." Dante stroked her hair.

"I'll have to go to work eventually."

"Only if you want to." He kissed her fingers one at a time. "But not right now, I'm not done with you." He pulled her in for a kiss, his passion for her not assuaged by the two days they had spent in bed. With an ease that surprised Geena, he lifted her into his arms and carried her upstairs to her bed. She was breathless with excitement. Never had she expected a man to be able to pick her up so effortlessly, let alone carry her any distance.

18

Leaving the warmth of Geena's arms and her bed were possibly the hardest things Dante had ever done. He had done many difficult things as a Palatine, as a wolf, but leaving his mate, voluntarily, was soul crushing. Geena had a hard time with it too, and she could not hide her sorrow. He tried to leave at least three different times. The first time, he took one look at the sadness in her eyes, then carried her upstairs and made love to her for the rest of the day and into the night.

He had to leave the next day. He could not afford to put it off any longer. The second time he thought he was leaving, he made it as far as the truck before he had to return to Geena. That time they didn't even make it all the way upstairs before he claimed her body one more time.

The third time, it was late morning, and Geena followed him out to the truck. He didn't want to stop kissing her, ever. Finally they let each other go, and he pulled away from her condo. From his love, from his home. Geena was brave, but tears still streamed down her cheeks. Dante didn't let her see how it affected him.

Geena's tears made him want to damage whatever it was that caused her pain. His brain turned into a rage monster. He wanted to punch and bite and scratch. The problem was—he was the cause of her pain. Internalizing his rage, he beat himself up mentally. He had hurt her once unintentionally; now he was causing it directly. It made him angry, and unfortunately, it came across as being aggravated with Geena, which made her sadder. The only way he knew to fix this was by kissing her more. But now, alone in the truck, all he could do was call her on the phone.

Dante had been gone for less than fifteen minutes the first time he called her. He could tell she had been crying. He desperately wanted to turn the truck around and bring her along. She was stronger than he was. The sound of her tears was all it took for him to want to give up and return to her. She had insisted that she stay at home. She needed to look for a job. She had wedding obligations.

Their first conversation over the phone was limited in its scope. Dante promised to return to her sooner than later, and professed his love for her repeatedly. Geena tried to stifle her crying and told Dante she would be fine.

Dante decided to drive straight through, stopping only for naps in his truck. The faster he could get this done, check in on the triplets, and deliver the Airstream to his cousin, the sooner he would be back home in Geena's embrace. She made him feel like he was a superhero, invincible. She gave him a purpose, a reason to be protective. He saw his future in her face, and knew within minutes of leaving Atlanta what he would be buying on this trip.

He made good time and was well into Texas by midmorning of the second day. He had waited to call Geena, knowing she liked to sleep in, especially if she had bad dreams the night before. He hated to think he may have caused her to have nightmares by leaving.

Geena did not sound good. Her voice was hoarse, and she had the hiccups. He could tell she had been crying for a long time.

"It's so cold and dark here without you." She sniffed.

"Geena, sweetheart, I miss you so much, and it's only been a day."

"You promise me you are coming back?"

"Of course. I love you. I'm sorry I'm not eloquent enough to express just how much I do love you. I can't even think of any corny song lyrics to quote for you right now."

"You'd walk five hundred miles?" She sniffed again.

"Of course, ain't no mountain high enough."

"I hurt without you here. I never knew I could miss someone this much. It's like you took part of me with you."

"I know exactly what you mean. You have my heart, and it's hard to breathe without you near."

"That sounded pretty eloquent to me, Dante."

"I love you." He chuckled.

"I'm going to be good for nothing while you're gone. At least there's food in the kitchen. I doubt I'll shower. I'll be smelly and gross when you return."

"Do I need to come get you? I will, you know."

"How far away are you?"

"I'm in Texas. There's a truck stop coming up. I can turn around there. I'll be back in two days. Can you hold on for two days?" All Dante needed was for her to say come, and he would turn around. He would bring her along, or he would call Shane to pick up the trailer. All he needed was for Geena to tell him she needed him, and he would drop all his responsibilities to be by her side.

"Really? You'd do that for me?"

"Sweetheart, it's not for you; it's for me. I can't stand the thought of you hurting because of something I did. And I did this. If coming home right now will make this right, I will."

"No, no. I think you just did make everything right by saying that. And you said you don't have the words to let me know just how much you love me. Those were some pretty terrific words."

"Geena," he sighed her name.

"I'll be fine. I just have to remember you love me. You. And you are doing what you have to so you can come back to me. Me. 'Cause you love me. It's not my imagination. It's not all one-sided. It's not me being hopelessly in love with you. You actually love me. Right?"

"I absolutely love you. You aren't making this easy."

"I'm sorry. I'll be all right. I will. You just have to call me when you can."

Their conversation was cut short by bad cell service. As soon as he was able, Dante called her back, not wanting Geena to think he hung up on her

"You okay?" Dante's voice was full of concern.

"I'm gonna be fine. You need to focus on driving safely. You'll call me again later?" Geena asked.

"I love you. I'll call you next time I pull over."

That night he pulled into the driveway of the triplet's mother's property much later than he'd intended. He sent Geena a short text to let her know he had arrived safely, and then he crawled onto the couch in the trailer.

In the morning a pounding on the trailer's door woke him.

That is a habit I need to break those kids of. Dante dragged himself off the couch and opened the door. As suspected, it was the boys, Jason, Percy, and AJ. They were dressed in jeans and wearing hooded sweat jackets with backpacks on their backs.

"Hey, man!"

"We didn't think you were coming back."

"Did you find Geena?"

Dante had forgotten how they climbed over each other while talking.

"Yeah, I found her." His voice was groggy with sleep. "You headed to school or something?"

Just then a dusty old Chevy pickup pulled into the end of their drive and honked. "Bye, man!"

"See you when we get home."

"Glad you found Geena; I like her." They ran, jumping into the back of the truck.

Dante shook his head, closed the door, and headed back to the couch. He needed to get more sleep. He picked up his phone and looked to see if Geena had texted him back. He smiled. She had sent a single heart emoji text. He fell back to sleep clutching the phone.

A light knock woke him a few hours later. Blinking, Dante opened the trailer door. Michelle, the triplets' mother, stood there holding a steaming cup of coffee.

"I figured since you got in late, you could use sleep. I hope the boys left you in peace on their way out."

"They stopped by to say hi." Dante groaned, stepped back, and indicated that she should enter.

"I can't thank you enough for letting me park this here for the past two weeks. I, ah…"

"The boys told me, you needed to go get your woman." She smiled. Michelle Haskie had a warm, friendly face, the same high cheekbones and eyes that the triplets had. She had her thick black hair pulled back into a neat braid. She was maybe five to ten years older than Dante, though she looked to be five to ten years younger.

"Yeah, my woman." He sighed. "More like the mother of my future children. I really do owe your boys a debt of gratitude in helping me find her."

"She say yes?"

"I haven't asked her yet. I have to find a ring." He grinned to himself. How was he ever going to find the perfect ring for her? Dante pressed his fingers into his eyebrows. He was going to have to call his mother and get her to help.

"Just ask; you won't need a ring if she really is the mother of your future children." Michelle took a sip of her coffee. "Well, let's not keep you here longer than you need to be."

Michelle continued to fill Dante in on all the information the triplets had shared with her. They had told her about the old wolf, and how he had cornered the girls. They also told her about how Dante knew exactly what they were, and how he, Dante, was the strongest wolf they had ever met.

"So you know other wolves?"

"No, not really."

"That's pretty noncommittal there, Michelle. Can you give me any more information than that?"

"When you left here, you told me you were looking up family lineage. Trying to see if you had any relatives around here. I liked how you called it a genetic anomaly. So I called my mother. My dad was a man named David Kee. He raised me. He's my sister's biological father, but he's not mine. I've always known that. I was never really interested in my biological father's family. There was a crazy old drunk who would show up every now and again. He called himself a skin-walker.

I thought he was just nuts. Mom was always nice to him, said he was my uncle, George, and we had to be nice to him since he was family. But he wasn't my dad's brother, and he wasn't Mom's brother. I was never quite sure where or how he fit in. I called again after you dropped the boys off. Mom was very helpful this time, now that I knew what questions to ask.

"George is... I haven't seen him for years. I don't know if he's alive, dead, or where he would be. Anyway, George is the brother of my biological father, my mother's first husband who died in Vietnam." She scoffed. "He was nineteen. She said he died before she even realized she was pregnant. That's so messed up." She shook her head and stared into her coffee. "Anyway, George is my uncle. Mom didn't know about any weird illnesses or skin conditions." She chuckled. "She still doesn't know about the boys' gift."

"So you don't have it?" Dante queried.

"I do not. But it was one hell of a shocker when those boys started shifting into puppies. I thought someone had slipped me some hallucinogenics." She rubbed her face, recalling the stress it had caused her temporarily aged her appearance. "I really don't know how I haven't lost my sanity over it." She shook her head and gave Dante a smile. She returned to looking younger than him.

"And their father?"

"He doesn't know!"

"How have you managed that one?"

"He travels for work, and it's been less than a year. So..." She shrugged and sighed; it was a deep sigh, letting stress go.

Dante pulled a box off the counter and placed it on the table. He began unpacking it.

"I think your biological father, and Uncle George, are the unknowns I've been looking for. These," he said, placing several plastic boxes in front of Michelle, "are DNA kits. They are all paid for, ready to go." Dante opened one of the boxes, showing Michelle the directions and talking her through the process. "I need you and the boys—I'll go over this with them this afternoon—to each complete one of these. I also want your husband to complete one next time he's home. I suspect you are the genetic link, but let's get him tested just in case. It's easy. You just spit in this tube." He held up a test tube. "Then you follow these instructions for sending them in. They will go to a lab we use for this all the time. The lab will send you the results. They will also send me a copy of the results." He started to package the tests back into the box. "We already know the boys have the gene and it's active. They are going to need support and training."

"Training?"

"Yeah, they are going to be stronger, bigger, faster than their contemporaries without the lupine gene. They need to learn to control their physical and emotional reactions. For now, that can be as easy as karate classes, judo, any martial art that emphasizes discipline."

"Oh, Dante, that's gonna be expensive." Concern was in her voice.

"It's paid for. Anything you need for them, it's covered."

"And what if your little spit DNA test shows that we aren't related?"

"Depending on if we know the family, I contact their people and let them know I found some pups, who and where you are. They will do the same, support your needs. If they aren't that kind of family, or we can't find a relation, the Palatines will continue to support you. You become family, related or not. Even if you are not a descendant of Margarita Palatine, as I suspect you are, you've got a huge family support system; you just need to ask.

"At some point, if you are Palatine, the boys will need to come spend some time at the house in Sonoma. You are welcome, of course, as their mother and keeper of their secret."

"My husband?"

"Depends on how you think he'll be able to handle all of this. If he needs to stay in the dark, we can work around that; if he can deal, then it makes things easier. But he has to be able to keep the secret."

Michelle nodded. "I'll have to think about that."

"You need to know, their education is covered. If they decide things are getting too hard at school, for any reason, I want you to call me. We have a private school, where they don't have to hide what they are. If they ever get in trouble with the law, I want you to call me. We have lawyers that won't necessarily get them out of trouble, but will keep them out of the local juvenile system. Get them to a place where we can work with them."

Dante's phone buzzed.

He picked it up. It was Geena. His face relaxed into a broad smile.

Seeing the look on his face, Michelle must have realized it was love. "It's your woman. I'll get going. We can discuss this more after the boys get home." She stood up and stepped out of the trailer.

Dante nodded in acknowledgment as she left.

"Hi, pretty girl."

"You sound like you're smiling."

"I am," he crooned.

"Why are you smiling?"

"Because you called me. And I am happy to hear your voice."

"You could see my face if I could get this stupid face-to-face feature to work."

"Still not working?"

"Nope, it keeps saying failed attempt. Hey, I called for more than just to hear your voice, but I will say you are making my ears happy."

"You sound better today, sweetheart."

"I am. I'm still sad, but better. I called because they just dropped off your car. Dante! Did you really order a Porsche?"

"Yeah, I got a Panamera Hybrid, figured that would be good for city driving."

Dante could hear Geena pause and breathe in. "You paid for that with a credit card over the phone?"

"Yeah, American Express."

"That's ridiculously expensive, Dante. Can you afford to do that? I mean, I know your money is none of my business, but sweetie, that's a really expensive car." Dante smiled at the level of awe mixed with concern in her voice.

"It's fine. I can afford it. I'm going to ditch this truck as soon as I get back to California. The Porsche is much more me. That's okay, isn't it? I mean, you didn't fall for me 'cause of the truck? Right?"

Geena giggled. "No, the truck had nothing to do with falling in love with you. Seriously, a Porsche?"

"You can take it for a spin if you like; will that make you feel better?"

"Ah, no. I made them park it. I was afraid to bump it."

"It's just a car, Geena. It's okay."

"Just a car? Wow. They are coming back next week to

install the plug-in thingy. That's what they said they had arranged with you."

"Sounds about right. And it's all paid for; you don't even have to tip these guys. They are well paid to do this. Okay?"

"I can handle that. How's it going? Have you seen the boys? How are they?"

Dante told her he'd seen them briefly earlier, and had spent the rest of his morning going over things with their mother.

"I'll probably be able to leave here tomorrow or day after at most. I won't be able to make as good of time hauling the trailer. I'm thinking I'll get the trailer back to Morgan two more days after that. Wrap up some loose ends. I should be able to catch a flight back in six, maybe seven days."

"Another week?" Geena's voice lowered.

"Another week at most. I want to be back with you as much as you want me back."

"All right. I love you. Tell the boys I said hey. Call me when its bedtime and you're alone. I have an idea." She giggled.

"Geena?" Dante dragged her name out. She giggled more on the other end of the line.

"I love you, Dante. Just call me later, all right?"

"Of course. I love you."

He rang off the line.

That afternoon Dante contacted the lawyer, Mr. Saganitso. He followed up on the records search he had requested. Saganitso was able to confirm the information Michelle had shared with him regarding family records. Her mother had been married to Joseph Tse-pe. He died in Vietnam. He had a brother, George. No known death records for him yet. The birth records for Michelle did not list Joe Tse-pe as father.

Dante went over the same information with the triplets

as he had with their mother. He included the specifics regarding the DNA testing, and he added extra details that only they would really appreciate, since they were the one to express the lupine gene and had shifting abilities. All three were eager to find and join a karate class. They agreed they wanted to visit the family in Sonoma over the summer. After an initial visit, they would discuss and make decisions regarding school and other opportunities.

Dante joined the family for dinner. The boys' mother made a large roast chicken. The atmosphere sitting around the family's kitchen table was warm and friendly. It reminded Dante of meals with his cousins and gave him a lump in his throat thinking about the family he wanted with Geena.

He spent the majority of his time answering questions about being in Atlanta with her. Dante was able to deflect the more seeking questions by telling them about Atlanta and what he was doing to get ready to move there to be with her.

Dante realized he had enjoyed hanging out with the boys while at the canyon. They were smart and goofy. They did not fit the stereotype of sullen, face-down-in-a-cell-phone teens. He hoped the kids he and Geena had would be more like them.

He decided with matters essentially wrapped up here, he would head out to California the next day. The sooner he left, the sooner he could get back to Geena.

He'd finished setting up the air mattress when his phone buzzed. Geena.

"Hello, pretty girl, I was just getting ready for bed." He heard Geena giggle. "What?"

"I can't. I thought I could, but I can't."

"Can't do what, sweetheart? And what's so funny?"

"I was gonna... Oh gee, I can't even admit it now."

"You're blushing. I can hear you blush. What?" Dante was beyond curious. It was going to make him crazy. Geena giggled her slightly embarrassed giggle, something that Dante found to be sexy. He always wanted to touch her and tickle her when she giggled that way.

"All right, I was going to try... um. I was going to try to be all seductive and do phone sex, but I can't." She giggled more.

Dante chuckled. "That you would even think about trying is a turn-on. Should I talk dirty to you instead?"

"I can't. I just can't." Clearly, she was unable to do anything more than giggle.

"I'm so embarrassed now. I love you. I'll talk to you tomorrow."

"I love you." Dante laughed as she ended the call.

In the morning he made sure everyone had his contact information, and he set up an online bank account for Michelle. This was so that someone from the family could provide her with the funds she would need for getting the boys their extra lessons and any other needs they might have.

Dante forgot that pulling the trailer shortened his driving days. He preferred to have it parked and settled before dark. Setting up the stabilizers and hooking up for water service after sunset was not his idea of fun. This made for long and restful nights. But now, without Geena, the nights were painfully long and tedious. Books didn't interest him. They weren't Geena. Movies could only distract him a little bit. He spent the first evening texting Geena silly emojis. She sent back photos of herself making silly faces.

Ohh that one was sexy. He typed.

Geena shocked him by sending back a photo of her nipple.

She was getting more bold after her embarrassment over the failed attempt at phone sex.

Not to be outdone, Dante sent a picture of his own nipple.

The next picture made Dante want to jump through the phone. Geena sent a photo of where her legs met, and the dark curls there.

Dante immediately called her. "What are you doing to me?"

"Delete that!"

"Never! My God, woman, you are evil."

"I shouldn't have sent that. Delete it, Dante."

"No, that's the sexiest thing I have ever gotten on my phone. Do you know how much I want you right now? And I can't touch you, and you send me that."

"Are you mad? 'Cause you sound, I don't know, angry."

"I'm frustrated, sweetheart. I'm frustrated 'cause I'm here and you're there, and you just gave me a raging hard-on."

Geena giggled. "I'm sorry. I was just trying to be playful."

"Then don't stop; tell me you want me."

"I want you, Dante. I miss you."

"Tell me how you would lick me." Dante pulled his erection free from his pants and began stroking himself as he listened to Geena. Her voice, no matter the words, was an aphrodisiac. Talking dirty, she was the most seductive thing in his existence.

"All right, I can do this. I can tell you I would take my tongue and lick you from the base to your tip."

Dante groaned. This encouraged Geena to be bolder. "I would place my mouth around your head and suck. I'd suck the rest of you into my mouth."

"Uh-huh." He continued to stroke, her voice and his imagination bringing him to a peak.

"I don't think I can do this, Dante." Her voice was calm, all giggles gone.

"Okay, you don't have to. Can I tell you what I'd do to you, and will you listen?"

"Sure," she answered tentatively. "I'll listen."

"Good, 'cause I want to feel your skin. My hands miss your breasts. My lips miss your mouth. And I miss driving into you when you're all wet and hot."

Geena gasped.

"Yeah, make noise for me. I do like your sounds. I miss your scent. Clean and lavender. Your hands on me, when you touch…" Dante's breath was growing ragged as he continued to stroke.

"Sweetie, you all right?"

"Just needing a bit more encouragement at the moment." He groaned.

"You can do it; yes, you can." Geena's voice was bright and obnoxiously high-pitched.

"Not the encouragement I needed, thank you. You sure you don't want to keep talking dirty to me?"

"Dante, are you…? Oh, you are."

Dante chuckled as she gasped again. He guessed she was blushing.

"Uh, imagine that's my hand."

"Oh, I am."

"What do I say?"

"Tell me to go slower or faster or…"

"Slow, go slow. I like to touch you slowly. That way I can feel how long and hard you are. You always like it when I squeeze a bit more at the bottom, then pull back up."

"Uh-huh, yeah, that's good." Dante changed his pattern to meet her directions and pace.

"Push your hand back down, and up again. You like to rock your hips when I'm doing this. And I like it when you try to finger me. I might lick you every now and again."

"Is your mouth warm?"

"Warm and wet. Shall I put my whole mouth on you? And slide my teeth up, and run my tongue back down. I can't get all of you in my mouth, you're too big, and I'd rather lick you like a lollipop anyway."

Dante let out a loud moan and a gasp.

"Did you just...? Did it work?"

"Oh yeah, baby, that worked. Thank you."

"Are you going to delete that picture now?"

"Never!"

19

Classic southern rock music and a hint of stale smoke wafted past Geena as she opened the door to the bar, the smell left over from years of smoking inside. Smoke that had become part of the woodwork and would never fully dissipate. Normally this was when Geena would have to mentally gird her loins to walk the rest of the way into the bar. It wasn't like she hadn't been here before, after all; she, Brooke, and Hannah liked to start off or end their nights out here. The bar had cheap beer and the best onion rings outside the Varsity drive-in. She was enough of a regular not to be nervous walking in, but not enough of a regular for anyone to know her name. Even so, Geena always felt the need to increase her mental fortitude to enter, but not tonight. Tonight Geena felt confident, pretty, and happy.

Dante had been gone for almost a week. The first two days had been hell. Geena had been convinced he would change his mind and never come back. The morning of his second day away he had asked if he needed to come back for her. She had told him not to, that she had things to do at home, but his willingness to turn around for her if she said the word had changed her mood considerably. They spoke daily on the phone, usually while he drove and had a signal, and they constantly texted when he wasn't driving. Dante reminded her every day how much he loved her and that he would return soon, even if she changed her mind about him. Dante's love provided her with the support that allowed her a new level of personal confidence she had never felt before.

Tonight she dressed up for no real reason other than she felt good, so why not also look good? The new clothes Dante had purchased for her fit well, and she felt pretty in them. She'd ordered them from her favorite online plus-size boutique. They had just released a new line, a modern take on vintage 1950's dresses with full skirts, scooped necklines, and waist-cincher belts. Dante had insisted she order what she wanted, and he'd paid for overnight delivery.

She hadn't had a chance to really wear them anyplace. Every time she and Dante had considered going out, and she put on the new clothes, he would declare how beautiful and sexy she was, then proceed to remove all her clothes and make love to her. More than once they hadn't even made it back to the bedroom. Stairs, Geena discovered, provided an excellent source of leverage and exciting angles. She smiled to herself over how much sex they'd had. Dante was insatiable, and around him, she was too. She had never had this level of sexual drive before. Dante's ability to recover and perform again astounded her. Her previous sexual encounters paled so much in comparison, she practically didn't count them anymore, especially since Dante's skills left her legs weak and feeling like limp noodles. She was surprised she could walk without wobbling.

Tonight Geena's dress was a rich peacock blue with a full skirt, featured a sweetheart neckline with a black lace overblouse, and a wide black belt. Geena made her way to the tall wood booth in the back where Hannah and Brooke were already seated. She scooted into her seat. A large basket of french fries sat in the middle of the table, and a tall beer waited for her.

"You dressed up. Going for that retro plus-size pinup look? I guess it suits your figure." Geena ignored Brooke; there was no mistaking the tone in her voice. That had been a barb, not a compliment. Geena did notice that tonight she was the one dressed well. Even if Geena dressed up, Hannah was impeccably dressed by default of the wardrobe she owned, and Brooke usually made an effort to look a certain way when they went out to bars. Tonight Brooke was actually dressed down. She typically didn't dress for an evening out in jeans. She played to her assets: long legs and cleavage. A night out would mean heels, miniskirts, exposed skin. Geena actually wondered if she felt well. Brooke looked tired—beautiful as always, but tired. Her hair hung loose and down, and she wore a gathered peasant blouse and jeans. This was Saturday flea market wear, not bar wear.

"So, how have y'all been? I haven't seen you since that fiasco called a road trip to the Grand Canyon." Hannah even did the finger air quotes as she said *road trip to the Grand Canyon*.

Geena pasted a false grin on her face. The only reason the trip had been a fiasco was due to Tim showing up and Hannah leaving with him, and because Brooke had scampered off with the bearded guy. They didn't know anything about Geena's time with Dante. And while Geena's trip had ranged from good, to bad, to terrifying, she didn't think Hannah had the right to call the road trip a fiasco. Her friend had no idea.

"Same old same old for me, just working." Brooke took a drink from her beer.

"Haven't heard from you at all. You've not even been online." Hannah nodded at Geena. "Have you been okay? I was kind of worried, you know, with everything."

"Yeah, how's the job hunt going?" The trip hadn't done Brooke any favors, and it looked like she hadn't slept well since returning home.

"It's not. I haven't even started looking," Geena answered merrily. She hadn't been about to spend a second of time job hunting when Dante was here, and she really hadn't felt like starting since he left. "I haven't really been worried about it."

"You know you really should start looking. Your severance package isn't going to last very long, and jobs take forever to get these days."

"Maybe I could ask Daddy if we have something?"

"What have you been doing then? Not hiding up in the dark, moping after that asshole?" Brooke sneered the last sentence.

"You mean Dante? Right?" Geena clarified. There had been plenty of assholes from the trip. She considered Brooke to be one of them.

"Yes, Dante. I had almost successfully forgotten his name, still just trying to get all of that behind me." Brooke scoffed, as if that particular traumatic event hadn't been her doing.

"Sorry you had a crappy time. I enjoyed the trip. And no, I'm not moping after Dante. As a matter of fact, I've been playing house with him." Geena smirked as Brooke choked on her beer.

Brooke wiped up the beer she'd spilled. "You've been

living with him? What did you do, find him online or something? I thought you didn't have his phone number?"

"Nope, he found me. Actually, he managed to find me and chase me home. He was waiting when I got back."

"Geena, are you sure? I mean, what Brooke told me and all..." Hannah's eyes went big with concern.

"Brooke, I know you don't like him. I don't really know why. Hannah, he's not like how Brooke paints him. He's the way he was when you met him, you know, nice. He really is one of the good ones."

"And so now he's living off you? What kind of freeloader is he? Geena, he's using you."

"He's not a freeloader, Brooke. I'm not sure how you missed it, but he's actually loaded. I mean, he's rich in a way I don't think any of us would understand."

"Even me?" asked Hannah. "Daddy is rich, and Timmy comes from money. I think I would understand money."

"Didn't either of you notice his truck was new, and so was that motorcycle? And it was a custom job."

"So he blew all his money on a motorcycle. Didn't he say the trailer was his cousin's?" Both women were shaking their heads, concern for Geena obvious on their faces. It was clear they were questioning her mental well-being.

"Look, Hannah, last time Tim bought a car..." Geena pointed at Hannah, who nodded. "He went to the dealership, right?" Hannah continued to nod. "He makes payments, right?" Hannah continued to nod.

"What's your point?" sniped Brooke. "That's how everyone buys cars."

"No, it's not. Right before Dante left, he called the dealership and ordered a car to be delivered. Like a pizza, but a car."

"What?"

"Yeah, the dealership delivered a Porsche Panamera Hybrid the other day. Just, you know, dropped off the car and handed me the keys."

"Oh my God, you didn't sign anything on that, did you? He's going to dump you with the payments."

"The only thing I signed was to say I received the keys. And no, he's not going to stick me with payments because he paid for it. Over. The. Phone. He said I could drive it and everything." Geena squeaked in excitement. "They are coming on Wednesday to install the recharging station. I've only sat in it so far, but wow, what an amazing car. I had no idea. And I thought my Civic was swank when I first got it."

"Why did they give you the keys? You just said he left. He's already gone? Where did he go?" Brooke snapped out the questions like this was an interrogation.

"He headed back to Arizona. He interrupted some work to come to Atlanta, so he's finishing that up, and he needs to deliver the Airstream back to his cousin in California."

"What kind of job does he do?"

"He's never coming back, you know." Hannah and Brooke spoke at once.

"He's an investigator for his family's business," Geena answered Hannah, then turned to Brooke. "Why do you keep saying things like that, Brooke, really? Why couldn't he be interested in me when he isn't interested in you?"

"Geena, you really..." Brooke let out an exacerbated sigh. "You really don't get it, do you? I mean, why would he be interested in you? Maybe he's got a really little dick and can't satisfy a real woman." She scoffed, then took another drink and wiggled her pinky finger.

"What? He can't think I'm sexy because I'm fat? Is that it?"

"Well frankly, yes. I'm sexy. Men are constantly hitting

on me, even when I'm dressed like this." She indicated her clothes, her expression making it clear she felt as if she was dressed like a schlepp. "How many men have you actually had? Two? Three? And how many of them did you get on your own? I'm pretty sure that all the dates you've had the past few years were with guys Hannah or I sent your way. So with a record like that, why would anyone believe you otherwise?"

"What's wrong with you? Why can't you be happy for me? Why am I not allowed to be happy? Hmm? Seriously." Geena arched a brow at Brooke.

"Geena, why are you with him anyway? He tried to attack me. He's dangerous." Brooke's voice was growing shrill.

Geena sat back. She carefully looked at Hannah as if to gain her bearings. Breathing deeply, she stared coldly at Brooke.

"Yes, he is dangerous, more than you know. Maybe it's the ultimate bad-boy appeal. But it doesn't matter, 'cause you are lying about him."

"Geena!" Hannah was shocked.

Geena continued, leaning into the table, staring down Brooke. "You never realized that I saw some of that. Did ya? And what you told me happened, what I saw, and what Dante told me happened does not add up for him being the aggressor. You're lying. What? You can't have him, so I can't either? He didn't attack you. He actually said no to you. You were kissing him, and he pushed you away."

"He tried to get me into the trailer, Geena," Brooke interrupted.

"No, he didn't. What you don't know, that I do, is that his cousins were with him. They were in the trailer. That's why I wasn't staying with him. So you are lying about that. I think you also lied about talking to Hannah." Turning to Hannah, Geena asked, "Did Brooke call you from the Grand Canyon just after you left?"

Hannah shook her head. "No, we didn't talk until you guys got back to Atlanta."

"I said I called Hannah, but I talked to Tim. He picked up her phone." Brooke's tone was sharp and defensive. Geena shook her head.

"Then why not just say you talked to Tim? Why lie? Dante has never said or done anything to make me have reason not to believe anything he has ever told me. You, on the other hand, I'm not so sure right now. And you know what?" She scooted out of the booth. "He loves me. Me, with the fat ass and everything." She took a long drink of her beer and tossed a ten-dollar bill on the table. "And he's got a really big dick, and he knows how to use it." Pointing to Hannah, she continued, "I'll see you at the rehearsal dinner. Text me."

Geena turned on her heel and left.

∽

It took Dante three long and tedious days of driving after he left the triplet's house to get the trailer back to the company's construction yard in Santa Rosa. Leaving the trailer and the pickup, he unloaded the motorcycle and rode home to Mission Run. Not home. The family estate. Home was with Geena. Home was where he needed to be heading after he wrapped up a few details here. This place just had all his stuff. He spent half a day packing a few belongings he would need in Atlanta. The condo was small, so he didn't want to bring too much stuff—clothes and electronics for now. If they decided to stay in Atlanta, he would buy a house, one with a large garage. Of course, it was all conjecture. She hadn't even agreed to accept him yet.

Dante spent another day typing up reports for Uncle Remi and Morgan regarding the triplets and the unknown identity of the old wolf at the Grand Canyon. His report included all the details of the family line, the family tree Saganitso had drawn; anticipated results from Saganitso's research, with action item recommendations based on the results; and a status report regarding DNA testing of the boys and their parents, and the skin sample he'd collected from the old wolf. Dante finalized his profiles on the boys, including all physical details, personality differences, wolf coloring, and having prints made of several photos he'd taken of them with his phone.

Dante knocked on the doorframe to Morgan's home office.

His cousin looked up. "Hey, c'mon in."

Dante had to admit, Morgan did look more like an older brother than a cousin. Then again, their fathers had looked like twins too. He dropped a small collection of file folders onto the edge of Morgan's desk.

"Here's all the info I have." He dug a USB drive from his pocket and placed it on the stack of files. "Margarita Palatine's line all wrapped up. I'm waiting on DNA results; then it's done."

Morgan pulled the stack toward him. "Nice family tree," he commented as he riffled through the first file folder. "Have you talked to Julia? I think we are going to need you to—"

"No." Dante cut Morgan off.

The other man's gaze locked with his.

"I've met my mate. I'm moving to Atlanta."

Morgan smiled. "She glows?"

Dante nodded. His eyes went out of focus as he played Geena's image across his memory. "Pink, her aura is a shimmery pink, and I can't function without her."

Morgan chuckled. "I know that one all too well. Honey still has that effect on me. What's her name?"

"Geena." Dante sighed.

"Okay then." Morgan understood the lure of finding his mate. Dante needed his wits about him when he was back on the job, and not pining after the arms of his love. They made arrangements for Dante to start off with a six-week leave. Hopefully he would be able to find his focus again after that much time devoted to his mate.

Dante left Morgan's office and searched for his mother. He found her on a shaded patio, nose deep in a book. "Mom, you want to go shopping? I need your help finding something."

20

Geena stared at the ring. It was beyond stunning. It had been on her finger for only three days. Three days, and she was still amazed and living in a dreamlike state. Three days ago Dante had slipped it on her finger, and she vowed it would never come off. She decided she really should keep the manicure just so her nails and her hands would look nice for the ring.

The polish on her short nails was a shiny old bronze color. It was the color Hannah had selected for her bridesmaids. Too make sure everyone matched perfectly, Hannah had bought everyone their own bottle of the nail polish. Geena had brought her bottle of the polish to the salon. The polish complemented the soft tones of the dresses they would be wearing tomorrow. The color, called gold-olive, wasn't the most flattering for Geena, Brooke, or Ashley. However, the three of them in that shiny khaki color surrounding Hannah made Hannah's complexion look perfect, and emphasized the ginger coloring in her auburn hair. It's why that color had been selected when they were dress shopping.

Geena hadn't been included in the appointment this afternoon with Hannah, Brooke, and Ashley. Hannah had said there was a mishap with the scheduling, and the salon didn't have time for all four of them. Geena suspected that Brooke "accidentally" on purpose forgot to book an appointment that would have included Geena. She was on her own for the manicure. Dante had accompanied her to the one she was able to get at a different salon, and the two of them got the full mani-pedi treatment. Dante had his nails painted black. He said it would fit his image for the weekend festivities. He was barely an invited guest, and really only as Geena's plus one. He figured that Tim would be far from pleased to see him at the wedding. Dante purposefully went for an intimidating appearance. Geena agreed that the black nails really fit the image—that and they looked sexy.

She looked from her ring to Dante. Sunglasses hid his eyes, his hair curled back from his brow, and dark stubble covered his jaw. A jaw set with concentration. He guided the car through traffic toward Callenwolde. It was a short drive, but rush-hour traffic started early on Fridays, lengthening their time in the car. A car with luxury she had never expected to experience in her life. A car that cost more than she'd made in two years when she was employed. The car purred its way through traffic like a sleek jungle predator.

She felt like one of the beautiful people. She knew she was with one of them. Dante's broad shoulders were dressed in a sleek, slender-fitting three-piece charcoal-gray suit. He looked like a movie star on the red carpet for a premier. He wore a deep purple shirt and matching tie. He had purchased the shirt and tie yesterday afternoon to coordinate with the dress she currently wore. He said he wanted everyone to know they belonged together, and he wouldn't be able to match her tomorrow, since he wasn't a member of the wedding party.

At some point someone was going to call her out for being an impostor. They would point out that she didn't belong in the beautiful car, with the beautiful man, dressed as if she too were beautiful. They would demand to know what she was doing in a corseted dress that emphasized her breasts and gave her an hourglass figure. They would demand she return the ring.

The ring was a true one-of-a-kind, artisan-crafted piece of fine jewelry. Dante had purchased it while he was in California, and he had slipped it on her finger moments after flying back to her, and she'd said yes. The ring was dark rose gold with a large flat face that framed two rows of rough cut diamonds. In total there were twelve square diamonds, all in the champagne range of colors. When Dante had slipped it on her finger, he told her he picked it out based on the jewelry she had admired so much at the various galleries and shops at the Grand Canyon. He had wanted to get her a diamond that was grand and full of sparkle, but he didn't think she would wear that. She cried when she saw the ring and Dante down on one knee. She had already been crying in anticipation of his return, scared that he really wouldn't be on the plane. It was the most perfect ring she had ever seen. No, she didn't need a big flashy ring; she just needed Dante. When he placed it on her finger the second time in front of Gran, her parents, and the judge, she'd agreed to tell him the second she wanted a flashy ring if she ever changed her mind.

Geena dabbed at her eyes. She knew she would probably cry this evening at Hannah's rehearsal dinner; she didn't need to ruin her makeup by starting early.

"You okay?" Dante reached over to squeeze her knee.

"More than. You gave me this, didn't you?" Geena admired the ring.

"I did."

"You aren't going to take it back, are you?"

"Not without teams of lawyers getting involved, or incurring the wrath of my mother."

Geena chuckled.

"You aren't planning on giving it back now, are you? I have signed documents, you know."

"No. It's mine. You're mine. I'm not giving either back."

∽

The great hall was full of people. Workers moved armfuls of folding chairs from a cart, placing them in rows, then placing white chair covers over them in preparation for the next day's wedding service. Small groups of well-dressed people mingled about. There seemed to be more people than were necessary for the actual rehearsal. Then again, this was Hannah's parents' idea of a wedding. The entire weekend would be one party after another. The rehearsal and subsequent dinner would include both complete families, all members of the bridal party, their guests, and various important guests of Hannah's and Tim's parents. The semiformal dinner was to be held at the exclusive La Trattoria de la Bellavita, one of Atlanta's top five-star restaurants. Hannah's father had reserved the entire restaurant.

The wedding would last all day Saturday, beginning with a wedding party brunch catered on-site for the bride, her family and her half of the wedding party. The groom, his groomsmen, and his family would have brunch catered for them at the Hillmore Bed-and-Breakfast. Scheduled morning activities would proceed to the actual ceremony, followed by a reception that would last until the facilities at Callenwolde closed. Hannah and Tim would be whisked away by limo to an undisclosed location for their first night together as husband and wife. Of course, everyone knew this to be back at the Hillmore B and B. They would return Sunday morning for a casual brunch being hosted by Hannah's family at their home. All members of the wedding party were expected to attend.

Hannah's mother flitted from group to group like the social butterfly she was, making sure everyone had been greeted and knew where she needed them to stand. She even wore a jewel-toned dress with deep dolman sleeves, giving her the appearance of wings. When she saw Geena and Dante, she came over and whisked Geena away to the far side of the room, leaving Dante to fend for himself. He found a wood-paneled wall out of the way to lean against. Mostly no one noticed him.

Hannah, Tim, and an elderly gentlemen, the pastor, were discussing some details. Dante watched as Geena joined the group. Hannah's mother waved a young lady over to join them. Dante assumed she was Ashley, Tim's sister. Brooke swished right past Dante on her way to joining the group, her black pencil skirt restricting her movement to an exaggerated wiggle.

Brooke's posturing and Geena's change in demeanor alerted Dante that Geena felt insecure. He wouldn't swoop in and save her, not right now. She had asked him to behave this evening. Geena had said she needed to be able to handle the confrontation with Brooke on her own. She knew there would be one. When they were getting their nails done, Geena had described her last meeting with Brooke and Hannah. Geena was amazed at herself; she had told Brooke to stuff it. She was tired of Brooke acting as if she was superior to Geena simply because of her looks. "Brooke thinks she is beautiful, and she is. But she thinks that I am not. And I've spent too many years agreeing with her. I'm beautiful, just in a different way."

Dante had agreed with her. "I think you are much more beautiful than Brooke will ever be. You not only have the outward beauty, but you also have a beautiful heart, Geena. Why do you think I love you so much?"

Geena glanced back at Dante as if seeing him would give her strength. He watched her stand a little taller and return to her conversation with Brooke. Everyone else also noticed Geena's improved fortitude, and they turned to see what she had been looking at. What they saw was Dante, well-groomed in an expensive designer suit, casually leaning against the wall.

It was like a riot broke out. Brooke began waving her arms angrily, Tim tried to bolt in Dante's direction, but Hannah grabbed him by the arm and was forcibly holding him back. A young man, presumably Tim's best man, had stepped forward and placed his hand on Tim's chest, restraining him. Geena shocked everyone. She put her hand on her hip and began wagging her finger, scolding everyone. Dante had to chuckle. She had found her strength and mixed it with the sass he knew she had.

Brooke harrumphed back into her role as bridesmaid. Tim, with coercion from the others around him, also obliged. He pulled his arms away from those restraining him and tugged on his suit. He shot glares of hatred toward Dante before turning back. Dante winked at Ashley, since she had been staring at him with her mouth agape the entire time, just before Hannah's mother spun her back around to face the pastor.

Hannah's mother made a beeline for Dante. "Young

man, I don't know who you are, but I think you might need to leave."

Dante stood up from the wall. He extended his hand. "Dante Palatine, Mrs. Harris. I'm with Geena."

Hannah's mother was fine-boned like her daughter, and in her younger days must have had similar coloring. Now her hair was frosted with blonde highlights to hide the gray. As if she could smell money, her blustery demeanor settled in his presence.

"Geena? With you?" Her tone was skeptical. She sounded like she subscribed to the Brooke school of thought that Geena would never end up with a man like Dante.

"Yes, Geena. I'm not sure what the problem is exactly. The groom doesn't like me much. I'll just go wander around the grounds. Please let Geena know where she can find me." Dante turned and walked out the side door.

Dante was in the gardens behind the mansion when Geena found him about thirty minutes later. "Hello, pretty girl," he said as she approached him. He wrapped his arms around her waist. Together they looked back at the mansion. "I can see why they are having the wedding here."

"It's beautiful, isn't it?"

"It is, but I think I prefer small weddings." Dante looked down at Geena, she filled his heart full of love and a bit of passion.

"Me too, tiny ones." Geena tipped her face up to kiss him. "Your eyes are glowing."

"Always for you, Geena."

She rested her head against his chest.

"You know I used to take dance lessons here after school?"

"Oh yeah?"

Geena grabbed Dante's hand and began to lead him

back to the mansion with the intention of wandering around the gardens and building together. "Yeah, they have all kinds of classes and concerts here. I can't imagine living in a place this big."

"You can't? Do you think you could get used to it if you had to?"

"Get used to living in a mansion? Maybe. It would have to come with staff. I mean, I have a hard enough time keeping the condo clean. I can't imagine what it takes to keep a place this big clean."

Dante laughed. "It takes an army. Maids, cooks, groundskeepers. Of course, other family members also live there."

Geena stopped. "Are you serious?" She knew Dante had money. But she hadn't asked details. She didn't know if he owned a house. He had a home in Northern California, but he had said wherever she was, was home now. She hadn't really thought about where he lived before; she guessed she'd assumed he lived in an apartment or a similar condo.

Dante squinted up at the building. He began gesturing to different areas along the roof. "Well, it's not this style, of course. And bigger." He turned, sweeping his arm along the west side of the mansion and back. "There is an extra wing." He looked down at Geena. "We don't have to live there if you don't want. But we'll always have rooms there available for us."

"You are serious?" Geena smiled with laughter. Dante nodded.

Shrieks from a loud argument pulled their attention away from discussions of living in a mansion. They walked around the side and headed toward the yelling they heard. Geena caught the flash of a black dress, and they saw Tim roughly running his hands through his hair. He had been arguing with someone. But there were too many women in black dresses this evening to begin to guess who it might have been.

Tim turned. He saw Dante and rushed him. There was no one there to restrain him this time. Dante gently pushed Geena out of the way and sidestepped Tim's charge.

"Tim! Tim! Stop it!" Geena began yelling.

Tim stopped himself and turned, charging back toward the taller man. Again, Dante smoothly moved at the last second, letting Tim pass right by him.

Tim's face was splotchy red, and he began to pant, his nostrils flared, his lip curled into a snarl. He was the one who looked like a wild animal, not Dante. Dante was calm, self-possessed.

Tim barreled straight into Dante, a tackling maneuver from his days as a football player. Dante took the attack and stepped back with the force. He reached over and pulled Tim's jacket up and over his head, shoving Tim back off him.

Geena yelled again. "Tim! Jesus, Tim, stop it!"

Someone had come out the door to see what the continued noise was. Geena heard the door close behind her, but she didn't pay attention. She wasn't worried for Dante; she knew what he was capable of. She was worried for Hannah. Tim didn't need to become injured the night before the wedding. Geena didn't want to lose Hannah as a friend if Dante seriously hurt Tim. Something he could easily do. Tim rushed Dante again. Dante boxed his ears, spun him around, and shoved him away.

Hannah ran out of the door and stood next to Geena. "What the hell?" She waved her practice bouquet at the two men fighting.

"He just attacked Dante. He won't stop. What's his problem?" Geena replied, also wildly waving her arms at the men fighting like animals.

Tim tackled Dante again. Dante spun him around, wrapping his arm across Tim's neck. More people came out to watch the fight. Tim dropped to one knee. It appeared that Dante had successfully restrained him, subduing him. Then with the force of two arms, Tim rammed an elbow into Dante's solar plexus. Dante let go, gasping.

Tim spun and threw a right hook. "That's for attacking my girlfriend!"

Dante easily blocked the blow and shoved Tim away from him.

"I never touched Hannah." He ducked, dodging another right hook.

Tim was an aggressive fighter but ineffectual. He continued lunging and missing. Sweating, he tore his jacket off and threw it to the ground. He lunged again. "Keep away from—" Tim growled a name, but it was garbled and impossible to understand.

Dante stepped to the side with the grace of a dancer and nailed Tim with a chop to the back of the neck. Tim stumbled but caught himself. He seemed oblivious to the gathering group of onlookers. All his rage focused on Dante. His failed attempts at actually hitting Dante amplified his blind hatred for the man. Tim lunged again and tried to reach out to grab at Dante. Again, Dante gracefully maneuvered out of his range. Tim changed his tactic of attack. Instead of lunging for Dante, he lifted his fists like a boxer, rolled his shoulders up, and began bouncing on the balls of his feet, darting back and forth.

Dante smoothly circled around. His eyes never left Tim's. Tim continued to punch and throw his fists at Dante. Dante countered by knocking Tim's punches off to the side, never giving Tim an opportunity to land a punch, never attempting to punch Tim in return.

"Tim, stop it. What are you talking about? He didn't do anything!" Hannah yelled. Tim wasn't listening.

There was now a crowd of guests witnessing the fight. Hannah's mother began pushing other men toward the two fighting, trying to get them to break it up.

Dante looked at Geena and mouthed, *I'm sorry.* She understood this to mean he was going to end the fight, Since Tim was not backing down, this meant he was going to have to hurt Tim enough to stop him. She bit her lip and nodded her head. She grabbed Hannah's arm and leaned in to tell her, warning her.

Hannah looked panic-stricken. "No!"

Brooke ran out of the door and stood next to Hannah. Her brow wrinkled with confusion as she looked back and forth between the two men fighting and Hannah and Geena.

Tim threw another punch at Dante. This time Dante caught Tim's fist, rotated him, locking the elbow straight, then punched him in the ribs just under his armpit. Tim staggered back, holding his side. He paused, trying to catch his breath. It appeared that he might actually stop attacking. He ran to tackle Dante again. He hit Dante in the ribs with his shoulder. Dante let himself be lifted. As he fell back to the ground, he pulled Tim with him, smashing Tim's face into his knee.

Tim stood, reeling back, grabbing the bridge of his nose. His nose was bleeding, and he looked a bit dazed. Tim reached for Dante. Instead Dante grabbed Tim by the throat and easily lifted him.

"Are we done?" he growled.

Tim's nose dripped blood and snot; his hair was wet with sweat. At some point his shirt had ripped at the shoulder seam. There was dirt on his knees. Dante barely looked ruffled, his hair a bit wilder. His suit remained unrumpled. If he had to continue fighting, his demeanor would soon change from one of cool possession to aggravated exertion.

Tim's feet barely touched the ground. He grabbed Dante's wrist and tried to gain purchase to support his weight. Dante dropped him. Tim landed, undignified, on his backside. Dante, thinking they were done, turned away slightly. Tim took this to be an opening and lunged again. Dante grabbed him by the arm as he passed. He whipped Tim around, pulling his arm up hard in a half nelson. He punched him in the shoulder. Tim let out a groan of pain. And dropped to his knees.

"I am done with you attacking me. I'm not here for your damned girlfriend." Dante shoved Tim away from him, causing Tim to catch himself on his hands.

Hannah and Brooke ran to Tim's assistance. "And I'm not here for your fiancée."

Hannah, Brooke, Hannah's parents, and Tim's parents all began talking at once. The rest of the onlookers stood in silent confusion.

"What are you doing here?" Brooke yelled at Dante.

"What does he mean, girlfriend?" Hannah asked. Her mother also asked a similar question of Tim's mother.

Dante stalked toward Tim, pointing menacingly. "Get your priorities straight. Stop fucking your fiancée's cousin. Be a man and pick one; you don't deserve to marry Hannah and ruin her life." He turned to Hannah. "I'm sorry, he and Brooke..." Dante made a fist as if he could crush the bad news he was delivering.

"He's lying. He's just saying that because I wouldn't have him," Brooke accused.

"I have never wanted you. You don't seem to get that." Dante's tone was full of annoyance.

"Of course you do. No one here believes that you are really with Geena." She pointed at Geena. She tried to walk to Dante, reaching out with her hand to smooth the suit across his chest.

He stepped away from her. "I'm not here for you. I'm here with my wife."

"Your wife? I'm what men want." She gesticulated wildly at Hannah. "Do any of you think Tim really wanted Hannah for anything more than her money? He wanted me. Just like you're supposed to." Brooke started to look like a crazy person. Her eyes were wide, and she flailed her arms about.

"You can't have married Geena; she's fat!"

Geena had enough. She grabbed Brooke by the shoulder and spun her around. "Shut up, you bitch!" Geena slapped her, leaving a bright red mark on Brooke's cheek.

∼

"When did you get married?" Hannah poured Geena another glass of champagne. "It's paid for, might as well enjoy it." She drank directly from the bottle. She and Geena sat on the steps of the Grand Staircase, the stairs on which Hannah was supposed to have made her dramatic entrance for the wedding ceremony.

Tim and his friends had already left. Hannah's mother had rallied and began directing the center's staff to put away all the tables and chairs. There would not be a wedding happening the next day. She had already sent Hannah's father and his guests, and all the extra family members on to the restaurant. The catering was paid for, no need to let it go to waste. Tim's parents and family had been invited, but neither Tim nor Brooke would be welcome. They had left together. Brooke helped a bleeding Tim limp off after Hannah's father yelled at him for wasting his money and breaking his little girl's heart. Tim's parents immediately offered their sincerest apologies to Hannah's mother.

"On Wednesday. At the nursing home. Just my parents and Gran."

Dante stood across the room talking quietly with the pastor. Geena watched as he massaged his ribs.

"So, were you going to tell me?"

"I didn't want to usurp your glory. We were going to have a big party next year and just tell everyone we eloped." She held up her flute for more champagne. "It wouldn't exactly be a lie, just delayed truth. You know how bad off Gran is. This way, she saw me get married. Something I know she never expected. She might even remember it."

Hannah patted her on the knee. She nodded her head and took another long pull on the champagne bottle.

"Gonna need another few of these if I'm gonna get properly drunk." Hannah began to stand.

Hannah's mother handed her a second open bottle. "Your friend... your husband," she corrected herself. "How did he know?"

Geena shrugged. "It's what he does."

"I watched that fight." She shook her head. "He could have hurt Tim at any time, couldn't he have?"

"I believe so." Geena nodded. She had known Hannah's mother for as long as she'd known Hannah, but she wasn't sure how upset Mrs. Harris was with her for having brought Dante.

"Well, I shouldn't say this. I wish he had done a bit more than break that asshole's nose."

"Mom!" Hannah began laughing. Her mother and Geena joined her.

"I'm sorry, Hannah." Dante approached the three women. "I understand if you need to hate me, but don't blame Geena for my actions."

Hannah shook her head. "How come none of us saw that?" Hannah squinted up at him, handing him the bottle of champagne.

He wiped the rim and took a drink.

"I had my suspicions based on some things Geena had just mentioned in passing. Honestly, I didn't have confirmation until we heard the fight right before he tried to jump me out there." He passed the bottle back.

"You know Brooke couldn't stand the idea of either of you having a man that she couldn't have. She said as much back at the Grand Canyon. She honestly thought I would leave Geena if she said she wanted me." Dante looked into his wife's eyes. He held out his hand to her. Standing, Geena took Dante's hand. He pulled her into an embrace. "As if I would want any other woman than my mate." He lowered his lips to hers, kissing her long and deep.

EPILOGUE

Geena stood in the middle of a large rec room. The entire room was bigger than the first floor of her condo. Dante had given up living here to be with her. The party Dante's mother was throwing to welcome Geena to the family was nothing she'd expected.

"You're looking a little poleaxed, dear," Karen, Dante's mother, said.

"I'm feeling a little poleaxed," Geena replied. "All these people, it's a bit overwhelming," Geena admitted.

"Well, I was about to say no one here bites. But you know better, don't you?"

Geena laughed with Karen. "Everyone has been so nice. I'm waiting for the other shoe to drop. I feel like someone is going to come up and tell me it's all a farce."

"Why would you say that?" Dante's sister, Ari, said as she joined Geena and her mother.

"I love Dante, but I'm waiting for him to wake up and change his mind."

"Why on earth would you think something like that, Geena? He loves you."

"Look at me, Ari. He's completely out of my league."

Ari stepped back and looked Geena up and down. Geena couldn't read her expression, but how could she not judge Geena's weight, her comfortable old jeans and T-shirt?

"You're beautiful, and I know I've only known you for a few days, but I do know my brother. You are out of his league, and he's well aware of it. Don't sell yourself short. Be happy you found each other. He's not going anywhere."

"Thanks, but it's a hard feeling to shake, like I'm an impostor. It overwhelms me from time to time."

"I think we all feel that way at times. But don't doubt Dante. I've never seen him happier. I am glad he found you." Ari leaned in and kissed Geena on the cheek. "Connie just put out more guacamole. You're going to want to get some before it's all gone."

Geena moved out to the patio where the cook, Connie, and the kitchen staff had set up a huge buffet and ran the grill.

Dante had described the estate, the house, the grounds, and the huge garage that used to be horse stables. But somewhere in her head, Geena had expected everyone to be formal and glamorous like on TV. She was in the middle of a large family barbecue with lots of food and even more wine, and kids running around screaming. Her idea of a large, rich family in Northern California was clearly based on her experiences of rich Southern families and television. The difference was radical. Well, at least in her experience it was. Parties of any kind at Hannah's were always formal. Even barbecues required dresses. Geena had packed expecting to have to dress to the nines at least once, if not twice. Instead, she'd met Dante's family while wearing jeans and the Santa Fe T-shirt she picked up on the trip when she met him.

"Hey, Geena, have you met Ethan yet?" Morgan's wife, Honey, a tall strawberry blonde, walked up to her balancing a baby on her hip.

"No, I haven't."

In an artful move Honey took the plate of food from Geena's hands and swept the baby into her arms.

Geena half expected Honey to comment on the food. After all, in her experience with anyone who ever worked as a model, they always made some comment on Geena's food or her weight in regards to food. But Honey was not Brooke. And Geena needed to not judge all thin blondes on Brooke's behavior.

"This is Caro's youngest, Ethan."

Geena cooed at the baby in her arms.

"Have you and Dante made any plans on having kids?" Honey asked.

Geena handed the baby back quickly, as if he was contagious. "Not really. We just got married; maybe in a few years, but not yet."

"Oh, I've got baby fever bad, but Morgan is dragging his heels. In the meantime, I keep borrowing this guy from Caro." As if on cue, Ethan started fussing. "Of course one of the benefits to borrowing a baby, is you can return him." She made a funny face at the baby. "Let's go find Mommy."

Geena turned and located her plate on a table where Honey had set it down.

"Hey, pretty girl." Dante sauntered up to Geena. His smile gleamed, and her heart skipped a beat.

"Hey, sweetie." Geena tilted her head for a kiss. His kisses curled her toes every time.

Dante reached onto her plate, stole a chip, and scooped up some of Connie's famous guacamole.

"Shane offered to buy the chopper."

"The one you just got? You sure you want to do that? You've barely had time to ride it."

"That's why I'm considering his offer." Dante took another chip full of guacamole. "I wanted to check with you first."

"Why? It's your bike."

"It's how we met. I thought you might feel, I dunno, sentimental about it."

Geena laughed. "I love you. Would you really keep that bike, even if you don't ride it, because you took me for a ride the first time we met?"

"Yeah."

"Dante, it's a motorcycle, not a shrine. What are you gonna do next, put the Grand Canyon under a glass dome?"

"For you? Anything." His expression was serious. Dark eyebrows slashed above intense hazel eyes.

Geena rested her hand against the side of his face. "I love you. Sell your bike if you want." She placed her hand on his chest above his heart. "This is the only shrine to our love that I need."

Geena heard applause and hollers as Dante kissed her. When they broke off the kiss and straightened, Geena found that everyone was watching and cheering them.

"To the bride and her groom!" a deep voice boomed from somewhere in the crowd.

"The bride and groom!" everyone repeated.

There was a collective gasp of appreciation as Connie rolled out a tall, multitiered cake, frosted to look like sunset over the Grand Canyon.

Geena blushed deeply. This was better than any planned wedding reception she could have asked for.

"Did you do this?" she whispered to Dante.

"No, you did when you married me," he answered before leaning down to kiss her again.

PREVIEW OF LONGING

Longing

Shane has to come face-to-face with his prejudices and his past in order to be able to truly love Lucy. He has been in love with her for as long as he can remember. He knew he would always do what was necessary to protect her when he was eight, and by the time he was sixteen he realized she was his ideal mate. The only problem was Lucy only ever saw Shane as her adopted little brother. Will time, and a life full of experiences change Lucy's mind when Shane shows up on her door step after the life she has made begins to fall apart, or will her family get in the way, again?

PREVIEW OF LONGING

Excerpt

Joe Diablo pushed the door to his apartment open. It wasn't locked. Warily he stepped inside, he figured one of the kids had broken in on a dare and was hiding. The rapid bam-bam-bam of video game assault rifles let him know whomever it was, they weren't hiding, at least not from him. A few more steps into the apartment and he could see a first person shooter video game dominating his TV screen. The reflection of the TV's blue light across the top of a bald head told him who it was. Shane. People were looking for him.

"So this is where you've holed up."

The reply Joe received from the man laying back in the recliner was a grunt.

"Wanna beer?"

Another grunt.

Joe made his way to the small kitchen, that he rarely used, since he typically ate up at the house. Why cook for yourself when Connie was a master chef, and fed everyone? His refrigerator, however, was always stocked with beer.

"What are you doing here Shane?"

The game figure on the TV screamed, and red splattered across the screen as if the viewer had been brutally shot.

Shane tossed the game control on the table, and grabbed the open beer Joe had set down for him.

"I'm shirking my responsibilities. You gonna nark on me?"

"What?" Joe chuckled, "the mighty Shane is in hiding cause he don't wanna?"

"Damn straight." Shane responded humorlessly.

"I'm not gonna narc on you, you are going to turn yourself in, or I have it on good authority that Connie will cut you off."

"Threatening me with food, that's low even for Morgan." Shane smirked.

Joe nodded. "Yep. My understanding is it's Honey's idea. That woman has a mean streak."

"Well she has to, she's playing with wolves. Anything to gain advantage over us, right? Between you and me, I don't think she plays fair."

"So you gonna call in?"

Shane stood, groaning. "I'll do one better. I'll go up to the house, put on my big-boy pants and deal with this."

Joe snorted at the term *big-boy pants*.

Shane shot him a glare. "I know, I know. Honey's terminology is rubbing off on all of us. But Morgan's never been happier. Can't really deny him that."

"No, but I swear its getting a little scary around here. Morgan, then Julia. Mates, hell even Dante got married. Dante."

"Naw, I wouldn't begrudge any of them their mates. That's something special there, man. You should be so lucky to ever find your mate. When you do, you'll do anything for them." Shane's mood turned sullen. He tipped his beer in thanks to Joe, then headed out the door.

"As if you have." Joe scoffed.

And I would do anything for her. Shane let the door close behind him. Including not being with her.

Shane had a choice, to continue to hide from his duties, or to man up and face this. To everyone else it looked like he had to suck up his personal prejudices. For Shane it meant facing down his past. He trotted down the stairs from Joe's apartment over the car barn into the vast space that housed the Palatines' vehicles: family vehicles in the middle, personal ones to the left, and on the opposite side of the garage, the bike collection.

A beautiful orange and green custom build-out chopper sat gleaming, waiting to be ridden in the golden hills of Northern California. He could turn right at the bottom of the stairs, get on his bike and... And what? He wasn't a coward. The family considered him to be one of their top men, an alpha even. Some alpha he was turning out to be, afraid to have a single meeting with a woman. Not just any woman, but a woman who represented everything he hated about his past.

He turned left. He knew what Morgan wanted of him. Time to man up, and get it taken care of.

ABOUT THE AUTHOR

Lulu is an aspiring best seller (it's on the list) who manages life in a series of to-lists. It should not surprise you she loves sticky notes, and they are posted all over her various offices (home and day job). Her not so scandalous past involves attending art school, teaching bellydance, earning too many degrees in education, and failing miserably at mastering the hula hoop and roller derby.

Her husband is tall, dark, and handsome, and really does wear kilts. Her children are bad-ass derby girls who have great plans on making this world a better place. The voices in her head come with complete character profiles and plot lines.

For more information, visit:
www.LuluMSylvian.com

Made in the USA
Columbia, SC
28 June 2018